TO
CHARM
A DARK
PRINCE

KATHRYN ANN KINGSLEY

FOREVER

NEW YORK   BOSTON

Forever
Hachette Book Group
1290 Avenue of the Americas, New York, NY 10104
read-forever.com
@readforeverpub

Originally published in 2023 by Second Sky, an imprint of Storyfire Ltd., Carmelite House, 50 Victoria Embankment, London EC4Y0DZ, United Kingdom
First Forever Edition: December 2024

Forever is an imprint of Grand Central Publishing. The Forever name and logo are registered trademarks of Hachette Book Group, Inc.

The publisher is not responsible for websites (or their content) that are not owned by the publisher.

The Hachette Speakers Bureau provides a wide range of authors for speaking events. To find out more, go to hachettespeakersbureau.com or email HachetteSpeakers@hbgusa.com.

Forever books may be purchased in bulk for business, educational, or promotional use. For information, please contact your local bookseller or the Hachette Book Group Special Markets Department at special.markets@hbgusa.com.

ISBN: 9781538769249 (paperback)

Printed in the United States of America

LSC-C

Printing 1, 2024

TO CHARM A DARK PRINCE

PROLOGUE

The nightmares had returned.

Mordred stalked the halls of his keep like a caged animal, his armored boots thumping on the wooden floor of his home as he moved from room to room like a shadowy nightmare. His dark cloak whispered upon the polished surface; the hood was pulled over his face to obscure his features, though it did not hide his emotions.

His servants knew better than to come near him when he was in one of his restless moods. He could not sleep. He could not rest. While his insomnia that night certainly was not uncommon, his anger this evening was.

He could not stop dwelling on the pure and simple truth that haunted his waking and unwaking hours.

He could feel his control of Avalon cracking. Literally and figuratively. It was just a matter of how much time he had left.

What was a soldier like him to do, without an enemy to fight? He was built for war—for *battle*. It was all he had ever known. It was what he had honed his body and his mind for over the centuries of life he had led. He was perhaps the greatest knight his world had ever known. Very few could best him in a contest of strength. And by rights, he *should* be king. But that was not why his mood was so foul.

It was because, despite all his efforts and sacrifices, Mordred was unsure if he could hold on. His furious wanderings sent him down the winding stone stairs, deep into the bowels of the cliff on which his keep had been built.

He had to see. He had to know. He had to make doubly sure that tonight would not be the night it all fell apart.

Like jagged, rusted, abandoned knives, the sharp claws of his gauntlet scraped against the stone walls as he descended into the darkness. It was a habit of his that brought him some manner of peace. The sensation somehow reminded him that this world belonged to him. That he wielded the power. That he *alone* held the destruction of the isle at bay.

The weight of his heavy iron armor was a comfort to him as well. It was familiar. Its burden was nothing to him anymore.

Pausing for a moment, he let out a breath and let his armor dissipate, save for the gauntlets he preferred to keep. As the iron in its liquid form receded, the chill of the lower levels met his bare skin. It was oddly comforting. It reminded him of what this place *really* was, in the end.

It was a tomb.

He studied the doors. They were the only guards he allowed to stand watch over the precious item within. No one else, not even his own creations, could be trusted.

The tangled, jagged spirals sculpted into the surface looked as though they had been guided by the hand of an artist whose work had been overgrown with wild vines. Natural and unnatural. Orderly and chaotic. There was no rhyme or reason to their appearance—only instinct. Pressing his metal palm to the surface, he sighed.

Upon his pushing the door, it answered its master and opened, gliding silently on its hinges despite its towering size.

No locks were needed. No locks would help. The doors would open for him, and him alone.

Stepping inside the chamber, he squinted against the glow as his eyes adjusted to the glare. The metal of his boots clinked against the floor as he walked, the sound mixing with the whispers that filled the air.

The whispers that wept and begged for freedom. That cursed his name and vowed revenge. The whispers that cried for justice. He sneered as he approached the glowing pool in the center of the room. He would *never* speak an answer to the words that surrounded him. They would not listen to reason. The Ancients knew how many times he had tried.

Pillars surrounded the circular pool in the center of the room, silhouetted harshly against the shimmering, crystalline substance within it. From each pillar ran a thick iron chain to the true quarry of the chamber.

His Crystal.

The prison for the magic of Avalon.

The cage for that which wished to tear his world to pieces.

Assembled from a trick of his magic—iron turned to a crystal-like quartz or amethyst—it hung suspended over the pool that collected the shards that leaked from it. No matter how hard Mordred worked to seal the cracks, some always seemed to form, like condensation upon a glass.

In a thousand of his nightmares, he had seen his creation crack, deform, and shatter. He had seen the terrible power within set free to wreak its havoc upon the world.

Lifting his hands, he began to work his will on the Iron Crystal, repairing the splits and reinforcing the sections that looked weaker than the others.

He watched as a small drop of the opalescent liquid formed upon the outside, coalescing from one of the seams in the metal panels, hardened into its solid form and fell from the surface into the pool with a quiet *tink*.

The Crystal was degrading faster and faster as time went on. Hence the nightmares that plagued him. But for now, it seemed it would hold fast. For now, he could take some peace in the fact that the end of Avalon was just a little longer delayed.

Turning on his heel to leave the room, he froze. And his second of hesitation might have cost him everything.

The Prince in Iron had come. The window for escape was narrowing. The man who stood and beheld his work was a nightmare and a dream in the same vision. The opalescent glow of the captive magic cast sharp shadows across his features. Features whose firm, handsome lines did nothing to belie his age but could not hide his coldness. Nor his resolve.

He had once been a knight in shining armor.

Now, darkened and corrupted by the toll of endless war.

Perhaps they were to blame.

Perhaps not.

But it did not matter anymore.

Armor—rusted and asymmetric like all the rest of his works of "art"—covered his muscular arms and shoulders. Yet he wore no breastplate over the black linen shirt that he left unlaced. He had no need. For no one would stand against him in this place. No one would dare.

For here, the Prince in Iron reigned.

He pulled the dark hood from his head, gazing up at the stone that was their prison. Molten eyes that swirled with shades of red, orange, yellow, and grayish blue held nothing but contempt and perhaps even worry as they gazed up at his masterpiece.

The terrible warden. The empty prince. The elemental who had betrayed them all. How they cried for mercy—for freedom—and how they had been ignored for so very long. But there was one amongst them who would not sit still. Who had not surrendered to the inevitability of their cage.

One voice whose scream was one of rage. Who deafened those who crowded him in the place that was so overcrowded and yet so desolate.

This is your chance.

Go.

Run!

Escape!

Mordred nearly missed the motion out of the corner of his eye.

A creature—small and feline, dark and matted fur still glowing from the magic of the Crystal—was bolting for the iron door he had left ajar. It was limping, but it was fleeing.

Something had escaped.

Snarling in rage, Mordred chased the creature into the hallway. "Stop!"

The creature did not heed his words. A portal through space, inelegant and ragged at the edges, resembling a tear in fabric, opened in front of the escapee. The feline did not hesitate as it jumped through the hole.

Before Mordred could reach it—before he could rip the small portal open wider and follow it to its destination...it was gone.

"*No!*"

Slamming his fist into the wall, he watched as the stone cracked and splintered beneath his rage, like a chaotic spiderweb around his knuckles. Schooling his anger, he took a deep breath and attempted to calm himself.

Perhaps it would not be so bad.

Or perhaps this spelled the end of Avalon, once and for all.

ONE

Gwen was having a shit day. A *really* shit day.

Looking down at her phone, she let out a sigh. Nothing quite like betrayal to get the whole thing off to the wrong start. This weekend was supposed to be fun. Her parents were away until late on Sunday, having gone off to Wichita to see a show.

It was supposed to be quiet. Easy. Simple.

She wasn't supposed to find out her boyfriend was cheating on her.

It'd never happened to her before. Mick had been such a good guy. The perfect boyfriend. Or at least that was what she had thought until one of their mutual friends had texted her a photo from where they were all off at college. Mick was sitting at a table with everyone else. And some blonde was sitting on his lap, kissing his cheek.

All her friends. Every single one.

Except her.

In her place had been a stranger.

God, the betrayal *hurt*. She had trusted him. Gwen had thought they were going to be together for the rest of their lives. But she really shouldn't have been surprised that their long-distance plan had lasted less than a week. She had called Mick right after seeing the photo of him with the other girl, and he had confessed.

So here she was. Alone. With nobody to talk to. Feeling like a knife had been stuck into her heart. She planned on having a day of self-care—order a pizza, text her dad to see if she could have a beer, watch a movie, light some candles, and bury herself in her favorite fluffy blankets.

But first, she had to check in on their farm animals. And one in particular.

"Merlin! Where are you?" Gwen nudged open the door to the barn with her shoulder, a bowl of cat food in her hand. She knew she wasn't supposed to feed the old, crotchety barn cat, but she couldn't help it. The ancient bastard was looking older by the day, and pretty soon he wouldn't be able to hunt birds and mice to feed himself.

That, and... well, she loved to spoil the evil thing.

"Merlin?"

Movement out of the corner of her eye caught her attention. She smiled. "There you are. Hey, buddy."

Sitting on a box in a pile of hay and a blanket she had put there for him ages ago, was the asshole cat himself. He was scrawny and always had been, no matter how much Gwen fed him. Fur that should have been black was sprinkled with gray. One of his ears was still torn to bits, nearly missing, and both his eyes had a milky film over them. The vet said he was probably blind in one eye, and probably would go blind in both before long.

He also only had one front fang, the other having fallen out before she found him ten years earlier. It gave him a kind of lopsided, snaggle-toothed expression. Honestly, everybody—the vet included—was shocked the cat was still alive.

Merlin swished his tail and glared at her. Like he always did. As she approached, he growled at her. Like he always did.

"Yeah, yeah." She put the bowl of wet cat food in front of him. "Eat it or don't, buddy."

If a cat could sigh, she swore he did. Lowering his head, he started gobbling up the wet food. She was tempted to pet him, but...the last time she did that, she wound up with stitches and, like, eighteen shots for rabies, just in case.

Merlin was an abject asshole.

But she loved him anyway.

"You know, you're lucky I'm here to give you treats. Mom and Dad aren't fans of cats. The only reason they let you live out here is because you're a murder machine and you take care of the mice." She sat down on a crate next to Merlin's little fort.

Leaning her head back against the wall, she sighed. "I guess that's one upside to not having gotten into college. I still get to spoil you." Well, that wasn't entirely true. She'd gotten into plenty of colleges. But her dad said they were too expensive, and she didn't get enough aid to be able to afford it.

Not to mention they were afraid that she couldn't handle it. She had started suffering panic attacks from a fairly young age. Every time she got too nervous or wound up, she'd lose the ability to breathe and black out. Sometimes, there wasn't even a reason. She'd just be sitting there, minding her own business, swiping through videos on her phone, and then the whole world would get too close.

That morning's betrayal had left her sitting on the floor, struggling to breathe, for nearly half an hour. At least she hadn't passed out.

She was in therapy for it. Her parents didn't believe in medication as a solution for "mental problems," so she wasn't taking anything. Which sucked. Maybe if she was, she could have gone to college with her boyfriend—*ex-boyfriend,* she corrected herself in her head. Damn it. *Damn it all, Mick.*

They had been friends since grade school. And like most young friendships, it bloomed into something romantic as they had gotten older.

She missed him. She missed having someone she could be with. Someone she could trust and rely on. But he went off to Boston and she didn't. There he went, and here she was.

She wanted to see the world. She wanted to learn. She wanted to find her place and where she belonged. Because she knew it wasn't here. Stuck. On a farm. In backwater Kansas.

"I was hoping to go to Boston University. Can you imagine it? A big city." Mournfully, she smiled. "It must be so much fun there. Noisy and crowded and...with *people* to talk to. Not just cats." She paused. "No offense."

Merlin didn't respond. It'd have been far worse if he had.

"I guess some people are just meant to stay where they're stuck, right?" She sighed. She had wanted to go major in... hell, she didn't even know. Maybe history? Literature and lore? Veterinary studies? To be truthful, she hadn't really cared. She had just wanted to get *away.* To get *out.* To find what she wanted to do with her life. "There's a whole world out there that doesn't involve growing corn and raising goats. But no. Here I am." She nudged a pebble across the dirt floor of the barn with her toe. "Talking to a cat."

Silence.

"Sometimes I wish I could just...*fly away.* Y'know?" She shut her eyes and leaned her head back against the wood wall behind her. "Sometimes I wish magic were real. That I could just..." She sighed. There wasn't any point in making stupid wishes. Magic wasn't real. She couldn't fly.

Corn. And goats. And an old asshole cat. That was her world.

"Whatever. I'm gonna go order a pizza."

Merlin was done with his food. He promptly shoved the empty bowl off the edge of his box.

"Hey!" She dove to catch it but missed. The bowl hit the ground and shattered. Sighing, she knelt down to pick up the pieces. "You're welcome, jackass."

Merlin loafed and stared at her, flicking his tail in irritation. She glared right back at him before giving up.

Pushing back to her feet, she dumped the pieces of the bowl in the trash. She hoped her mom wouldn't notice it was missing. She wasn't supposed to be feeding Merlin in the first place. If she did say something, Gwen could pretend she was the one who had broken it.

Shoving her hands into the pockets of her hoodie, she left the barn without saying goodbye to the cat. Not like the animal cared. Gwen wasn't dumb—she knew the animal hated her. But he was easily over twenty years old and seemed to hate everything. As far as she was concerned, the old bastard had earned it.

Pulling out her phone, she texted her dad. *Hey Dad. Mick and I broke up. Can I have a beer?*

A few seconds later, the little dancing dots appeared, before she got her reply. *Oh no! What happened?*

He cheated on me.

More dots. *You can totally have a beer. Mom says you should have two. Just be safe. Are you okay?*

Gwen loved her parents. She smiled. They knew how

miserable she was to be left behind, and this was just an insult added to injury. Or more like injury added to injury. They let her get away with a lot, as long as she was being responsible. *Yeah. I'll be all right. Enjoy your show. Love you.*

Love you too, sweetie.

Heading to the fridge, she pulled out a bottle of the amber liquid and popped the cap. Her parents had always let her have one now and then for special occasions. They trusted her. And she was too much of a goody two-shoes to do anything without their permission, anyway. She called the pizza place on her phone—there was only one joint that delivered this far out into the middle of nowhere—and she settled down on the sofa to watch a movie.

After lighting a candle, she kicked up her feet, turned down the lights, and watched the opening scrawl to one of her favorite Disney movies start up.

Forty-five minutes later, the pizza arrived. Opening the door and the screen, she thanked the guy and took the box. It smelled fantastic.

Just as the door was about to swing shut, she yelped as a small, furry black object whipped past her, nearly tripping her as it bolted into the house. "Hey!"

Oh no.

Merlin stood in the middle of the kitchen. He looked back at her and, with his single-toothed fang, took off into the house.

"No! Merlin, come back! You know you're not supposed to be in here!" No, the cat probably very much didn't know that. Nor did he care. Nor had he ever once tried to get inside. The cat was in the living room, knocking things over with a series of thuds and crashes.

Gwen chased him. For a geriatric, scrawny, near-death animal, he was *fast*. Everything that had been on the coffee table was on the ground. The lit candle, three books, her bottle of beer that was now spilling everywhere, and a few coasters.

He was already on to the next room, knocking over a lamp. The bulb shattered.

"Mom's gonna *kill* me—" Her parents were going to be livid if they found the cat inside. Let alone all the damage. Dad was allergic to cats, and he'd already probably be sneezing for a week just having Merlin run through the place. "Come back!"

The cat ran upstairs. So did she. If he went under a bed, maybe she could at least corner him. He led her on a wild chase through each of the rooms. More lamps broke. One curtain was now on the ground. But she *finally* had the bastard cornered.

"Okay, you little fucker." She rolled down her hoodie sleeves and prepared to grab a very angry, very snarling cat. She was going to bleed from this, she was certain. "Time to go back outside."

Merlin hissed.

The fire alarm went off.

Blinking, she turned toward the direction of the stairs. "What the—"

The candle!

Running to the stairs, she let out a wail. Black smoke was already curling up along the ceiling. "I'm dead. I'm *so* dead."

Bolting down the stairs, she came to a screeching halt. She hadn't been upstairs that long—it'd only been maybe a minute that she'd been chasing Merlin around the house like an idiot.

But the house was an *inferno*. The walls were curling with fire that arched up along the ceiling. The smell of it was nearly choking.

Her money was suddenly on the fire.

Very much on the fire.

"Fuck-fuck-fuck-fuck-*fuck-fuck-fuck!*"

Gwen ran into the kitchen, but it was in the same condition as the living room. A total, impassable inferno. How was that even possible? She knew fire could spread quickly, but this was insane!

She tried to make it to the door. But just as she thought she might see an open path, a line of fire roared up in front of her, blocking her. Every time she ran to a window, the fire seemed to outsmart her.

Which wasn't possible.

It was just fire.

Pretty soon, Gwen's only option was to go back upstairs. Maybe she could jump out of a window—she'd break her ankles or her wrists, but at least she wouldn't *burn to death*. She was crying, her heart stuck in her throat like a rock as she raced from room to room trying to find a way out. But the exterior of the house was ablaze.

There was no escape.

Oh god, I'm gonna die. I'm gonna die!

She wound up in her bedroom, panic having led her there with nowhere else to go. Standing in the middle of the room, she laced her hands into her chestnut hair. The heat from the fire was nearly overwhelming.

This was it. This was the end. Gwen was only nineteen

years old, and she was gonna die in a fire that made no sense. The room was engulfed. Coughing at the smoke that stung her eyes and her lungs, she wept.

Stepping through the flames as if they weren't real…was a scrawny, battered-up old black cat.

Merlin.

The bastard just *walked* through the wall of fire as if he didn't feel a damn thing! He wasn't smoldering. He wasn't burning. He yawned as if it were the most casual thing in the world.

"What the—"

Gwen's confusion only deepened as the cat walked over to an open area of the floor and, with a swipe of his paw through the air, seemed to open up a hole.

A hole.

In space.

It looked almost like it had been drawn there. It was jagged at the edges, as if actually caused by the cat's claws. It was also only a few feet in diameter. The space on the other side was only a swirl of darkness—she couldn't make out anything that she was looking at.

"I'm having a panic attack. That's all. Just a panic attack. I'm—I'm hallucinating this, because I'm probably already burning to death—" Gwen was shaking now. She didn't know who she was talking to. Herself, or the cat, or nobody.

Merlin looked back at her, swished his tail once, and jumped through the portal. Because that's what it was, wasn't it? A magic portal. The cat was gone. Through a *magic portal.*

Letting out an undignified noise, she realized she had a choice. Jump head-first through the tiny *magic portal* or burn to death.

Not really much of a choice. "I hate you, Merlin!" Putting out her arms like she was going to jump off a diving board, she leapt into the hole. She really hoped she wasn't going to end up face-planting wherever she was jumping into. That was, if she wasn't going to just jump into more fire.

Nope.

That wasn't the problem.

Gwen screamed as she fell, hundreds of feet above land. She had gone from fire into frying pan. She wasn't going to burn to death, but she was going to splatter all over wherever-the-hell-she-now-was.

Screaming, however, seemed to help the situation.

As she plummeted toward the ground, Gwen blacked out.

TWO

"My liege?"

Mordred had not been paying attention. He had not been sleeping well of late—though that was not uncommon. He was tempted to use the sleeping powder that the cook made for him, but the concoction often left him drowsy and clouded the following day. He had placed his head back against his throne and shut his eyes, and had apparently lost track of time.

Turning his focus back to the knight in front of him, he arched an eyebrow. "Yes?"

The man in question sighed. He was older by appearance than Mordred, though looks were always deceiving in this world. The knight stood head and shoulders over the rest of Mordred's servants, looking almost frail due to his proportions. Which was, once more, deceiving. The Knight in Gold was one of the fiercest fighters that Avalon could boast. More than once, Mordred had found himself counting his blessings that Galahad was on *his* side.

Even if Galahad had no choice in the matter.

"There has been…an incident." Galahad frowned, his expression hidden mostly under his gray mustache. The creases at his eyes were pronounced as a result of his obvious concern.

Rolling his eyes, Mordred braced himself for whatever the so-called incident was. "What village has decided to wage a rebellion this time?" He rubbed his fingers along his temple, already feeling a headache beginning to take up residence. He disliked it when he had to raze a town, but it had to be done now and then in the name of keeping the peace.

"No, prince." Galahad's fingers flexed and clenched at his side, the gold detailing of his armor reflecting the candlelight. "It is more serious than that, I fear."

Mordred blinked. "Well, out with it."

The Knight in Gold pondered his words for a moment before resigning himself to whatever chaos was about to follow. "A fiery meteor fell from the sky and struck Ellainwood."

Grimacing, Mordred stood from his throne. Summoning his armor in mid-stride, it spread over him, welcome and familiar. The iron formed the jagged points and elaborate, tangled patterns that he favored. Beautiful but frightening. And it was by design. Let all others fear him—he had long since given up earning their love.

Clenching his clawed gauntlets into fists, he headed for the door. There was no time to waste. Galahad would have known to already fit up their drakes for the ride. Ellainwood was several hours away, even by flight.

He could only hope that they would not arrive too late.

Too late for what, he did not know.

But it would spell disaster if they did not. Of that, he was certain.

Gwen groaned. Her head hurt. A lot. Screw that, everything hurt a lot. Pressing a hand to her head, she was at least mildly impressed that she was alive. She could feel her legs, for better or worse, and could wiggle her toes.

She hadn't broken her neck, which was good. Or snapped her spine in half. But how? She remembered falling, seeing the ground hundreds upon hundreds of feet below her. There had been fire—wait, wasn't that *before* she had jumped through a portal and fallen through the air?

What the hell was happening to her?

Sitting up, she rubbed her hands over her face and struggled to see straight. She felt dizzy at best, and nauseous at worst.

And entirely naked.

"What the *fuck*?"

But that was, somehow, not the most alarming thing she saw. Not only was she entirely naked, she was sitting at the bottom of a flaming crater. Shooting up to her feet, she stumbled and fell again, squeaking in surprise as her hand landed in the flames. Scrambling back, she waved the hand to try to stop it from burning, but it was all around her and suddenly she—

She realized it didn't hurt.

Okay, fine, she hurt, but not from the fire. She was sitting on her butt in the middle of a flaming crater, surrounded by crackling logs and debris, and...she wasn't burning. Reaching out, she tentatively stuck her fingers into a particularly large flame next to her.

The fire curled around her hand as if it wasn't there. She felt nothing. Her skin didn't blacken or char. "How...?"

"Can we get a move on, or do you plan on sitting there like an idiot all night?"

Jolting in surprise at the voice, she looked up. There, sitting at the edge of the crater at the top, was Merlin. The cat was flicking his tail from side to side, glaring at her like he always was. "Well?" His mouth didn't move. But it was clear where the voice was coming from. His voice was deep, raspy, and *mean*.

Boyfriend's betrayal. House on fire. Portal to somewhere. Falling to her death. Waking up in a flaming crater unable to burn. Naked. And now her cat could talk. Sure. Okay. Fine. Why not? Why the *hell* not. "Am I dead?"

"Not yet." He sighed. "Are you going to get up?"

"I— But—" She shook her head. "What's happening? How is any of this happening? Where am I? How am I not dead? How can you talk? Why am I naked?" She felt panic begin welling up in her chest, and she struggled to breathe. Shutting her eyes, she began counting backwards from ten. That was a trick her therapist taught her years ago, and it always seemed to help.

Hopefully, this time wouldn't be any different. But normally she wasn't dealing with so much insanity—maybe literal insanity—all at once.

The cat let out an exasperated groan. "You are such a child."

"Well *excuse me*, but I don't know what's going on!" She put her head in her hands and tried again to count back from ten.

"We can discuss things on the way out of these woods. Sitting there fretting will solve nothing. And if we do not leave quickly, we will both regret it."

Looking up, she arched an eyebrow at the cat. "Why?"

"Because then the Prince in Iron or his bastard knights will find you. And if that happens, you'll be dead. And if he doesn't kill you, what he'll do instead will be far worse." He bared his teeth—one fang and all. "Trust me."

"The Prince in Iron?"

"Must you ask stupid questions? Yes! That is what I said. Now *get up*, and let's *go*." The fur on Merlin's back rose as he stalked away from the edge of the crater and toward the line of trees.

Oh. Woods. Yeah. They were in the woods. Standing on wavering legs, she looked down at her naked self and decided it was pointless to try and cover up. She couldn't climb out of a hole and hide her boobs at the same time. And running around the woods pretending to be Eve from some dumb painting was going to cause more trouble than it was worth.

With her luck, she'd end up finding poison ivy.

But she took her long hair—which she usually kept in pony-tails or a braid, but her tie was gone with everything else—and brushed it down over her chest. It was a sad attempt. Espe-cially since she had no *pants*.

Wait.

Holding up a piece of her hair, she stared at it. Her hair was supposed to be brown. Not dark red. But there it was, in the light of the full moon—an unnatural shade of almost crimson. "What the—"

"*Now*, you child!"

"I'm being ordered around by my asshole cat. And my hair is the wrong color. And I'm in a hole. That's on fire." Climbing out of the crater was easier said than done. The sides didn't look steep, but the dirt and gravel was loose, and she slid back down more times than she'd care to admit. But finally—now scraped and dirty along with naked, wrong-color-haired, confused, and terrified—she made it out of the blast zone.

It was only when she looked back at it that she realized... Oh. She had been the one who had made that hole. When she had hit the ground. And she wasn't dead. Or on fire.

Sitting at the edge of the forest, looking just as angry as ever, was Merlin. With a sigh, she walked after him. "What hap-pened to my clothes?"

"They burned. Obviously." The cat began walking.

With nothing else to do, she followed him. "There's nothing obvious about any of what's happening." Wrapping her arms around herself, she frowned. "Where are we?"

"I think we landed in Ellainwood." He huffed. "Not that it means much to you."

She shook her head and didn't know what to say. What was she supposed to do? How was she supposed to handle this? Her mind just kept going round and round in circles over the same things.

Fire.

Falling.

Talking cat.

Naked.

No, she had to focus. She took a moment and tried to reconcile what had happened. She could process everything later once she was safe. Taking a deep breath again, she held it and slowly let it out. It was going to be okay. She wasn't hurt. She was just naked in a forest with her talking cat. No broken bones, no giant wounds, no burns. She could solve this. She could get through it.

She shivered. Damn it, it was chilly. It looked like it was autumn. The trees around her *looked* normal, but she wasn't going to trust anything as far as she could throw it until informed otherwise. They looked like birch trees, with their white and black strips of bark. Some of the branches were bare, but most had leaves on them in every shade of orange, red, and yellow. It was hard to see in the darkness, but the moon was bright overhead. If maybe just a little too large to be normal.

She could see bits and pieces of the starry sky beyond. None of them looked familiar to her. Just more proof that she wasn't in Kansas anymore. She sniffled.

"Don't you dare start crying." The cat sighed. "That's all I need."

"Why not? What've I got to lose?"

"Salt. Water." He glanced over his shoulder at her. "Dignity."

"What dignity?" She gestured down at herself.

"Good point." He looked back ahead on the path they were walking on. The dirt was at least fairly smooth beneath her feet, even if she did find a rock here or there in the worst way possible. "At least you admit how pathetic you are."

"It's nice to know you're as much of an asshole as I thought you were." She hopped a little to pull a pebble from where it had stuck onto her foot before continuing after him. "Have you always been able to talk?"

"Yes."

"Why haven't you said anything before?"

He snorted in laughter, but didn't reply.

Frowning, she tried a new tactic. "Where're we going?"

"There is a village not far from here. I saw it as we fell. Unless you want to starve or die from exposure to the elements, I thought it might be a good idea to steal some supplies before moving on." He said it as though it were all perfectly normal. That this was the kind of thing he did all the time.

"Are you going to tell me why I'm here? Or who you are? Or anything?" She glared at the animal. "Literally anything. And that there's some Iron Prince or some shit that's running around and might kill me."

"I am afraid I might overwhelm you and your delicate sensibilities."

"Look, just because I have panic attacks, doesn't mean—"

"Delicate. Sensibilities." He bounded ahead five or so feet before slowing back down to a walk. It made her jog to catch up with him.

What a jackass.

"So, what will you tell me? I'm not going to just follow you through the woods not knowing anything."

"And where else will you go? Hm? What else will you do? Sit about and starve? Perhaps be attacked by the direwolves that call this wood home? No. You're going to follow me because you don't have a choice." He paused. "Especially if you ever want to go back."

"Wait—" She jogged to catch up with him again. "Can you send me back?"

"No. Bringing us both here used up almost all my power. I am not strong enough as I am now. If you want to go back to Earth and that pathetic, flea-ridden farm you called 'home' with those equally pathetic humans who spawned you, you will have to help me regain my power. Until then, consider it mutually beneficial to follow along. You help me and I will help you."

"You set my house on fire."

"I did what I had to do. Tell me you aren't going to whine about that for the rest of the walk."

"I have plenty else to whine about."

"Fantastic." The cat swished his tail behind him from left to right.

"Can you at least tell me where we are?" She shivered and hugged herself a little tighter. She really wished she had clothes.

"I told you. The Ellainwood."

"Which has direwolves. Great. We've established that. But like, zoom out. Is this Earth?"

"No."

And he didn't give her anything more than that. She wanted

to kick him, but that was mean—he was still a cat, even if he was an asshole cat. "Want to tell me where we are then?"

"Only if you promise not to have one of your 'panic attacks.' We don't have time for you to weep into a paper bag."

Yeah, now she really wanted to kick him. Rolling her eyes, she let out a long breath. "I'll do my best. Where are we? Hell?"

"No. We are somewhere far worse than the hells." His fur on his back rose up again. "Somewhere far more dangerous, far more destructive. And far more chaotic."

Where could be worse than hell? Somewhere she'd probably never heard of, she supposed. "Does this super-nasty place have a name, or are you just going to keep being obtuse?"

He paused for a long moment as if debating not answering. Finally, just when she was going to ask again, he replied with all the joy of a lead balloon.

"Welcome to Avalon, Gwendolyn."

Three

Mordred stared down into the charred crater that must have been the site of the "meteor" impact. He knew it was not a natural phenomenon. He could sense it in the air around him.

This was the work of magic.

Brushing a strand of his long hair out of his face, he pulled the hood of his black cloak over his head to obscure his features. He did not wish either of the knights who had joined him to see his expression.

He did not want them to see his fear. Or his rage.

He knew this magic that simmered in the air—the feeling of it. This was the shard that had escaped not so long ago. It had returned...

And now he needed to find it. "Where is the nearest village?"

"There are four within walking distance. Do you think whatever caused this...got up and walked away?" Galahad asked, clearly confused.

"Yes. I do." *On four or two legs is what I still do not yet know.* "Mount up. We will have to search them one at a time."

His Knight in Silver, Lancelot, sighed heavily from where he stood by one tree, leaning against it with his arms folded over his plate armor. "Must we? It was a rock that fell from the stars. It happens."

"No. It was *not*." Mordred turned on his heel, heading back toward the direction of his dragon. His cloak whirled around him as he moved, the panels resembling jagged blades.

"You are being paranoid," Lancelot argued. "We should go b—"

Mordred stormed up to him and snapped his clawed gaunt-let around the other man's neck. He hefted the other man easily up off his feet, sliding him up the tree and pinning him there. Lancelot gagged and grabbed hold of his arm—but it did no good.

Mordred resisted the urge to dig his claws into the man's flesh and rip out his throat. "Do not speak to me of paranoia, knight." He grimaced. "Or perhaps you should. You know plenty of what inspires it in me." He dropped the man to the ground.

Lancelot kept his footing, to his credit, and coughed. "I meant no insult—"

Mordred did not bother replying. Yes. Lancelot very much *did*. But it was not new. And they had critical work to do.

Magic had escaped Avalon and now it had returned.

Whoever or whatever it was who had disappeared through that portal ten years ago had come back, and Mordred knew better than to think they would seek peace. No, the odds were good that their mystery escapee would seek revenge—the downfall of all that Mordred had worked to achieve. And what would inevitably follow . . . would be the ruination of all Avalon.

And it was up to him to stop it before it was too late.

Gwen knew Merlin had just told her not to have a panic attack. But it wasn't like it was something she could control. She felt dizzy for a moment before she made herself focus on breathing again.

"Wait. Wait—wait—wait. Avalon? *Avalon, Avalon?*" Maybe she really had died. Maybe this was just her fucked-up version of an afterlife, or her dying brain going through some random synapsis bullshit. "Like, King Arthur's Avalon?" She tried to focus on the legends. She had loved the stories growing up— the history that mixed with myth that had become the backbone of an entire civilization's culture.

"Don't be ridiculous. This place was here long before he reigned, and it's existed for thousands of years since he died." Merlin jogged ahead, as if trying to disassociate himself from her ignorance by sheer distance.

Okay. That was cool, right? *Don't focus on the scary shit. Focus on the cool shit. You're on Avalon. The real Avalon. That means they were more than just stories. You wanted an adventure—here it is!* "But. But he was real? King Arthur was real? And this—this is the same Avalon?" She cringed. "You're not the real Merlin, are you?"

"*No.*"

"Jesus, sorry." Frowning, she paused for a long second. He had been so emphatic about that, it had felt personal. She opted not to poke the angry cat's buttons as much as she could help it. "So...you need to get your power back and then you can send me home?"

"Yes."

"How do we get your power back?" Rubbing a hand over her face, she couldn't believe what she was saying. She was talking about restoring some wacky magical power to her asshole cat so that she could go home. From Avalon.

He laughed. It wasn't a pleasant sound. Come to think of

it, Merlin sounded like he smoked a case a day and chased it with rubbing alcohol. He sounded just as old and scruffy as he looked. "Let's focus on one thing at a time, shall we?"

"I guess. Can one of the things we focus on soon be getting me some clothes, though? This is *weird*."

"It isn't as strange in Avalon as you might think. But yes. I would appreciate it as well if you weren't nude. Namely, because it will be one less thing for you to whine about."

"Do you have to be so mean? None of this is my fault. You dragged me here."

"I dragged you here because I had no other choice." He glanced back at her again. "When I came to Earth all those years ago, I could either die or join our life forces together. I chose to live. Now, you and I are bound together until I can *fix* this."

"What do you mean, 'join our life forces together'? What did you do to me?" Fear ran down her spine at the notion.

"It means our lives are shared. If you grow sick, we share the illness. If I were to suffer a fatal wound, you would bear half of it." He sounded so annoyed. Either because of the situation they were in, or because he had to explain it to her like she was a kid. Her vote was both.

"So that's why you're so damn old and mangy and haven't died yet." If he was going to be a pain in the ass for her, she was going to be a pain in the ass for him.

"I am not—" He grunted. "Never mind. The fact remains. I need to regain my power. If I do that, you will go home, and I will finally be free of you."

"Gee, I'm so sorry I'm such an inconvenience." But there was a part of her that was so curious about being in *Avalon*. Magic was real! That would be incredible, if it weren't so terrifying.

She wondered how old Avalon really was. Or who lived there. Or why. Or who this Iron Prince was and why he was so scary.

Maybe once she got clothes and had a chance to figure things out, she might get the opportunity to talk to someone who was a bit nicer than Merlin.

Speaking of. The cat huffed. "Apology accepted."

She rolled her eyes. "And you won't tell me how we're supposed to get your power back?"

"No. Not yet. Not until I have a better sense of the situation. I have not been to Avalon in ten years. And while things rarely change here"—he snorted, as if it were some sort of inside reference—"who knows what has transpired in my absence. Also, the less you know, the better."

"Look, I know you think I'm pathetic, but—"

"You are."

She glared at him. "But don't you think I should know exactly what we're supposed to be doing here?"

"No."

"Why not?"

"Because if—no, perhaps it is a when—you are captured and tortured, the less you know, the better."

"*What?*" She stopped walking. "Torture? They're gonna torture me?" Waving her hands in front of her as if to shake them off, she tried to breathe. In. Out. In. Out.

"See? This is precisely why I'm not telling you anything." The cat sat down in the path and looked at her, the end of his tail flicking with his irritation.

"You—gee, I'm sorry I'm reacting to the idea of being *tortured*, you shitstain." She put her hands over her eyes and felt herself on the edge of panic again. Now wasn't the time. In. Out. In. Out. She focused on her breathing until she could hear the world around her again and not just her pounding heartbeat.

When she didn't feel like she was going to pass out, she dropped her hands and let out a long exhale.

"Better?" The cat set off again. "Try to keep up."

"Why do you have to be so mean to me?" She followed after him, feeling more and more like she was going to cry.

"You are slowing me down. I have waited long enough." He jumped over a tree that had fallen into the path.

She climbed over it, cringing at the reminder that, yep, she was still *really* naked. "Why today? Why now?"

"Those of us who tap into the magic of Avalon must stay within it to survive. I could not stay away for much longer without becoming trapped like this forever." He huffed. "I would rather die."

"You're not supposed to be a cat?"

"Of course not." He snarled.

"I don't know! You aren't telling me anything, so as far as I know you've always been a talking cat." She jogged a little to catch up with him. She really was done with walking. Especially in the cold.

"I have not always been a talking cat."

"Great. I'm glad we have that established." They walked in silence for what could have been half an hour. Or ten minutes. She honestly had no way of knowing. She couldn't resist the urge to needle the animal. If he was going to be a jerk, she was going to enjoy annoying him. "Are we there yet?"

Merlin groaned.

Smirking at how easy it was to give the cat a hard time, she started singing. "Ninety-nine bottles of beer on the wall, ninety-nine bottles of *beeer*."

The cat did nothing. She kept going. It seemed somewhere around sixty-five, he couldn't take any more.

"Stop! Please, stop."

Snickering, she stopped singing. "Only because you asked nicely." Suddenly, hope lit up her heart as she saw lights through the line of trees ahead. "Oh! Are we there?"

"It seems so." The cat grumbled something under his breath, but she didn't catch it. That was fine by her. She was going to have to get used to being insulted by the animal, it seemed. She could go without hearing every little detail.

As they reached the edge of the forest, Gwen let out a breath. "Whoa." She didn't know what she was expecting, but it wasn't that. What stood in front of her was a small village straight out of some kind of Renaissance fair. That was, if the designers had done a few lines of speed and the architects had decided that straight lines were for losers.

Everything looked kind of . . . twisted. Maybe the houses had all settled into their strange, haphazard shapes. The exterior walls were a mixture of all sorts of materials—wood, plaster, thatch; some looked made out of metal, even. Lanterns glowed atop wooden posts, illuminating the center roadway that was little more than two carriage ruts through the dirt. The light that came from the lanterns and the windows all seemed a little washed out, however. There appeared to be a mist in the air that dulled the colors. Or maybe it was just a trick of the eye.

The village was cute. Quaint, even. The lack of color made it all look a little dreary and forlorn, but it probably looked better in the daytime.

Merlin was already walking ahead toward the stone wall at the back of one of the properties nearby. She followed, suddenly now much more self-conscious about her nudity. But she couldn't help but smile as she saw there was a clothesline on the back of the house he was leading her toward—and on it were *clothes*.

Finally, clothes!

"I feel bad just stealing from people." She kept her voice quiet as she hopped over the rock wall.

"Then you can stay naked. I don't care," the cat whispered back. He jumped up onto a barrel by the back of the house. The windows were covered by leather from the inside. Some of the homes looked like they had glass windows, but most either just had open holes or were covered up with something or other.

Finding a pair of dark blue cotton britches and a linen shirt, she pulled them on and tied the waist off as best she could. They weren't the right size at all, but it was better than nothing. She let out a sigh of relief. Clothes. Check. "Now what?"

He jumped back off the barrel. "We should leave before we are discovered."

"Leave...the village?" She blinked. "But we just got here."

"Yes, obviously."

"Shouldn't we, like...ask for help? Or something?"

He snorted as if that were the dumbest idea he'd ever heard. "Do you remember my comment about torture? Because that's how—"

The back door to the home opened. "Hello? Who is out there?" It was a woman, maybe in her fifties. Short and round, with a wide face and curly hair. Gwen couldn't make much else out about her, as she was silhouetted from behind by the glow of a pale fire.

Gwen froze. She was right in full view. "Um—" She didn't know what to do. Or say. She had been caught red-handed. And to make matters worse, Merlin had *vanished*. Straight up disappeared into thin air. "I—I'm sorry, I didn't— I'm—uh— lost, and—"

"Oh!" The woman stepped out of the home. Her eyes were huge and dark. "Who are you? Why are you wearing my husband's clothes?"

"I—I woke up in the woods—" Not technically a lie. "And I'm sorry, I'll give them back, I just—I was naked and cold, and—" Also not a lie. "And I don't know where I am." Okay, she knew, just not in any meaningful way. "I'm so sorry, I don't—"

"You *poor* thing! Look at you, you're shaking. One of the s'lei must've gotten you." She huffed. "Those monsters are always stealing pretty girls, wiping their memories. I don't know why those damnable knights don't do their *one* job and hunt the rest of them down. Come in, dear. Come in." The woman waved her inside, glancing around as if worried someone else might have seen or she might not be alone. "Quickly now."

Suddenly, Gwen really didn't want to know what the s'lei were. Or what else they did besides steal pretty girls and wipe their memories. Gwen smiled nervously but accepted the woman's invitation. The inside of the small single-room home was warm and cozy, if just as tilted and wacky as the exterior.

The woman stuck her head outside to search around one more time and then shut the door and locked it. Wherever her husband was, he wasn't there.

"Sit by the fire, dear." The woman patted her shoulder. "My name is Valessa. Do you remember your name?"

"Gwen. I . . . I don't know if I was attacked or not." Kind of? Sort of? Her asshole cat-who-wasn't-a-cat burned down her home. She walked over to the fire and took one of the seats, glad to warm her hands. The fire still looked like the wrong color. It was too whitish yellow. Which was weird because the *other* fire from the crater had looked normally orangey-red.

She wasn't going to ask. Even if she was boiling over with

questions—which was pretty normal for her, to be fair—this situation was weird enough that she knew when to keep her mouth shut.

"The s'lei are bastards at best. Our neighbors down the street lost their son to them a few years ago. Poor boy never came back. Just magical enough to exist, not enough to be caught, those ugly bastards." Valessa poured some liquid into a wooden mug and handed it to her.

It looked like wine. "You—you really don't need to go through the trouble..."

"Quite all right. Trust me, dear. Wilhelm is on watch with the guard tonight. I can put some blankets down here by the fire. Once the morning comes, we'll talk to the mayor and see if he can help you." Valessa patted Gwen's shoulder again before settling down by the fire in the other chair. "Can you tell me what else you remember? It might give us some clues on where your home is."

Gwen had a choice. She could lie and play dumb. That was probably what Merlin would tell her to do. Pretend she had no memories at all until morning, then make a break for it.

But Merlin was also a jackass. A mean-spirited, cruel jackass.

Valessa seemed very nice and sweet.

What was the worst that could happen? Gwen should have known not to jinx it.

"Well, um...see, here's the thing...I'm not from here. I'm from Earth." She smiled nervously.

Valessa jumped to her feet, ran to the front door, and threw it open as if it was *her* home that was on fire. The older woman screamed as she ran out of the home. "Guards! *Guards!*"

Gwen groaned and put her head in her hands. "Oh, I'm so screwed."

FOUR

- · ҉ · ҈ ·

Gwen ran for the back door. Maybe she could still make it to the woods before they caught her.

She scrambled at the bar holding the back door shut, but in her panic, she kept slipping and couldn't wedge it out from the latch. Maybe she could still escape out the front. If she was lucky, she could run faster than them.

She made it about four steps out the front door when hands grabbed her by the upper arms. She yelped as she was dragged backwards. "Hey! Hey, let me go!"

She kicked at them, but there were two of them and one of her. And she wasn't exactly a fighter. Before she knew it, she was out in the street, being pushed ahead by the two men who had snagged her.

Taking one look at the first guy, she screamed and staggered back.

He had horns.

Legit, literal *horns*.

"Oooh, shit—ooh, this is too fucking weird," she said through a wail, as she threaded her hands into her hair and tried desperately to keep her lungs functional. Maybe Avalon wasn't going to be as cool as she had hoped. "Please, let me go, there's been a terrible mistake, and—"

"Calm down, miss." Someone spoke to her from her left.

Someone who wasn't the guards. She turned. This guy looked normal at first, except for the fact that he had deer legs.

Deer legs.

Deer guy was also wearing a fancy, grayish blue coat. He had a long thin goatee, and a pair of very small circular glasses perched on the end of his thin nose. "We mean you no harm. Valessa was just frightened. We have not had any visitors here in . . . hundreds of years."

Gwen was shaking from adrenaline, but it was slowly starting to simmer down. She was really sick of the nonsense she was being put through, but she had a feeling it was only just the beginning. "I—I—" She felt dizzy. She stopped talking before she passed out. *Breathe in, breathe out. Breathe in, breathe out.*

"I am the mayor of this town. My name is Grigory Lamor." He reached out a hand to her. His nails were black and kind of pointed.

Taking his hand, even though she was still trembling, she nodded once, weakly. "Gwen. Gwendolyn Wright."

"Good to meet you, Gwendolyn Wright from Earth. Please, come with me. I would like to offer you my hospitality until we can get to the bottom of what has transpired. Tell me, did you have anything to do with the fireball in the sky?"

"It wasn't my fault . . ."

He smiled. "I believe you. Well, you caused no damage. Come. I will have someone fetch you new clothes and I will see Wilhelm's clothes returned. Are you hungry, Miss Wright?" He began to walk down the street toward where she could see some larger homes clustered together. They looked more modern than the others—if only barely.

She fell in step beside him, noticing that the guards were still following them both. "You can just call me Gwen, and

I—I'm okay, really. Just scared. I don't know what's going on." Frowning at the guard with horns, she ducked her head. "Sorry I screamed."

The guard looked extremely worried, but she didn't know why. He didn't reply, but Grigory did. "Coming from Earth, I expect you have had little exposure to anything mystical." He clasped his hands behind his back.

"None. Magic isn't real where I'm from."

"It used to be." Grigory sighed darkly. He had long brown hair pulled back in a ponytail, tied with a white silk ribbon at the base of his neck. He would have looked like somebody from *Hamilton* if it weren't for the fact that he had deer legs.

"What happened?"

"That is a story for another night. Or at least best told over a glass or two of wine." He smiled at her again and waved a hand through the air as if to dismiss the thought. "It is neither here nor there. I am far more curious about you and how you came to join us." He approached the front door to what she assumed was his home. It was beautiful, if still full of weird angles. It had a wooden fence out front that she mistook for wrought iron because of its shapes, but upon getting closer, she realized it looked like it...grew that way. As if a series of trees and vines had just decided to *become* a fence.

Avalon was weird.

Maybe if she knew she was safe and wasn't going to be tortured by some terrible Iron Prince, or if she wasn't lost, confused, and out of her league, she'd be able to appreciate how beautiful it all was.

But she was too scared. She felt like at any second she was going to have a breakdown—if something didn't murder her first. She followed Grigory inside his home. The manor had what looked like hand-painted murals above the wainscoting. It depicted a colorful field in bloom with summer flowers, a glade, and an adorable village she could recognize as the one she was in.

Creatures of every kind imaginable were painted amongst the trees and buildings. Dragons, griffins, sea serpents, and more. Women with butterfly wings danced with centaurs. Creatures big and small seemed to frolic before her eyes.

Walking up to it, she marveled at the artwork. It was old and faded, and clearly had once been much brighter. But even still, it was gorgeous. "Whoa..." A sea monster in a lake that looked like it was playing with a woman on the shore caught her eye.

A billion questions ran through her head at once. Who had painted it? When? How old was it? Who were the people in the art, were they real? Did this place really have centaurs and sea monsters? Could she meet one? Did she *want* to meet one?

"A depiction of Avalon when it was whole. Before the prince..." Grigory trailed off. "Come, Miss Wright." He hummed. "Gwen. If you are truly a stranger to Avalon, there is much you should know." He brought her into a sitting room. Lavish—well, colonially lavish—furniture was arranged around a flickering, still-too-pale fire. A young woman in a servant's gown was setting down two glasses on a tray in the center of an ornate stone coffee table.

Grigory gestured for Gwen to sit and took a spot in the chair across from her. She sat down, but perched at the edge of the chair nervously, ready to run at the first loud sound.

"Tell me everything that happened. But first, please." He picked up a glass and offered it to her. "To calm your nerves."

That sounded like a good plan. She took a sip from the glass. It wasn't a harsh flavor, though it tasted a little odd. Maybe it was just an Avalon thing, that wine here tasted different than what she remembered from home. She took another sip. She figured with everything that had happened, she was allowed a glass of wine. It wasn't like she was planning on getting smashed. "Thanks."

"Of course." Grigory sat back. He had sharp features that were accented by the light of the fire and cast stark, flickering shadows.

"Is the fire always that color?"

"Hm?" He glanced at the flame, and sadness creased the corner of his eyes. "You know, I hardly even notice anymore. No, Gwen. The fire should not be that color. Avalon is only a shadow of its former self. And so are we all, I am afraid." He took a sip of his own glass of wine.

"What do you mean?"

"Do you know anything of this isle and its history?"

"I saw *The Sword in the Stone* when I was a kid, and kind of got obsessed with it, so I guess I know all the legends, but something tells me it's really different than the Disney flick"—she stopped at his blank stare—"sorry, Earth thing. Movies. Moving pictures. Whatever." Now she felt stupid. "I know about King Arthur, and Excalibur, and Merlin. Lady of the Lake, magic and faeries. But all the stories are pretty conflicted."

"I see." He chuckled. "So you know nothing true about Avalon." When he was smiling, he didn't look nearly so severe. She could almost forget the fact that he was so clearly inhuman.

"Only the myths and the legends." She took another sip of the wine. "Sorry."

"It is not your fault. Believe me. It is not by your hand that Avalon has been cut off from the worlds around us." Grigory's expression grew grim as he stared into the fire. "Avalon is unwell. We suffer a blight set upon us by the Prince in Iron. We languish like this, broken and devoid of the magic that should sustain us."

She didn't know what to say to that. So she fidgeted with the glass. "That . . . sounds terrible."

"It is. He was not without his reasons, I suppose. But at what cost?" Grigory tapped his black, pointed fingernails on the wood trim of his chair. "He has captured all the magic—stripping it from those of us who could tap into the wellspring of our gifts. And those who were too tightly wound to the essence of our world suffered a worse fate."

"Death?"

He huffed. "They likely wish for such mercy. No. They are imprisoned. And have been for three hundred years."

Cringing, she stared down into her wine. "That's just awful."

"No one has come or gone from Avalon in all those years. The way was closed. That is why poor Valessa was so frightened when you said you came from Earth." He curled the fingers of his other hand beneath his chin and watched her curiously over the rim of his circular glasses. "Tell me, how did this all come to pass?"

She had another choice in front of her. Tell Grigory the whole story, or . . . leave out some parts. Namely, the thing with Merlin. She could almost hear the cat reaming her a new one for having gotten into this much trouble already.

Gwen wasn't going to make the same mistake twice in less than twenty minutes. "My house caught fire. I ran upstairs, and there was just a . . . portal thingy. I could either go through the hole, or burn to death, so I jumped through the hole. I was falling. I woke up in a crater."

"*You* were the meteor." His eyes went a little wide for a moment. "By the Ancients. Continue, please."

She sipped the wine. It was helping her relax. At least there were some small favors. "I woke up and...I was naked, and I just found a path and started walking. I wound up at Valessa's house, and you know what happens from there."

"That's all?" He pondered her curiously for a moment, as if trying to find her lie.

She nodded and hoped her ears weren't turning red. "Oh. My hair wasn't always this color." She picked up the end of one of her long wavy curls. She could see the crimson color in more detail now, even in the faded light of the fire.

"Was there fire in the crater when you landed?" He arched a thin eyebrow.

"Yeah."

"It did not burn you, did it?" He sipped his own glass of wine. "You can tell me the truth."

Frowning, she let out a sigh. He already guessed it anyway, so there was no point in hiding it. "No. The fire didn't burn me."

"Can you do me a favor? Reach your hand into the flame, if you would. I wish to see this for myself, if you do not mind." He gestured to the fireplace.

"I—um—"

"Withdraw the instant you feel any discomfort or pain, of course."

Taking in a deep breath, she held it, and let it all out in a rush. "Okay, sure. Whatever." Standing, she walked to the fireplace and, crouching down, reached her hand out toward the fire.

It felt warm, but not uncomfortably so. As she moved her fingers closer, she waited for the burning to start. But it never did. She placed her hand atop one of the logs. It felt like the temperature of a hot bath. Kind of pleasant, actually.

Grigory muttered something that wasn't English. Welsh, maybe? Did Avalon have its own languages? Now she wanted to know. But she couldn't spare the time to ask, as whatever Grigory said didn't sound happy either. In fact, he sounded *extremely* upset. Straightening up, she brushed her hands off together and saw him staring at her with a mixture of awe and maybe just a bit of fear.

"I'm sorry. I don't...I don't know why, or how, or what this means."

"It means you should sit, my dear girl. We have much to discuss."

She saw no harm in that, she supposed. Picking up her glass, she sat back down and took another drink of it. "I really am sorry. Is this fixable? Whatever 'this' is?"

"I am not an expert in such things. We may need to take you to someone who is. Would you be willing to do that?" Grigory placed his empty wine glass down on the table in front of him. "It would be a hard journey."

"Great. A quest." She snickered. "I'm going on a *quest*." She loved those kinds of video games. Hey, hadn't she just been wishing her life was more interesting? Here she was. She finished her glass of wine, and refused a second as she put the glass down in front of her. "Thank you for helping me."

His expression turned sad and regretful. "You seem like a kind soul. I am sorry for all that has transpired until now. And I am even more sorry for all that will follow after this."

She shrugged. "It's not your fault." No, it wasn't *his* fault. It was her stupid asshole cat's fault. The cat that wasn't a cat, whose name wasn't even Merlin. She wondered what his real name was, actually. She hadn't had the chance to ask him. And she also had no clue where the hell he had gotten off to.

"I fear that some portion of it will be."

"What do you—" She blinked. The room looked a little out of focus. That was odd. Rubbing her eyes, she blinked again. No, that only seemed to make it worse. The fire was suddenly too bright.

She didn't feel so good. "What did you . . . the wine?"

"I am very sorry, Miss Wright. But the prince will have seen the meteor, the same as us. He will be on his way. I cannot let him think that I am harboring a fugitive."

"I'm not—I didn't do anything—" She tried to get to her feet, but only successfully slumped to the ground. Her legs were as good as jelly. Something told her she wasn't going on a quest. "I . . ."

"But you have committed a grievous sin, young one. Even if you did not intend to. Please forgive my deception—I needed to buy some time while it took effect."

Gwen's eyes slipped shut of their own accord.

"You are an elemental. I am afraid you are bound for the Crystal."

Gwen couldn't find the strength to respond as everything went dark.

FIVE

Gwen was getting sick of waking up in weird situations. And in pain. She groaned. Her arms *hurt*. Like, a lot. Like a whole lot. It took her a hot second to realize why. She was hanging from them.

Whelp. That'd do it.

Pushing up onto her feet, she whined at the burn in her shoulders. She had shackles—literal metal shackles—around her wrists. They were attached to chains that ran over her head to a rusted iron post that was shoved deep into the ground behind her.

Yanking on her wrists, she instantly regretted it. Her shoulders twitched and spasmed in protest. They weren't so happy about the extra strain. "Ow, ow, *ow*—" She tried to wriggle her hands out, but the damn things were tight enough that her fingers were tingly. There wouldn't be any squirming out of them without breaking all the bones in her hands first.

Which might be on the table.

"Let me go!" She decided to try shouting. "Help! Somebody help!"

There were people gathered around nearby. She could see them at the edges of the center of the town where the post was stuck. Where she was stuck.

"I am sorry, Miss Wright." It was Grigory. He was walking

over, flanked by the same two guards she had met before. "This is the only way. The prince will be here soon."

"What—why? What is happening? What're you going to do to me?" Now she really *was* going to have a panic attack. "I didn't do anything!"

"You do not deserve this, and you have my sincerest apologies. But I must protect my people. Surely, you understand that." He clasped his hands behind his back. "The prince's dragons were sighted on the horizon. You will not be here for long."

"That's not a good thing!" She kicked at the post and swore. Right. She didn't have shoes on. "Let me go. Please, let me go—I'll leave. I'll run into the woods. I won't be a problem, just *please*, let me go."

"I cannot. If he discovered I had a hand in your escape, my life would be forfeit. And those of everyone under my care. Forgive me, Miss Wright." He bowed his head to her and walked away again, leaving her there alone. In the middle of a field. Chained to a metal post.

"This *sucks!*" She flailed again. Maybe she'd get lucky. Maybe the prince wouldn't be so bad. Maybe he'd listen to reason, and—

The sound of metal creaking filled the air. On a trip to the East Coast for vacation, her dad brought her onto an old World War Two battleship. She distinctly remembered the old iron ship groaning as it shifted in the waves, even just tied to the docks as it was.

This sounded exactly like that.

Like something enormous and metal moving in ways that metal shouldn't.

When something crashed down to the ground in front of her, Gwen screamed at the top of her lungs.

She screamed.

And burst into flames.

"Shit-shit-shit-*shit!*"

Now she was also screaming because she was on fire.

It only got worse when she saw what landed in front of her. The damn thing was the size of two or three school buses stuck together. It took her a few seconds to focus on it, considering everything else that was happening.

It was a dragon wearing twisted, warped, and bizarre armor.

No. It wasn't a dragon wearing armor—it was a dragon *made out of armor.*

It was hollow on the inside, with gaping exposed "ribs" made out of panels of plate armor that looked more like they were made from overgrown weeds painted iron than hammered out of flat shapes. It towered above her, its eyes glowing a strange, eerie white that seemed to shimmer with color like an opal or an oil slick. In its chest was a crystal of the same color, suspended where its heart should have been by chains that kept it tethered to the monster's ribs.

It stepped closer to her, its limbs seemingly being puppeteered by the rest of it, as tendrils of metal oozed and stretched to yank it along, its movements halting, jerky, and... well, terrifying.

At some point, Gwen had lost the ability to scream, instead staring up at the thing and waiting for it to open its enormous, jagged-toothed maw and tear her to shreds.

The sight of the thing had also made her forget, however temporarily, that she was *on fucking fire.*

She had wanted to see a dragon.

Now she really wished she hadn't had that thought.

Because she was probably going to get to see the inside of a dragon in the worst way possible. Hollow as it was, it was the ride there via its sharp and pointy teeth that she was worried about. The dragon peered down at her with its glowing eyes, the creak and groan of metal growing louder as it approached.

She was going to die.

She was going to die.

She was going to die.

Her panic attack was now in full *go mode*, her breathing shallow and rapid as she stared up at the thing, waiting for it to open its mouth and rip her apart.

It dropped down to its elbows with a resounding *thud*. It was only then she noticed that the thing had a rider. A man was climbing off the dragon's back. Gwen couldn't decide if this made the situation better or worse. She could barely see the figure in the darkness. But as he stepped closer, into the glow of her fire, she decided it was definitely worse.

This had to be the Prince in Iron. It *had* to be. There was no possible way it wasn't.

The man was huge. Towering in height and broad-shouldered, he looked like something out of a nightmare. He wore elaborate, ornate, and chaotic plate armor that seemed to be made of the same strangely organic rusted metal as the dragon. Over which, he had a long cape cut into pointed sections that reminded her of feathers, or maybe blades.

He wore a black hood that obscured most of his face. All she could see of his features were a few locks of hair that looked gray—not white, but literally *gray* in the dim light.

His armor clanked as he walked up to her. As he drew closer, she wished she could run and hide. She wished she could do anything. But the man was heading straight for her, and she was chained to a post.

And also on fire.

It wasn't like she was blending in anytime soon.

The man must have been pushing seven feet and was built like a professional wrestler. Or at least, she assumed so with how wide he was, even accounting for the armor. He stopped a few feet in front of her, tilting his head to the side slightly as if studying her.

Even in the flickering light from the fire that burned all over her, as if she was actually *made* of it, she couldn't see much of his face. Just sharp shadows and a flash of pale skin.

The man was wearing armored gauntlets, the fingertips ending in claws that looked almost like rusted knives. The points were all sharp and impossibly thin, but the blades themselves were jagged and missing chunks as if they had corroded that way.

The man had knives for hands.

Knives. For. Hands.

Gwen was wondering if death-by-dragon wasn't the better option.

Her stomach was twisted up in knots. She couldn't breathe. She felt like she was going to puke. There was a dragon. She was on fire. So she did the only logical thing—she started blabbering. "I'm sorry I didn't mean to. I shouldn't be here, but I didn't have a choice and now I'm on fire and I don't want to die and I'm so very sorry and I don't want to die, and I don't know why I'm on fire, but now I can't stop and—"

Something very sharp and pointed touched the end of her nose, breaking off her words as quick as a light switch. The man had lifted up one of his gauntleted hands and placed the end of his pointer finger there.

"Remember to breathe now and then." His voice was deep and smooth. "You may find it helpful."

Shudderingly, she filled her lungs, listening to his advice without really meaning to. Her head instantly felt a little less foggy. But not by much. "Please, I—I don't want to die." She was crying. When had that started? She supposed it didn't matter. When something hissed on the ground by her feet, she glanced down to see the tears that fell from her hit the dirt as tiny black puddles of lava.

She was crying *lava*. Fear gripped her like an iron vise. No pun intended. "What's happening to me? I don't understand."

The backs of those terrible pointed claws stroked over her cheek before they uncurled and his metal-covered palm cupped her chin. He watched her as if she were some kind of fascinating anomaly. "From where do you hail, firefly?" God, that voice of his. It was like velvet. It shouldn't calm her down, but it did. It felt like a warm blanket on a cold night. Not that she needed one right now, because she was *still on fire!*

Wait. Did he just call her firefly? Everything was happening too fast. It was all too much. She wanted to crawl into a hole and have everyone leave her alone for a second.

He seemed patient in waiting for her answer at least.

She sniffled. There wasn't any point in lying. Grigory was going to tell him anyway, she was certain. "Earth..."

He let out a deep sigh. "I see. And how is it that you have come to be chained to a post?"

"The—the mayor tricked me. Drugged my wine." She felt so damn small standing in front of him. Never mind the fact that she was—*oh damn it all*. She was naked again. The clothes must have burned up when she caught on fire.

Glancing down at herself again, Gwen realized that she wasn't just on fire now, she was made out of fire. She really wished she could take the time to appreciate that fact, but there was a giant spooky guy standing in front of her who had knives for hands and an enormous rusty dragon.

Both of which were probably going to kill her.

And the man still had his palm resting against her cheek.

Dropping her head, she gave up. "Please just make it quick..." Her voice sounded as small as she felt.

When he placed the back of one of his claws beneath her chin and lifted her head back up to look at him, she wasn't sure what to do but go along with it. His touch was gentle, even if it was strange.

"What is your name, firefly?"

"Gw—Gwendolyn Wright. But j—just Gwen, is fine—" Now she was stammering all over herself like a total idiot. She swallowed, and tried to follow his earlier advice. Breathe. Just breathe.

"Well met, Gwendolyn Wright." He lowered his hand. "I am Mordred, the Prince in Iron. And I—" Without warning, he flicked his arm up to his side, the cape that was made of sections of fabric suddenly stiffening and turning to metal in a split second, almost like a wing. He was using it to shield them. She heard something *tink* off the outside surface. He lowered his hand, the panels returning to fabric and falling to his side. "Treacherous imbeciles," he said through a snarl.

It took her literally that long to realize Mordred wasn't alone. She hadn't dared take her eyes off him or his enormous dragon. But there were two other dragons gathered farther away—one made of gold and one made of silver that had patinated a deep gray in sections.

A man in golden armor was already stalking toward a man in tattered linen clothes, barely visible in the darkness. The villager who was being approached by the knight had a bow held in his hands. The villager dropped it to the ground as he turned and ran away in terror. He must have shot an arrow at them. But that made no sense. Why would he shoot at someone wearing full armor?

Oh.

He hadn't been shooting at the prince. He must have been shooting at *her*.

The prince lifted his arm and swept wide with it, gesturing strangely. She didn't realize what he was doing until a sword shimmered out of the air and appeared floating next to him—floating in midair.

The blade was almost as long as she was tall. It was just as twisted and bizarre as the rest of his armor, looking more like it came out of a fever dream than reality. He flicked his wrist, and she watched as the blade shot through the air.

It whipped past the man in the gold armor, straight for the man holding the bow. The man was still running away, but he wasn't as fast as the flying sword. It punched straight through his rib cage.

Gwen looked away, a choked noise escaping her. She was glad the man was far enough away that she didn't hear much of the impact. Shutting her eyes tight, she felt more tears run down her cheeks and heard the drops of lava hiss into the dirt.

Magic. Flying swords. Dragons. Mordred of King Arthur fame. Men in strange armor. She was made of flame. But a man just died like it was nothing.

Avalon was strange and interesting—but she was quickly realizing it was just as equally deadly.

"Bring me the mayor."

She decided very quickly she didn't like the prince's tone of voice when he was angry. What was once velvet and soothing was now hard and cold. It made her shiver. She knew her life was forfeit now. Whatever happened, she had no control over it. Even if she was on fire.

When she felt brave enough to look, she saw the man in gold—who might as well have been a streetlamp wearing armor for how tall and thin he was—was now ushering Grigory forward toward the prince.

Grigory looked as terrified as she was. He bowed low at the waist. "M—my liege, my prince—I am Grigory Lamor, mayor of this—"

"I do not care." The Prince in Iron stepped toward the cowering mayor. "Explain."

"I—I apologize for the rash actions of the man you have executed for his treasonous—"

"Not him." The prince snapped a gauntleted hand around Grigory's throat and dragged him closer. *"Her."*

"I—I do not know much more than—than you do, my liege. She confesses to be the source of the meteor. It was she who fell to Avalon from above. She is an elemental, somehow escaped from—"

"I can see that."

Grigory looked like he was going to be sick. "—I took the liberty to sedate her in order to—"

"Sedate her how?"

"Through—through poisoned wine, I—" Grigory gagged as the prince tightened his grasp on his throat. He grabbed at the metal gauntlet, trying to pull it off him, but it was useless.

"We have strict laws of hospitality in Avalon, Lamor. It is some of the only meager scraps of decency we might boast on this destitute isle. You took her in under the auspices of providing shelter to a frightened young woman. You betrayed this covenant of trust."

"But—but she—" Grigory coughed, his eyes growing wide as saucers. "I did not mean to break the laws, I was only thinking of—"

The prince was not having any of it. "If she cannot trust you, how am I to trust you? Hm?"

When the prince grabbed Grigory's head with his other hand, Gwen had the presence of mind to look away. But the sound of crunching bone was worse than witnessing the details, and she couldn't help but see what had happened.

The prince dropped Grigory's crumpled body to the ground. His head was on *backwards*. The Prince in Iron must have snapped the man's neck so hard it swiveled all the way around.

Gwen wailed and started yanking on the chains harder, desperately trying to free herself. It was pointless. But her panic didn't know that.

The prince walked back to her, wiping the claws of his armor off on his cape. "Where were we?"

"I don't want to die, I don't want to die!"

"Ah, yes. That was where we left off. Thank you for reminding me." He stopped in front of her again, only a foot away from her. She could smell the tinge of metal. He sounded vaguely amused—as if he hadn't just snapped a man's neck.

He reached out a hand, trailing his claws through her hair. When he brought a strand of it forward, it was as though it were also made entirely of fire. It flowed like usual, but fire licked up from it like she was a bonfire.

"Would you kindly extinguish yourself?"

She blinked up at him. "I—what?"

"Extinguish yourself." He let go of the lock of her hair. "Kindly."

"I—I can't." She was shaking again. She really didn't want to have her head ripped off. Or to have a sword fly through her rib cage.

He tilted his head slightly to the side. "Oh?"

"I—I don't know how, and I know it's probably not important, but I'm also naked again, and I—" There she went, babbling again. "And I know you could probably kill me anyway, so it doesn't matter if I'm on fire or not, but I figure it doesn't hurt to try to—"

He chuckled. "Calm yourself. I do not plan to kill you."

"I don't wanna go into the Crystal either..." She cringed.

"Ah. The mayor told you of that, I see."

"Kinda?"

"Kine-dah." He repeated the word as if it was foreign to him. When he clearly figured it out a second later, he grunted. He pulled the hood back from his face.

Gwen felt the breath get pushed straight out of her lungs. What little air she had, anyway.

His long hair was in fact the color of iron—gray, but not glossy enough to be silver. His features were strong and sharp, with a jaw that looked like he had been carved out of stone. But it was his eyes that struck her. They were the color of rust—every shade of orange, yellow, and red, mixed with a little brown and bluish gray. Like the trees in the forest. And even as she watched, the markings shifted and changed, as if his eyes were made of molten, rusted metal.

He was gorgeous.

There wasn't any way she could deny it.

Even if he had just twisted a man's head around with his bare hands after killing a dude with a giant, floating sword.

She stared at him in awe, forgetting her terror for a moment, as she tried to wrap her head around what was happening.

At least if he's going to kill me, he's super hot.

He smirked, as if knowing exactly what was going on in her head. She didn't know if she could blush while she was on fire, but damn it if she wasn't trying.

"Lady Gwendolyn, I am going to remove your chains. If you run, I will catch you. Do you understand?" His tone left no room for argument. The man was clearly used to being in charge.

She had no clue where she'd go, even if she tried. And she was kind of a lit torch. She wouldn't exactly blend into the woods very well. *I'd probably burn it all down.* "Why did you kill those men?"

"The mayor betrayed a sacred law of Avalon. And the other fool was making an attempt on your life." The prince arched an eyebrow. "Are you trying to defend their choices?"

"I'm saying that maybe you didn't have to kill them." She shouldn't be talking back to the man. But she was probably dead, anyway—even if he did say he didn't plan on killing her. She didn't exactly trust him. "It seems harsh."

"Luckily, that is for me to decide. Not you." He reached over her head. Looking up, she watched as he touched the chains that held her to the post. The metal . . . dissolved. Just turned to liquid goo that began to swirl in the air around his hand.

Rubbing her wrists, she took a second to marvel at the fact that she was literally made of fire. It was so bizarre to see. She kept her back to the iron post, unsure of what to do now that she was free. He had warned her not to run.

She was going to do the smart thing and listen to somebody for once.

The prince began to work the iron that floated in the air around him like a sculptor crafting clay. It wasn't hard to forget about all the strangeness with how beautiful it was to watch. Little by little, she could see what he was crafting. It was a necklace made of wide panels of metal. It almost looked like a—

A collar.

Complete with a little circle at the front where someone could attach a chain.

She stared at him flatly. "You've got to be kidding me."

He huffed a single laugh. "Extinguish yourself, and I will not have to make you wear this."

"But I don't know *how.*"

"Therefore, this is required." He was smiling at her, in that faint way someone smiled at someone being incredibly silly. It wasn't a cruel expression. It just made her feel stupid. Well, more stupid than she already did. She felt pretty damn dumb at the moment, all things considered.

"Could it be a little less…I don't know, creepy?" She wrinkled her nose.

"Creepy."

"Collar-y." Unless he really was considering her his slave. The image left her weirdly conflicted. It was both horrifying and…uh…well, wow. That was something she didn't know about herself.

I'm learning all sorts of new things in Avalon.

"Hm. Very well." He studied his creation. At his gesturing, the iron collar shifted and changed until it could be mistaken for a very thick necklace with a hard V in the front. While the pieces were broad, the detail was beautiful and delicate. It was a stunning work of art.

He brought her back to the moment. "Does this better suit your sensibilities?"

She nodded silently. She didn't know what it was supposed to do, really, but it at least didn't look like he was about to slap a leash on her. "Thanks." Didn't hurt to be polite.

He brushed her hair back away from her shoulders and stepped in closer to her. The touch of his metal claws sent a shiver down her spine. She should be terrified of him. She shouldn't be reflexively stepping closer as he carefully clasped the iron behind her neck. The points of his fingertips grazed over her shoulders as he let the weight of it settle onto her. It was smooth and cold.

"Perfect," he murmured.

Suddenly, the fire that was burning all around her...just snuffed out. She was normal again. She squeaked and quickly covered herself.

"Iron is the foil to all the magic of the world. With it, one can control—and contain—the wild energy of this isle," he quietly explained. He reached out again, and she flinched as he gathered up a lock of her hair. She saw it had changed colors again—now it was a series of oranges, yellows, and reds—like fire. Almost like the color of his eyes. "To an extent. While a skilled elemental such as myself could find a way around the limiting nature of the necklace you wear, I doubt you will."

Hot *and* egotistical. Great.

The knight in the silver armor quickly approached and pulled a cloak off his shoulders. It was made of thick, white fur. He handed it to the prince, who draped it around Gwen's shoulders, covering her nudity. His arms lingered there for a moment, and she wondered for a second if he was going to pull her close.

She wondered if she'd mind. "Thanks…" Well, there was that problem solved at least. But she felt like this was going to get worse before it got better.

"You are welcome. Now, if you will." He gestured toward his enormous metal dragon, who was still sitting on the ground like an enormous loafing cat.

"Wait. What? You want me to ride *that?*"

"Do you want to walk?" He smirked. "You will be safe."

"Uh-huh. Sure. Says the guy who just killed two people. And who owns a giant stabby dragon. And who has knives for hands."

He laughed. One of his hands settled on her shoulder, fingers curled around the back of her neck. "I can be a bit intimidating, I admit."

"Understatement of the year," she muttered under her breath. "Where are you taking me?"

"To my home." Simple question, simple answer. He gestured wide with his other arm toward the big rusty metal dragon.

She started walking at his insistence, and tried not to get too distracted by the sensation of his hand on her mid-back, guiding her. "This might be a stupid question. Am I your prisoner?"

He smiled. It wasn't an unpleasant expression, perhaps even a little bit pitying of her situation. "Yes."

That wasn't anything to laugh about. She glanced back at the body of Grigory on the ground, and winced. "I really wish you hadn't killed him."

"I have killed thousands in my day. And I will kill thousands more. Such is the way of Avalon. Now…please." He gestured to the dragon. She could see a saddle way up on its back. She pulled the cloak tighter around herself and hesitated.

The dragon tilted its head around to look at her. Its head alone was the size of a damn car. It peered at her with those strange, glowing, eerie white eyes.

"Um. Hi. Hello, Mr. Dragon. N—nice to meet you."

It made a strange clicking sound, like metal tapping against metal.

"He says hello. And he is impatient to go home. As am I." The prince gestured at the dragon. "Do you need assistance?"

"N—no. I think I—I think I can do it." She chewed her lip, and started climbing up the side of the monster. It was easier said than done, but luckily the dragon was covered in jagged, pointy bits. It gave her things to hold on to. It was made even more difficult by the cloak she was wearing, which she was definitely prioritizing over a speedy climb. She reached the saddle and sat there, nervously waiting.

Now what?

Then she realized what, and her cheeks went warm. She'd ridden enough horses to know what was about to happen. *Ah, shit.*

The prince climbed up after her, much more quickly and smoothly than she had. He sat behind her and, before she could even process what was happening, she found herself between his knees, his arm wrapped firmly around her.

It was like being held by a truck. She went rigid, and felt her breathing start to grow fast and shallow again.

"Calm yourself, firefly." He held her firmly to his chest. It felt reassuring, even if he was the reason she was about to have a panic attack. "Lest you pass out."

"Probably too late for that, thanks for—" She broke off in a scream as the dragon stood.

She kept screaming as the dragon spread its wings and jumped into the air.

The last thing she remembered was the prince laughing behind her.

SIX

Mordred held the unconscious young woman in his arms as they flew back to his keep. It was likely for the best. Avalon was not what it used to be in days gone by. While flying through the sky at night had once treated the viewer to an array of lights and wonders, now the world beneath him was bleak and dark.

But there was no other choice.

What a curious little marvel he held to his chest, ensuring she did not fall from his dragon as they returned home. She nestled so neatly into him, her cheek resting against his breastplate. She was a welcome distraction.

At least her appearance had finally solved the mystery of where that errant magic had escaped to ten years prior. Now, he simply wanted to know *how* and, perhaps more importantly, *why* it had chosen her. And why it had chosen to return here and drag the poor young woman along with it.

There was a spark of pity in him for her. She was frightened beyond her wits. When the gates were open between the worlds, he had seen more than one human lose their composure over the monsters and wonders that Avalon had to offer. It was not wholly unexpected.

But those were days long dead and gone. No one had come to Avalon in hundreds of years—he had seen to it personally.

Not until this one. Why? How? And why *her*? What an adorable little creature she was at least, he had to admit.

She had a spark to her, buried beneath the terror, that he had seen briefly come to the surface. He found himself wishing to see more of it. Her eyes had been the size of saucers as she had stared at him in abject terror. He wondered what color her eyes had been before they turned a fiery ember. That was, when they were not actually made of flame.

What a sight that had been. A beautiful young woman, chained like a sacrifice to some ancient god, and entirely ablaze with a power that she could not control, nor understand. And despite it all, she had the gall to scold him for executing two fools who had sought to do her harm and to reprimand him for his choice of shackle for her.

Gwendolyn Wright from Earth. An elemental of fire. An escapee by no fault of her own. He should take her to the Crystal and put her with the others. But...

He looked down at her. He could feel the warmth of her through his armor that was not truly armor at all. Even bundled up in Lancelot's cloak, she was naked beneath and he worried that she might catch a cold. He pulled his cape around them both, hoping to further insulate her from the wind. Creatures of fire could catch such a chill sometimes.

He let out a sigh. He could not help himself. Lifting a hand, he traced the back of one of his claws over her cheek.

Innocent. Naive. *Terrified.* He smirked. All offered a thrill in their own right. He would not claim that he did not enjoy his intimidating appearance. It was always amusing to see someone gaze at him for the first time in a mix of awe and fear.

But he had also noticed fascination in those red eyes of hers.

There was a mystery to be solved.

If there was treachery involved—if any of his knights or subjects had been to blame for the escape of the magic and now its return—he had to know. Or, even worse, whatever power had escaped from the Crystal had chosen this young woman for its own means. It was clear there was a sentient force behind it. It was clear to him now that it was not merely random energy that had disappeared. But who was it? Who was inspiring all this?

Their goal was obvious—to destroy him and the Crystal. To free those who must, at all costs, remain imprisoned. He could not fully stop them until he knew who they were. She must know something of how she came to Avalon or who was behind it.

No, he would not put her in the Crystal until the player moving their pieces upon the board made themselves known. Mordred could not fight an enemy he did not recognize.

For now, he would keep her safe until the enemy had revealed himself and his path forward was clear.

He could not say he was not a little bit relieved. She would not have been the first soul to go into the Crystal that he regretted condemning to an eternity in confinement. But he could avoid it this time for a short while.

He tucked a strand of her hair carefully behind her ear. It was such a beautiful array of colors. He assumed it would change again, along with the rest of her form. Elementals were bound to change their shape.

An errant thought entered his mind, and he pushed it away as quickly as it had come.

No.

He would not let himself hope.

He would *not* allow it.

He did not know Gwendolyn Wright. She could be a spy. He could not trust her. He could *not* allow himself to believe that he...

No.

Grimacing, he stared into the cold wind and let the iciness of it force his thoughts elsewhere. Gwendolyn Wright would be an amusing distraction and a clue to a mystery he had puzzled over for a decade. That was all.

I'm so sick of this shit.

Gwen woke up slowly with a huff. She was lying on something soft, and buried underneath what felt like heavy blankets. The last thing she remembered was a giant dragon taking off with her on it. She screamed. A whole lot. Again. And blacked out.

Again.

She really hated her panic attacks. At least the stupid necklace that the prince had put on her was keeping her from *bursting into flames.* She had so many questions. How much of the legend of Arthur was real? Which version was real? Was he really *the* Mordred?

Don't be an idiot. He can't be the same Mordred. He'd be over a thousand years old, and super dead. He's probably just named after Mordred.

A billion questions she had nobody to ask. This was why she had always loved history and literature. It always blended together in weird and fascinating ways. For now, she was warm and cozy. She was sore and exhausted. She had no idea how long it had been since Merlin had opened that hole into Avalon, but it had felt like weeks. As far as she knew, it was only a few hours.

She buried herself deeper in the warmth and shut her eyes, trying to process everything that had happened and come up with a plan. She had to *do* something. Besides kick Merlin across the room for having gotten her into this mess.

"Congratulations, you've screwed everything up."

Speaking of...

Lifting her head, she squinted. Sitting in the corner of a jail cell was the cat in question.

Wait.

She sat up so quickly her head spun and for a second she thought she might be sick. Groaning, she leaned against the wall and tried to take stock of where she was.

Her parents had taken her to Disney on a trip when she was young. She had gone on the *Pirates of the Caribbean* ride and seen the animatronic prisoners inside a janky, ancient-looking jail. And now she found herself in one.

Iron bars separated her from a hallway and the cell next to her. She was in the corner of a small room. Across from her were two more cells and a guard's station that sat empty. Candles burned in sconces bolted onto the walls, and there wasn't a window to be seen. There was only one doorway in or out of the space.

She was alone in the room, except for the cat.

She glared at him. "Where the hell have you been?"

"Hiding! Do you know what kind of trouble you've gotten us *both* into?" He bared his single tooth and snarled at her. "You're going to get us both put in that Crystal. I won't go back. I *won't!*"

She blinked, stunned at his outburst. He had sounded almost frantic at the end. "I...I'm sorry."

"You should be." The fur on his back settled down. Picking up one paw, he licked it before wiping it over his brow. "And you have that blasted thing around your neck. Your first step is to get that thing off."

"Okay, but why? It's keeping me from setting things on fire." It made perfect sense, really. She couldn't say she blamed Mordred for putting it on her.

"Do you want to get into a brawl with him? Engage in fisticuffs, perhaps?" He shook his head.

"I—I guess not, but I don't understand what—"

"If you want to defend yourself, then you will need to be able to summon fire. And you cannot do that with that thing around your neck." His tail thwacked against the stone floor.

"I didn't let him do *anything*, he—"

The cat kept interrupting her. "I need to restore my full power if I am going to return you home. And you heard what Grigory said, didn't you?"

She stared at him silently.

Merlin let out a long, suffering sigh.

"Give me a break!" She picked up a pebble and tossed it at him. "I've had a lot to deal with, and you aren't telling me the whole story. I'm trying to deal with everything that's being thrown at me a mile a minute, and—" Then it hit her. "Oh. All the magic in Avalon is in the Crystal and that means..." Her shoulders drooped. "Your power is in the Crystal."

"She *can* learn. How wonderful." He huffed. "Yes, girl. You were meant to help me overthrow the prince and break the Crystal. But you cannot do that if you are trapped *inside* the blasted thing."

"I can't overthrow anybody." She gestured at herself. "Look at me."

"Well, now we may never have to learn if that's true. All hope might already be lost. The guard has gone to tell the prince you've woken up. He'll lock you in the Crystal for certain, and I will likely be dragged in there with you." Merlin hissed.

"I ... I mean, there has to be a way—"

"No. No, there *doesn't* have to be a way, you idiot child. That is not how the world works. You are the prisoner of the exact person you were supposed to help me defeat. He's—" Merlin looked over at the door, his one good ear twitching. "*Shit.* Tell him nothing. It might be the one thing that'll save us both from that fate."

"Wait—"

The door opened with a creak just as Merlin disappeared into thin air with little more than a wisp of smoke. She pulled the blankets tightly around herself and cowered in the corner of the cell. Like it'd do any good. There wasn't anybody else in there with her.

The thing that stepped into the room might have been a man. But it looked more like cobbled-together, mismatched, and deformed armor than a human as it lumbered toward her. It was chaotic but angular and strangely beautiful, like a Picasso painting. From within the seams of its breastplate she could see a dim, opalescent glow.

"Whoa." That was the best she could do.

It stopped at the door to her cell. "The prince would like you to join him." It was a man, judging by the voice. And it sounded normal, considering the circumstances. Nothing on the armor creature moved when it spoke, kind of like Merlin.

"Um ..." She looked down at herself. Under the blanket, she was wearing the white cloak that the silver knight had handed over. Whatever. She tried to balance her brief interaction with the prince with the warning from Merlin. Furrowing her brow, she thought it over for a second. "And if I say no?"

"I'm supposed to drag you there. Without the cloak, specifically." The thing sniffed dismissively. "Doesn't matter to me either way."

"Had to ask." She sighed. Standing, she wrapped the cape around herself tightly and made sure she was as covered as she could be. It reached to the floor, and she felt more like she was wearing somebody's queen-sized comforter than a cape. At least she wasn't going to freeze to death. "I'll go."

"Good." The armor turned and led her out of the room. She followed after him, trying to take everything in around her.

Never once in her life had she ever set foot inside a medieval castle. It was a lot less rustic than she would have expected. The ceiling had high, gothic arches and wooden beams crossing between them. The walls were made of various materials as she wandered through—some wood, some stone, and some made unsurprisingly out of metal.

She passed people who paused to stare at her. She fought the urge to stare right back. Every single one of them looked like the guard leading her—made out of metal. Some appeared more or less human than others. They were beautiful and artistic, each one slightly different than the next. But they gave her the willies all the same.

Something about them just felt *wrong*.

Frowning to herself, she pulled the cloak around her tighter as they passed rows of hallways, stanchions with pale-colored flames, tapestries, and beautiful but faded works of art. When the guard took her to a large, shut double door, he pushed it open and gestured for her to go inside.

Stepping into the room, she heard the door click behind her.

The guard had shut it behind her without following. That only meant one thing. *Ah, shit.*

"Come in, Lady Gwendolyn."

Ah, double shit.

Swallowing the lump in her throat, she turned to look into the room. It was an enormous great hall. A fire burned brightly in the gigantic hearth that dominated one wall. She had seen pictures of walk-in fireplaces in history books and magazines of architecture, but they weren't exactly common in Kansas.

The table that stretched through the room was made of gleaming metal that had all the appearance of an elaborately carved antique. Atop the table were plates of food, a jug, and a gold goblet filled with what looked like wine from where she was standing.

Great. More wine.

Standing in front of the fire, his back to her, was the prince. He wasn't wearing most of his armor, though his arms were still covered up to the shoulders. The plates didn't look nearly as bulky as before—it took her a second to realize they weren't part of the same set. But one thing remained . . . the claws.

The pale flickering light cast him in a sharp silhouette, not helping how intimidating he was. He held a second gold goblet perched between the talons of one of his hands. Lifting it to his lips, he downed the contents before finally turning and setting it on the table next to a throne at the head of it.

She froze as the man approached her, watching him with wide eyes. Slowly, as if afraid that he was going to spook a frightened animal, he walked toward her, his hands clasped behind his back. He watched her closely with those searing, rust-colored eyes. She fought the urge to turn and run, so she settled on retreating away from him.

When she backed into a large wooden table, she squeaked,

startled. In the space of time it took her to glance down at the offending piece of furniture and back up, he had closed the distance between them, and was only a foot or two away.

She had never felt so small in her life. God, he was *huge*. He was wearing an unbleached linen shirt with the V of the neck unlaced, tucked into a pair of black canvas trousers that disappeared into knee-high black leather boots. It seemed shockingly casual for someone who was a prince—but she supposed she knew extremely little about what people in Avalon wore.

She couldn't help but stare.

And it seemed he noticed.

The back of a claw rested underneath her chin and tilted her head up to him. It would be so easy for him to rip out her throat. Swallowing thickly, she had to know whether or not that was going to be the case. "Can...can we get something out of the way, like, first?"

He arched an eyebrow—it was the same odd gray tone as his hair. "Oh?"

"Are you planning on murdering, maiming, torturing, or traumatizing me? Or throwing me into the Crystal?" She did her best to stay standing up straight, even if she wanted to hide under the table she had bumped into. "I just—I just want to know what to expect."

He chuckled. A deep sound that resonated in his chest. She had heard his laugh before, but she had been a bit distracted with everything else going on to really appreciate it. It sounded like thunder on the horizon. "Tonight? No."

Well, that was better than a yes. "And what about tomorrow?"

"Tomorrow remains to be seen." Using the same sharp talon, he deftly brushed a strand of her hair behind her ear. "To be frank, firefly, I do not know what to do with you."

That was fair, she guessed. Frowning, she nodded, accepting that answer for now. "Just, um, if you make up your mind, will you tell me? On second thought—if you're gonna kill me, don't warn me. Just do it when I'm not paying attention." She wrinkled her nose at the idea. "Not that I'm asking you to, or anything."

That drew out another laugh from him, louder than the first. "I will do what I can." He gestured to one end of the table where a stack of clothing was folded up. "I had my servants fetch you clothing. That is…unless you wish to remain in nothing but a cloak." He tilted his head to the side slightly as his gaze wandered down her body. "I certainly do not mind."

Her cheeks felt like they had burst into flames, which was now apparently a thing that could happen. She knew she must be blushing solid crimson. "I—um—" She cleared her throat and stepped to the side, escaping from him. "No, normal clothes would be lovely, thank you."

"Damn."

She tried not to laugh. She at least managed to hide her smile. All right, that was kind of funny. And flattering. She just wasn't used to people flirting with her, especially not someone like him. Walking to the end of the table to the folded clothes, she found a chemise and a deep crimson dress that looked like it had a bodice that laced up in the front. It smelled a little bit dusty, but it looked in good condition. The fabric was thin wool and it seemed like it would help keep her plenty warm.

Mordred walked to the head of the table and poured himself another goblet of wine. "I apologize for the lack of undergarments. My servants do not have need for clothing, being made of metal as they are. I had to send one into storage to locate anything at all."

That would explain the dust. "Thank you. It'll do fine." She looked over to him, and realized he was watching her. "I'm not going to change with you staring at me."

He smirked. "What if I told you it was customary in Avalon?"

"I wouldn't believe you." She glared at him half-heartedly. It was clear he was teasing her. She gestured for him to face away from her.

"I have already seen you naked once." His smirk broadened into a playful grin.

"No."

"Pah! Being a prince is good for nothing." He turned his back to her, facing the fire. "Does that suffice?"

She shook her head, once more smiling. She didn't expect him to be cracking jokes with her. "Yeah. Thanks. I'll let you know when you can turn around." She took off the cloak and draped it over the back of the chair, quickly pulling the chemise on. It wasn't the softest material in the world, but it wasn't the worst either. The dress was easy enough to pull on, and it honestly fit her pretty well, all things considered. She began lacing up the front, starting at the bottom and working her way up. She knew she was meant to cinch the thing up like crazy— but she liked breathing. "Done."

He turned and watched her finish lacing up her dress. "Red looks wonderful on you."

Her cheeks went warm again. Damn it, she really wished she would stop blushing. "I guess it goes with my hair, now."

"What color was it before?"

"Brown." She shrugged. "Nothing exciting."

"I prefer it this way. Though I understand your confusion. I was once blond." He waved a hand at his own head. "The magic of Avalon is often strange in its manifestations."

"No kidding." Why was he so easy to talk to? It made no sense. *I mean, look at him.*

He gestured at the chair beside the throne that was set for a guest. "Will you join me for dinner, firefly? You must be starving."

She was, now that she thought about it. "What time is it? I guess I missed dinner."

"More like that you missed breakfast and lunch. You slept through the day." He glanced at the window. "We reached my keep just as the dawn broke, and now it is a few hours after sunset."

She blinked. She had no sense of how much time had passed. "I was exhausted."

"With good reason. Come, sit with me." With a scrape of wood on wood, he pulled out the chair for her.

Damn that voice of his. It made her more conflicted than she already was. With a shuddering breath, she walked to the table and sat down. She stayed perfectly still, afraid of making any sudden movements.

Standing beside the chair, he leaned over her to reach for the jug and poured the wine into the gold goblet. He was so close that a strand of his long, metallic hair brushed against her shoulder. She shivered.

It was obvious that he sensed his nearness was affecting her, as he lingered there as he spoke, his words quiet next to her ear. "Eat. Drink. I give you my word, I only intend to speak to you tonight."

"You sure?" She had a hard time believing that. From her limited interactions with people in Avalon, everybody made him out to be a monster. Merlin's warning rang in her head. "You're positive you aren't planning on torturing me or anything?"

"Not unless you ask nicely." His expression turned a little playful for a moment, and even just a little bit wicked. It made her cheeks go warm. She wasn't used to being flirted with. And she was pretty sure that was him flirting.

Luckily, he took pity on her and sat down in his own chair. It was basically a throne, really. There was no way around it.

Clearing her throat, she reached for the wine and went to sip from it before hesitating.

"I promise it is not poisoned this time." Leaning back in his chair, he watched her, curling his metal-clad fingers and resting his temple against them.

"Great. Thanks." She took a sip. He might be lying. But then again, he might be doing a lot of things. If he wanted to knock her out or slip her truth serum, she supposed she couldn't exactly stop him.

For a moment, he studied her in silence as she put some food onto her plate and began to eat. Her stomach grumbled in impatient gratitude. A billion questions were burning away in her head, and she had no idea where to start. "You're a prince, huh?"

"Last I checked." It must be funny for a guy like him to have some bright-eyed and bushy-tailed girl from Earth running around like a total fish out of water. It was clear how amused he was by her.

"Is there a king?"

"That would have required the elementals ever agreeing on anything." He huffed, clearly having an extremely low opinion of them. "No. There has only ever once been a true crowned king of Avalon, and it was a posthumous honor to a hero. He barely lived for two weeks before he passed from his wounds."

Fascinated, she turned in her seat to face him. "Who was it? King Arthur?"

"Correct." He sipped his wine. "He was brought here with mortal wounds, in search of magic that could heal him. Unfortunately, Avalon did not see fit to spare him."

It was still so *cool* that he had been real. She sighed wistfully. "I wonder what he was like."

"Just, and firm. A true king the likes of which had not been seen before or since. I would not say that he was kind, but he certainly was not cruel." He studied the wine in his glass. "Snored like a sawmill. Sharing a tent with him was an experience in patience. I sometimes wonder if that was not where I developed my sleeplessness."

"Wait." She blinked. "You *knew* him?"

"One would think so." His lips twisted into that lopsided smile of his that seemed to come so easily to him. "He was my uncle, after all."

SEVEN

"You're shitting me!" Gwen shoved Mordred's metal-clad arm.

"I—" He arched an eyebrow. "I fear I am having trouble parsing that one... Either you are expressing disbelief, or this conversation has taken a *very* strange turn."

Her cheeks went hot. "That's—it was the first one. I didn't mean that literally." She laughed.

He chuckled along with her. "I would hope not. I am telling you the truth. I came here with Arthur and his knights in search of the power to save his life. Sadly, we were... unsuccessful."

"Whoa." It was clear there was way more of a story there than what he was telling her. All her questions burst out at once. "How old are you? How did you know to come here? I bet it was Merlin. Oh shit, did you know Merlin? Was he awesome? Is he still around somewhere? Did Arthur really have a magical sword? Was there really a lady in the lake? Or did it come out of a stone? And—"

He was laughing, waving a clawed hand at her. "I surrender, I surrender. One at a time, please."

She sat back. "Sorry. This is just exciting."

"I am glad. Here, I was afraid you would be cowering in terror all night. I much prefer to be besieged by questions." He reached over and refilled her goblet.

"Are you going to answer any of them?" She smiled, teasing him back for once.

He leaned back and hooked his leg over the arm of his throne. He didn't seem much like a stuffy, tyrannical asshole to her. But maybe he was just being nice. "What will I get in exchange?"

"I really don't have much to bargain with."

"I would beg to differ." There was that mischievous glint in his eyes.

It took her a second to realize what he meant. "Oh my God, you're terrible." Picking up a grape from the table, she threw it at him. She didn't really know where she got the gall. For a moment, she panicked. What had she just done?

He caught it in midair before it hit him. Seemingly untroubled by her harmless violence, he ate the grape in question. "Projectile fruit was not what I had in mind, but suit yourself."

What an odd man. She had seen him twist a man's head around backwards. He had impaled somebody with his giant floating sword. And he was playful and flirty. And…being kind of *nice* to her.

It was all too weird. She needed to not get hung up on the details. She had a bigger picture to worry about. Even if the details were *super* cool. "So. What does being an elemental *mean*? The mayor didn't quite tell me the whole story. What am I?"

"The magic that fueled Avalon is chaotic at best. It chooses conduits, for lack of a better term. You and I, and those imprisoned, are those whose nature has been consumed by its power. Each of us is gifted in one way or another. You, with flame. I, with iron. The knights who you saw beside me are elementals as well, though their conditions are…" He paused, a darkness crossing over his expression. "Unique. And a story for another night."

He had so many secrets. But she supposed being sixteen hundred years old would do that. "And you won't tell me why you've imprisoned all the other elementals?"

"The story is long and unpleasant. Bluntly, I am not in the mood to tell you, as I am enjoying your company." His expression stayed dark, but now it had grown cold. "For the little time you remain willingly in my presence."

Sure, *that* wasn't foreboding as fuck or anything. What the hell was she supposed to do with that? "Um...okay?"

"I did it not for my own thirst for power, I can assure you. I did it to protect Avalon from itself. That is as much as I have the stomach to recite at the moment." And there was the tone of the man she had been expecting to meet. Not the friendly, flirty one. This was the man that the asshole cat had made him out to be. Mordred's tone left no room for argument. It was clear he was used to being in charge and expected her to obey.

And she wasn't about to push his buttons if she could help it. Nodding, she decided to try to change the subject. "You said you don't know what to do with me. What do you mean?"

"Well," he began, as he finished off his goblet of wine and refilled it from the jug. "Quite simply...here you sit, the product of escaped magic. Magic I have sworn to imprison and contain for the betterment of Avalon. I should put you with the rest of the elementals. And yet, I find myself deeply curious as to *why* and *how* you were chosen. Especially if the force behind this strange turn of events is malignant."

She didn't know much about "Merlin" the cat, but she would call him pretty malignant. But if she told Mordred the whole story, she was going to wind up trapped in the Crystal. She didn't want to lie to the man—even if he was dangerous—but she didn't know how to tell him the truth.

As if seeing her conflict, he shut his eyes. "Yes, I understand that this means you cannot tell me what you know without putting yourself at risk."

"Which is why I keep bringing up the topic of torture." She wrinkled her nose. "It'd make sense."

"Contrary to what others might have told you, I am not a monster. I abide by the rules of this land. You are my prisoner of war, Gwendolyn Wright." Those rust-colored eyes met hers. "And prisoners of war are honored guests, and not to be harmed."

She supposed that was some small measure of relief. "But at some point, you'll get frustrated and chuck me into the rock with everybody else."

"Most likely, yes."

She sighed and rubbed a hand over her face. "I want to go home."

"Would that I could." He shook his head. "Sadly, I cannot without shattering the Crystal. And even still, with your power linked to Avalon, so is your life. In time, you would wither and fade."

That was what Merlin had told her. At least the cat wasn't feeding her total bullshit. "Is there any way to...un-elemental myself? To give this up?"

"If there was, I would have stripped the power from my compatriots instead. It would have been a kinder fate." He studied his metal gauntlet for a moment, turning it over and flexing his fingers one at a time. "We are what we are...as unjust as it may be."

"How did you become an elemental?"

"Avalon simply chose me." His expression went somehow colder than before. "It was power that should have gone to my uncle. I am not meant to be—there has never once before been an elemental of iron. Nor shall there be one after me, I suspect, when I have failed and been rendered to dust."

Cheery.

She swallowed the lump in her throat.

"Forgive me." He shut his eyes again, looking suddenly exhausted, like the weight of the whole world was on his shoulders. "I am told I make for miserable company."

Something in her heart broke for him unexpectedly. There was so much tiredness in that statement—so much loneliness and sadness. She reached out before she could stop herself, and placed her hand atop his metal gauntlet where it rested on the table.

Rust-colored eyes met hers, his expression unreadable. But perhaps just a little surprised.

Shyly, she pulled her hand away and bit back an apology. She'd already made an ass out of herself, no need to keep digging that hole. "I mean, this—um—you're a lot better than what I was expecting." *Way to go, idiot.* She cringed and slapped a hand over her eyes. "I'm sorry, that came out wrong."

He laughed quietly, and his hand was then over hers, the cold of the metal against her skin strange but not unpleasant. "I will take that as a compliment and thank you for judging me on your own and not from the words of others."

She smiled at him faintly.

The moment ended, and he withdrew his hand to serve himself more food. "Eat, firefly."

"Why do you keep calling me that?" Not that she really minded.

"I suspect calling you by your true title will earn me more incredulous laughter."

Tilting her head to the side slightly, she furrowed her brow. "I have a title? What is it?"

He lifted his goblet to her. "Hail to you, Princess in Flames."

EIGHT

Snorting in laughter, Gwen proved him right. "Nope, bullshit. I'm not a princess. It'd be cool, but nope."

"We are given rank and title from our power and the number of those we command. As you are currently the only other true elemental free from the Crystal, that makes you a princess."

"That's dumb." She shook her head. "That doesn't make any sense."

"And yet, here we are." Mordred impaled a few potatoes with a fork and ate them.

"If I'm a princess, does that get me anything?"

"Not really, no. If you were not my prisoner of war, you would be free to etch out your own domain if you wished. But as it stands, sadly, you are princess in title only."

"Damn." She ate a piece of bread and some cheese before she couldn't resist the allure of the turkey and the potatoes. She watched as Mordred reached over and stabbed a strawberry with one of his jagged talons and ate it from his finger. "Why're you wearing those things?" She had to know. Even if it was vaguely insulting to ask.

"Wearing what?" He seemed genuinely confused.

She wiggled her fingers at him. "You don't need them to be spooky or intimidating, trust me."

"Hm? Oh." He chuckled and looked down at his hand. "Ah,

yes. I forget that I am wearing them. I fear it is simply more natural for me now to have them than to not. I could see how they could be troubling. Or...spooky."

Mordred lifted his hand, and she watched as the iron claws simply melted away. They dissolved into nothingness, or rather they merged back into him. And a second later, the armor was simply gone, revealing a perfectly normal-looking hand. "Is that better?"

"Whoa." She blinked. "How—okay that's awesome. How did you do that? Magic? Or like, is that elemental stuff? Wait. That's the same thing, isn't it?"

"Yes." He was smiling with a strange amount of amusement. As if he had just shown a card trick to a toddler. "I, too, am an elemental. We are shapeshifters, you and I. That is how you transformed into flame."

"Shapeshifters." She blinked. "That's why my hair keeps changing colors."

"And your eyes. Indeed. You choose your appearance, as do I."

"Wait—you *want* to look like that?" She winced. "Oh, God, that came out meaner than I meant it, that's not what I—"

He cackled with laughter and slapped his hand on the metal table. It clearly didn't offend him. "I take it you find me hideous and unappealing! Woe to me, the tragic prince."

"No! That's not what I meant!"

"So you do find me appealing then?" Now he had a wicked smirk on his face. He was playing with her.

She glared at him. "Knock it off. Stop teasing me."

"No, I do not think I shall. This is far too much fun." He leaned back and hooked his leg over the arm of the chair again. "And to answer your question, to a point, yes, I do choose to look this way. But the face in the mirror is my own. It is hard for our souls to forget who we are, though it has happened to some over time."

"But your armor isn't really armor."

"It is. It is simply part of me, the same way the fire is now part of you."

She shook her head. It was still so hard to believe.

Reaching over the table, he picked up a candle and placed it down next to her. When she looked at him quizzically, he gestured at it. "You know it shall not burn you."

"Yeah, I mean..." She reached out and put her finger into the flame. It was comfortably warm. "Sure, I understand what you're saying. But I don't know what it really means, or what this means for my life."

"We will worry about all that in time. For now, you must adjust to this new state of being. I remember when I was chosen, I was beyond livid over the whole ordeal." He huffed a laugh. "Believe you me, you are not the first person to react poorly to becoming an elemental."

She sat back in the chair and stared down at her hand, remembering how it had looked when she had been made of fire. "Do I get to learn how to control it? Y'know, so I can walk around without burning everything down?"

He studied her for a long moment. "I suppose it would help ensure the safety of my home. Do you wish for me to teach you?"

Merlin had told her to figure out how to get the necklace back off. And if fighting this guy—which she didn't even know if she wanted to do—was the only way to get home—which she didn't even know if she wanted to do yet—then she'd have to be able to control the fire.

This was a chance at real adventure. At having the thing she had been wanting for so very long—to become something. Someone.

And . . . being around Mordred wasn't as terrifying or miserable as she thought it might be. She smiled at him. "I think I'd like that. At least until you make the decision to snap my head around backwards."

He huffed a laugh and joined her playful half-sarcasm. "Yes, I do suppose it will pass the time before your inevitable murder at my hands."

Gwen laughed again. She didn't mean to. It was just all ridiculous. She covered her eyes with her hand again.

"Are you quite all right?"

"Oh, I'm great. I'm fine. I'm just fuckin' thrilled. I'm stuck in a magical world with a guy with murder hands and I can burst into flames randomly. Albert Einstein and Darth Vader could sit here debating the merits of blueberry muffins and it'd be all the same to me right now."

"Blueberry muffins?"

He didn't question the names, but he questioned the breakfast option? She looked at him curiously. "Have you never had muffins before?"

"No. I cannot say that I have. I fear they likely did not have them in my day. Perhaps I could talk you into making them for me."

"If you ask nicely."

"Or threaten you with torture." He grinned teasingly. "Whichever comes first."

She wanted to throw another grape at his head, but decided it was probably smart not to try her luck a second time. They sat there in silence again, simply watching each other once more. She had so many things she wanted to ask. So much she wanted to know.

As if once more reading her mind, he hummed. "Tomorrow, we shall trade stories. You will tell me how you came to Avalon, and I will tell you why all the others despise me. That sounds like a fair exchange, does it not?"

"Sure." She paused. "Thank you for the clothes. And dinner."

"You are very welcome." He walked up to her, and she watched as his armor melded back onto his body, including his pointed claws. That was so fascinating. It was graceful, and more than a little sensual. She wanted to see him do it again but was distracted by his hand hovering in front of her, palm up, asking for hers. "Shall I show you to your chambers?"

"You're not going to keep me locked up?"

"You are quite locked up, I assure you. Whether or not I keep you in chains"—he hooked his pointer finger into the front of the necklace she wore—"is another matter entirely."

The sound of metal sliding on metal sent a shiver down her spine. Yeah. That was why she shivered. Totally why she shivered. Totally why she felt like her face was bursting into flames again.

Totally.

He smiled, faint but devious, and she knew he saw straight through her. But he took pity on her and lowered his hand. "You will be under guard and supervision. But no. I shall not keep you locked away. That was merely a precaution in case you...did not take to this situation gracefully."

She took a step away from him and rubbed a hand up and down her arm. "I mean. I don't really have a choice."

"You would be surprised. Come, firefly. Will you let me walk with you?"

He was asking? Seriously? She blinked. "Um—y—yeah. Sure."

He bowed his head and led her to the door before heading down the hallway, walking beside her. More of those strange armor-people stopped and bowed as they passed. She couldn't help but glance nervously at them.

"Do they trouble you?"

"They're...weird." She didn't want to insult Mordred any more than she already had. "But everything is weird here."

"They will not harm you. They are all of my making and obey me in all things." He didn't sound proud or thrilled about it.

"You created them?"

"I cannot trust the other denizens of Avalon not to slit my throat in my sleep." He grimaced, the bitterness thick in his tone. "But I am unable to maintain the keep by myself. Nor would I truly wish to."

"I suppose it'd get lonely being here all by yourself."

He went silent for a long moment. "Indeed."

"What about the other two guys who were with you?"

"Hm? Ah. Galahad and Lancelot. There is one other who is here, Percival. The others are off hunting magic and keeping the peace. Their situations are...complicated. I would prefer to explain it another time."

That was fair. He was telling her a lot, and she supposed he was right. She was already pretty overwhelmed. Galahad and Lancelot. Percival and the knights of Arthur. It was all so surreal, it almost felt like a dream. It was, despite the predicament she had found herself in, damn exciting. "Do you, like—have a round table and everything?"

"What? I have a table that is round, if that is what you are asking me. Oh! Yes. The silly stories." He chuckled. "No, they are my knights, and I am their prince."

"I figured all the stories were made up."

"The best stories are."

She stifled a yawn. Poorly.

"And as if on cue, here we are." He stopped at a single door. There were two more of those weird armored people standing outside of the room, each one holding a spear. "The guards can fetch you anything you may need."

"You don't happen to have, like...indoor plumbing, do you?" Man, a shower sounded fantastic.

"You needn't go outdoors to use the privy, if that is what you mean. And if you desire to bathe, the servants can fetch you hot water." He opened the door and gestured for her to go in first.

That'd be a nope. "I can wait. I think I'm too tired for all the fuss." She stepped inside. The room was beautiful if...well, really archaic. There was an enormous bed covered in fur blankets. Fabric draped from the four posters, likely to help insulate the space and keep more warmth inside. A fire was lit in the much-more-moderately-sized hearth by the wall. It felt... cozy, all things considered.

"Will this suffice?"

"I. Um. Yeah. Thank you." It was much nicer than a jail cell, that was for sure. Even if she would kill for Wi-Fi and her phone. She could at least tell everyone she was alive. But there was no chance of any of that.

"Of course. Sleep well, my lady." He lifted her hand and kissed the back of her knuckles again.

"Y—you too."

He bowed and left the room, shutting the door with a click. All at once, she realized exactly how exhausted she was. It had been a wild "day." Or two days. Whatever.

Stripping off the clothes, she folded them and draped them on the chest at the bottom of the bed. She figured she probably wasn't going to burst into flames in her sleep while wearing the iron necklace, but if that happened, the whole room was going to go up in smoke anyway. And sleeping in that much fabric was going to be uncomfortable. She found a slip in a wardrobe and pulled it on over her head.

Climbing under the covers, she sank into the plush mattress. It didn't exactly have springs, but it wasn't as uncomfortable as she was afraid of. She was also way too tired to care.

Avalon. Elementals. An iron Crystal. Dragons, and monsters, flying swords, and talking armor.

As she fell asleep, her thoughts circled one thing more than the rest, however.

Mordred, the Prince in Iron.

NINE

"Are you certain about this, my liege?"

Mordred shrugged as he pulled his cape around his shoulders. Galahad was always one to express concern for everything. Especially in matters that involved change or uncertainty. Holding his hands out in front of him to warm them by the fire of his library, he finally responded to the knight's question. "Of course not. But I fear I do not have a better path forward. Do you?"

Galahad sighed. "No. I am not one for wanton cruelty. But to let her stay free from the Crystal seems to run counter to your goals. I am merely surprised."

"It wasn't just power that escaped the Crystal that day, Galahad. It was driven by a sentience. I know it. And whatever—*whoever*—escaped, is still pulling her strings. Rightfully, she does not trust me with the truth. I must spend the time to earn it. Though I must admit, I am enjoying the nature of the distraction."

"Sir?"

He chuckled. "What? Am I not allowed to enjoy someone's company for a change? Please, old friend. You are wonderful for companionship, but you lack a certain...quality." He grinned at the knight.

"Now I am quite convinced you have lost your mind."

Galahad walked to the wall to pour himself a glass of liquor. He was considerate as always and poured two. "You cannot have taken to her so quickly. And, if she is deceiving you, she is dangerous."

"I am unsure if she is deceiving me out of treachery or if she is hiding the full truth of it for her own safety." He took the glass that Galahad offered as the tall, lanky knight approached. "And if it is the latter, I cannot very well judge her for it."

Gwendolyn was safe from him for the moment . . . for as long as the mystery remained of who forced the power upon her, he would not act. And there was no kind end for the young woman ahead of her, no matter how Mordred might wish to paint it otherwise for her benefit.

"She is bound for the Crystal." Galahad's words were not harsh. Simply stating facts.

Mordred sighed and took a drink from the glass. "I know." There was sense in not permitting himself to enjoy Gwendolyn's company. He should not allow himself to see in her a spark of hope for something that he had been devoid of for so very long.

Hope that perhaps he would not forever be alone.

His knights were tolerable, and he was grateful for their presence. But they were his creations, the same as the sculptured armor that served him. It was not the same. He shut his eyes.

"Then, I will counsel you against becoming . . . entangled with the young woman."

"Believe me, I know." He vanished one of his metal gauntlets so he could rub at his temple. "But I must gain her trust to learn the truth. And I cannot do so by being aloof and distant."

"Then guard yourself against what will happen when she must

inevitably join the rest." Galahad put his hand on Mordred's shoulder. "I do not wish to see you bring yourself such pain."

"Truly? Considering the irony of the situation?" He sneered and decided to down the rest of his glass in one gulp before putting it on the mantel. "Seeing what you lost to the Crystal when I waged my war?"

Galahad dropped his hand. "We have been through this. I am loyal to you, my liege."

"Because you must be. Because it cannot matter to you what I have robbed from you, for I have not given you the ability to act against me." Mordred walked away to sit down in his large, upholstered chair by the fire. "Would that you had the freedom to choose, perhaps our friendship would be more fulfilling."

"Yet it is a moot point of discussion. And simply because I am incapable of the desire for revenge upon you does not make it also equally true that I do not wish to see you suffer the same pain I have endured at your hand." Galahad turned to leave the room. "But do as you will, my liege."

"I always do."

Galahad shut the door behind him with a click, leaving Mordred alone with his thoughts.

Which, perhaps, was keen enough revenge on its own.

Gwen woke up when something bit her hand. "Ow! Sonova—" She rolled onto her back and waved her hand, glaring at the offending creature. Which was, entirely unsurprisingly, Merlin. "Why do you have to be so mean?"

"Why do you have to be so stupid?" He was sitting on her pillow, swishing his tail. "And keep your damn voice down, will you? We do not want the guards to hear."

Sighing, she stuck her finger in her mouth for a second. "Whatever. Jerk." She rolled onto her side, facing away from the cat. "What do you want?"

"I have decided on a plan of action in order to get that bastard to take the necklace off you."

"Oh?"

"You will seduce him."

"What?" She sat up.

"Shut *up*, girl," the cat said through a hiss. "Keep your voice down."

A knock on the door. "Are you all right, my lady?" It must be one of the guards outside the room.

"Y—yeah, I'm fine, thanks," she called back. "Just stubbed my toe." She laughed nervously.

Silence. The door didn't open.

Letting out a breath, she put her hand over her face. "I hate this so damn much." At least she remembered to keep her voice down. Hugging the sheets to her chest, she glared at the cat. "And I'm not going to seduce him."

"He seems to be doing all the work for you already." Merlin walked to the foot of the bed and sat there. If a cat could look disgusted, he did. "He must have a particular attraction to imbeciles."

"You know, I don't really want to help you when you're being such a jackass." She lay back down, not wanting to deal with him. There was gray light streaming in through the windows between the cracks in the heavy curtains.

"You have no choice. I am your only way home. And your only other path leads to imprisonment within the Crystal."

"Mordred said I couldn't go home."

"And you believed him? You really are a fool."

She resisted the temptation to throw a pillow at the cat's head. But barely. "Okay, so explain to me how helping you gets me home then. In detail. Because he said it couldn't be done."

"For a normal elemental, yes. But you're borrowing my power. It doesn't belong to you. If I am restored to my full strength, I can break the bond between us. You'll be a normal mortal human again, and I can open a portal back to Earth and send you on your way."

"Was that so hard?"

"What?"

She lifted her head to shoot him a look. "Telling me useful information."

"Yes, in fact. Because now you might turn around and blather it all to our enemies." He thumped his tail against the comforter. "Better to keep you in the dark as much as possible."

"Whatever." She lay back down and turned her back to him. The bed was warm. She was achy and tired. "Dumb cat."

"I am *not* a cat."

"Until you tell me what you are, you're a dumb cat." She shut her eyes. Maybe he'd just go away. "And I'm not going to *seduce* him. He has knives for hands." Besides, what would a sixteen-hundred-year-old immortal, who was basically a demigod, and a *prince*, want with a woman like her?

Well, he did call her a princess.

No, no, no. Bad Gwen. Bad, she scolded herself. She was not considering it. She wasn't. Mordred was dangerous. He had killed people. A lot of people. He was keeping the magic of Avalon prisoner in the Crystal-thingy. She was not going to entertain the idea of—

Merlin bit her foot through the comforter.

"*Ow!*" Somehow she managed to keep her voice down. She

kicked at him reflexively, but he jumped away. "What was that for?"

"Ignoring me." Angry tail swish.

She sighed and pulled the blanket up over her shoulder. "Go away. I'm not going to seduce him."

"Well, you certainly aren't going to outwit him."

"I might want to help you more if you were nicer to me, y'know. Flies with honey instead of vinegar, and all that." It was clear that she wasn't going to get back to sleep. Flopping onto her back, she stared up at the wood ceiling of the room she was in. The exposed beams and rough-sawn planks reminded her of the barn at home.

Home.

That was why she had to help the dumb cat. *Home.* Avalon meant adventure, excitement, and magic. But also death and danger. Home was safe, even if it was probably a burnt pile of rubble. But she didn't need to make the choice yet. She didn't even have a choice to make. "He said he'll train me to use my power. That's a start, right? Maybe if I can control the fire, he'll leave the necklace off."

"My power. Not yours. But he's egotistical enough that it might work. And if it does not, you can attempt to use your feminine wiles against him."

"Ew, do not *ever* say that again." She glared at the cat. "Nobody says shit like that."

"Yes, they prefer to turn every other word into an obscenity." The cat walked to the edge of the bed. "The fact remains. Get up and get to work. The longer we wait, the more likely he will put you in the Crystal and be done with you." He jumped off the bed, vanishing into a wisp of black smoke.

She really hated that damn cat.

For a minute, she shut her eyes and wondered if she would be allowed to just go back to sleep. Her stomach growled. With a surrendering sigh, she gave up. "All right, all right..."

Maybe the guards would let her explore the castle. Maybe she could even explore on her own. That honestly sounded fun—she loved poking around cool places. And she'd never been in a castle before.

Oh! And maybe she'd find breakfast while she was at it. Or lunch. Or dinner. Or whatever meal it was. At least it was daylight. Maybe Mordred would be there.

No, no, no! Bad Gwen!

Climbing out of bed, she pulled on her dress. In the wardrobe by the wall, she located some sandals that she could strap onto her feet and a fur cape that was much more "her size" than the one she had been loaned earlier.

Heading over to the door, she experimentally pulled on it and was a little surprised when it opened. Weren't prisoners supposed to be kept locked up?

The guards turned to look at her, and she couldn't help but shrink back an inch at the sight of them. They were just still so *weird.* Sculpted sentient armor wasn't supposed to be a thing. Magic wasn't supposed to be a thing. But here they were. Beautiful works of art—and more than a little creepy.

"Do you need anything, my lady?" one asked. She honestly wasn't sure which of them it was, since their mouths didn't move.

"I—um. I was wondering if I could go for a walk?" It sounded dumb, now that she said it. "I didn't know if I was...supposed to stay here or not."

The two guards glanced at each other. One shrugged with a quiet clank. The other, who must be the one who spoke the first time, looked back at her. "I would ask that you stay within the keep unless you are escorted."

"Sounds fair." She pulled the cape closer around herself. It was chilly. "Do you have any idea what time it is?"

"Midmorning," the second one responded.

"Thanks." She smiled. No reason to be rude. They were being perfectly nice to her. She stepped past them, still feeling a little odd. "I—um. Have a nice day?"

They stared at her silently. Perfectly nice but perfectly weird.

"Good talk," she muttered, as she headed down the hallway. It was amazing how a few hours of sleep could brighten her mood, even just a little. She didn't think everything around every corner was going to kill her immediately, which was also helping.

Besides, the idea of exploring a big, spooky old building was *exciting*. The place was filled with a billion little nooks and crannies, she was sure of it. She wondered if there were hidden passages—all castles had cool hidden passages, right?

Stopping by a window, she looked out to see where she was. The glass was that kind of wavy, bubbly texture that made it hard to see, but she could make out enough details. The sky was gray and overcast. The castle overlooked a cliff that went out into the ocean, the water so dark blue it was almost black. If she focused, she could hear the waves hitting the cliffs down below them.

A castle on a cliff. How oddly romantic, if a little forlorn. *Seems to be the vibe of the place. And its owner.* She shooed those thoughts away.

Continuing on her walk, she marveled at the wall-sized tapestries and the enormous paintings that depicted monsters and warriors. Some looked medieval—well, she assumed anyway, she wasn't a history buff—but some looked more modern. Ish. Give or take. Some of the oil paintings were so dark it was hard to make out what was in them. She wondered if they had aged that way naturally or if it was the intention.

It was in one of the larger rooms that she found someone who didn't look like sculpted armor. Well, not entirely, anyway. It was the guy from before—the gold one. He wasn't wearing full plate armor this time, but she figured there were only a few people in the castle who had to be seven feet or more.

The man was sitting down at a table by a window, reading. He had gray hair—actually gray from age, not gray from being *metal* like Mordred—and holy hell if the guy wasn't just *long*. As if sensing her, he looked over at her, and she felt her eyes go wide.

He stood and bowed. "Good morning, my lady."

There were parts of his skin that were embedded with gold. Not like paint—but like there were parts of him that were just made out of golden armor. It shifted and moved in all the ways that she expected skin to move.

"I—um. Hello." She smiled nervously. "Sorry to interrupt."

"No, no. Not at all." He walked up to her, and she found herself craning her neck to look up at him. He was a few inches taller than Mordred—which was a trick—but a third the width.

"Aren't you a tall glass of water," she said through a chuckle. She extended her hand to him. "Gwen. Nice to meet you."

He took her hand and bowed to kiss her knuckles. "Sir Galahad, the Knight in Gold." He had a kind voice. Soft. But there was strength in his grip and his fingers were calloused. She was pretty damn sure he could kick ass with the best of them. Even if he did look like a string bean. "What brings you to this wing of the keep?"

"Just wandering and exploring." Her stomach audibly growled. She sighed. "And attempting to feed the beast."

He laughed, his expression crinkling into a gentle smile. "Would you allow me the pleasure of escorting you to the kitchen?"

"Well, you'd be doing me a favor, so sure." She smiled back at him. "Thanks."

"Of course. It has been a very, very long time since we have entertained any manner of guests." He began to walk, and she fell in step beside him. "You will have to forgive me if my manners are out of practice."

"I have zero manners. Don't worry about it."

Chuckling, he clasped his hands behind his back. "It can be jarring to come from Earth to Avalon. Especially with how much time has passed between then and now. What year is it on Earth?"

"Twenty twenty-three."

He grunted. "Goodness. It does not feel as though that much time has passed. Sometimes, time here passes differently than in other realms. But that is not to blame here, I fear."

"Realms? Plural? Mordred mentioned this world used to be a gate."

"Indeed. Avalon exists in a space between many worlds. Earth is merely one of them. I myself hail from elsewhere."

"Really? That's awesome. Where're you from?" It was amazing how less terrifying magic could be when it wasn't trying to kill you or set you on fire.

"A world named Tir n'Aill. It is a land of the fae. I traveled from there to Earth to fight alongside King Arthur. When we came here to Avalon with him and the others, I stayed at Mordred's side." He shrugged as though that were no big deal at all.

"Fae. Like. Fairies?"

He smiled. "Yes. Fae as in 'like' fairies. This world was also rife with my kind before..." He trailed off, his expression falling.

"Before the Crystal?"

"Yes. Before the Crystal." He shook his head. "Forgive me. I should not burden you with our tales of woe. You should not be a victim of our history."

"I think I already am." She pulled the fur cape around herself a little tighter. It was cozy and warm, and she was still chilly in the autumn air. She assumed it was autumn, anyway. She honestly had no clue.

"Yes, I suppose you are." He didn't look thrilled by the idea at all. He looked so damn sad that she almost wanted to hug him and tell him that everything was going to be okay. She wanted to ask him more questions about the Crystal, but with how clearly upsetting it was to him, she opted not to.

Luckily, a change of subject happened pretty quickly. They reached a doorway in the depths of the castle. Keep. Whatever.

"Out, out, *out!*" a woman shrieked. A frying pan flew out of the doorway and smashed against the wall, clattering to the floor.

Gwen jumped almost a foot in the air, leaping backwards. An armored figure, looking a bit more haphazard than some of the ones she'd seen around the castle, ran out of the room a second later. That suit of armor looked like it was missing entire sections, and one of his arms was floating, detached from his body, in the space next to him.

Gwen hid behind Galahad as the armor ran away, clanking as it went past them.

A collection of armor and... kitchenware stepped out of the

room. It was shaped like a woman wearing an apron. She was wielding a rolling pin like a weapon. It kind of reminded Gwen of her aunt Lucy, who was rounder than she was tall. "And don't come back, you broken half-wit!" the woman screamed after the armor that was running away. "I *swear*."

Galahad sighed. "Good morn, Maewenn. I have brought our visitor to see you."

"Oh!" the armor-that-looked-like-Gwen's-aunt squeaked. "It's you, Galahad. And—oh, look at you, you poor thing. Come in, come in. You must be *starving*. Missed breakfast, did you? Must have been so tired. I hope the prince didn't keep you up all night yammering. He doesn't talk frequently, but when he does? Come come, in in, let me rustle you up some food!"

"I—" Gwen didn't get another word out before Maewenn grabbed her by the hand and was tugging her into the kitchen. She looked back at Galahad and mouthed the words *"Help me."*

Chuckling, the tall knight bowed his head and turned on his heel to walk away. "Enjoy, Lady Gwendolyn."

Why did she feel like she just got hazed? Oh, she was going to get him back for this.

Once she escaped the kitchen, anyway.

TEN

"You may wish to go rescue our visitor."

Mordred looked up at Galahad as he walked into the room before arching an eyebrow at the tall knight. He hadn't slept—not that his inability to rest was all that shocking or unusual—and he wasn't in the mood to deal with the scolding Knight in Gold.

But a mention of rescue was not what he was expecting. "Oh?" He sat back from the table. He was poring over notes and books to see if he could discern the source of Gwendolyn's power. But there was little to base his search upon.

"She is trapped in the kitchens with Maewenn." Galahad smiled thinly, revealing his game. It was very intentional on his part, it seemed.

Mordred shook his head. "You are a right bastard."

"She complained of being hungry. What else was I meant to do?" But his expression revealed the knight's mischief.

"You could have summoned a servant to fetch food from the kitchens, not send Gwendolyn into the lion's den. No, more specifically, to make *me* go rescue her from said lion's den." He sighed and pushed up from the table. There was no point in prolonging the inevitable. He could send guards to fetch Gwendolyn from the kitchens, but Maewenn would likely just scream at them and chase them away.

No, Mordred would have to go get the young elemental himself. Which was entirely Galahad's goal. "If you are trying to counsel me to keep my distance from the young woman, this is not helping."

"Hm. I suppose not. But it is nice to see you outside your chambers. This is the most life I have seen from you in years." Galahad lifted a shoulder in an idle shrug. "And I fear your entanglement with her is inevitable at this point. Besides, Maewenn has been asking to speak with you for months, yet you avoid her."

"And you know why I avoid her."

"I do." The knight's smile widened. "And here we are."

"You are a right *ass*," Mordred amended his previous statement.

"If that poor young woman must suffer a tragic fate, I would have her time here at least provide *some* light of purpose. I have not seen you smile in...a very long time, my liege." Galahad clasped his hands behind his back.

Mordred shot him an unkind look. "I do not need you mothering me."

"Someone must." The knight turned to depart. "You should fetch the girl before she is fed so many pasties that she explodes, however. You know how Maewenn can be."

"Yes. I do. Thank you." Mordred wanted to whip his mug at the back of the knight's head. But there was no point. He sighed. Galahad was right, he should rescue Gwendolyn.

Summoning his armor—as Maewenn was likely to hit him with some cooking implement—he headed down to the kitchens. As he approached, he tried not to laugh at the conversation he overheard from inside. It was extremely one-sided, as was to be expected.

"—and there's only four. Four! Four and the damn dogs he keeps. Do you know how pointless it is to be a cook with an enormous place like this and only be expected to feed *four* mouths? Pah! Waste of metal, I am."

"I—"

"Eat up, dear. Eat up! Gives me meaning to whatever life I'm supposed to have. You wouldn't want old Maewenn to rust away down here, would you? Eat."

"Thanks, but I couldn't—"

"Try not to kill her, would you, you old bat?" Mordred stood in the doorway, leaning against the wood jamb. Gwendolyn was sitting on a stool at the large center island, a veritable feast arranged in front of her.

"Old bat! Why, I—" Maewenn turned from the stove, ready to unleash hell on him, before pausing. "Oh, my prince!" She curtsied with a quiet clank. "You never come down here."

"I thought perhaps I should save our new friend from being fed until she is sick." He crossed his arms over his chest.

"I would *never.*" The cook placed her hand on her chest. "She said she was hungry, and she just looks so thin!"

"Comparatively," he muttered under his breath. Luckily, Maewenn did not hear him. "I intended to fetch our new friend regardless. It is time to begin her training." He looked to Gwen, who was now watching him in wide-eyed fascination and curiosity.

What a precious thing, that. There was no disgust. No disdain. No revulsion.

Yet.

"If the lady wishes, of course." He smiled lopsidedly.

"I—well, yes, that sounds great, I—um." Gwen turned her attention to Maewenn even as she was climbing off the stool.

"Thank you so much for all the wonderful food. I'll take one for the walk." She picked up one of the baked meat pies.

"Bring a second for the prince." Maewenn waved a hand in his direction. "Rare that he remembers to eat, that one."

"Not that you often let me forget." Mordred pushed off from the jamb.

Gwendolyn obediently grabbed a second meat pie, and headed rapidly toward the exit where he was standing. "It was really nice to meet you, Maewenn. I'll make sure to stop by next time I'm starving."

"Please do! I do get so lonely down here. Only four mouths to feed. Four!"

"Five, now," Mordred corrected the woman. He stepped back to allow Gwendolyn into the hall, resisting the temptation to place his hand on her back to guide her. The way the young woman blushed at his nearness was alluring. She was a temptation.

"Five. Hardly enough." Maewenn sighed mournfully and went back to stirring a pot of whatever stew she was making. "You could at the very least—"

He stopped listening. Gwendolyn was already making a hasty retreat up the stairs. He followed her, also eager to escape the cook, who was still talking to herself as though they were still there.

Gwen was standing atop the stairs, staring down at the two meat pies she was holding. "Do you actually want one of these?"

"No." He smiled.

"I think if I eat any more, I'll blow up. I mean, they're good—they're great, actually, just—wow." She chuckled.

"That is how she shows affection. It has been a long time since she has had a guest to tend to." Mordred could not help but find her smile addicting. Oh, she was adorable when she was frightened. But there was something else about her easy, friendly expression that made him wish to see it more.

Galahad was right. He was already doomed.

He hated when that bastard was right.

"So—you're going to train me?" She seemed almost eager. "I get to learn how to control my fire?"

"Yes. But first, we must get you a more appropriate set of clothing." He smirked. "Unless you wish to incinerate what you are wearing again. I would not mind a second show."

Her expression of frustration mixed perfectly with the blush on her cheeks. "No, I think I'm good, sorry to disappoint."

He huffed, purposefully laying on the drama for effect. It succeeded in making the girl chuckle, and that brought a smile to his face. Galahad's words returned to him—that this was the most life he had shown in years. And perhaps the Knight in Gold was not wrong.

But at what cost?

He led her to a courtyard in the center of the keep—a small open-air section of packed dirt and sand. Racks of weapons and shields were arranged by the wall. And on the table, his next gift to the young fire elemental. He gestured for her to follow him. "You might find these a bit more suitable for your gifts."

Watching her expression, he could not deny that there was some joy in him as she examined his handiwork. He had made her two metallic garments—a top and a wrap-around skirt, made from the finest and smallest chainmail that he could summon. At first glance, it looked almost like fabric.

Her eyes lit up in wonder as she ran her hand over the surface. "It's beautiful."

"More importantly, it is also not flammable." He could not help but crack a half-hearted joke. He turned his back to her so she could change without his prying eyes.

"Done."

Turning, he did his best to hide how his breath caught in his chest. Perhaps he should not have designed the top to be so very low-cut in the front. But he also could not say that he did not deeply enjoy how she looked in the chainmail clothing.

She looked as if she belonged in Avalon.

Like a true elemental.

And just like that, his mood came crashing back down to reality. *A true elemental who will betray me. Who will pitch this world into bloody chaos like all the rest. It is just a matter of time.*

But by the Ancients, she was beautiful, even shy as she was, blushing, sheepishly staring down at her sandaled feet. Beautiful and tempting. Too tempting.

That was likely why he had foolishly agreed to train her. She could be his enemy before long. She could be standing across from him on the battlefield. So why, by any stretch of the imagination, was he standing here, readying to teach her how to control her power?

He was gaining her trust so that she told him the true story of her arrival to Avalon.

That was the excuse he had made for himself.

But perhaps it was far more insidious than that.

"I will warn you now." He grazed the back of one of his claws over her cheek. He trailed down the line of her neck before hooking the blade underneath her iron necklace. The latch in the back let go upon his silent command. He placed the necklace on the table beside them. "I do not plan to take pity upon you."

"I—oh. Um. I mean. Okay?" Her cheeks reddened, much to his delight. It was clear to him that the attraction was mutual. But he would not be a brute. The young thing was overwhelmed enough as it was.

He took a step back from her. He needed to put distance between them. He needed her to understand who he was. He shrugged out of his cloak and threw it over the table and picked up a sword from the rack. It was small and light—it would suit her well enough.

He knew he was being harsh with her. But perhaps it was best to force a wedge between them earlier rather than later. Galahad was right—entanglements with the young woman would lead to painful complications. "You are eager to know of my history with my uncle, are you not?"

"I—I mean, yeah, he was King Arthur." She chuckled.

"Well. You know of his legendary sword?"

"Excalibur?"

"Caliburn. What that Frenchman did to the story I will never quite understand." He gestured his hand in the air. He summoned his blade and it shimmered into existence beside him, floating and awaiting his command. "But it is the same blade. My uncle gifted it to me when he passed."

Gwendolyn's eyes went as wide as saucers. "Whoa . . ." She blinked as she started to put two and two together. "What does this have to do with training me?"

He threw the smaller blade to the ground at her feet. "Pick it up."

Hesitating for a moment, she reached down and did as he said. By the Ancients, her form was *atrocious*. They would have a lot of work to do. "I—but—okay, but what's this have to do with—me being trained as an elemental?"

"Discipline." In more ways than one.

"I don't know how to fight."

"That is about to change." He flicked his wrist, and Caliburn spun in the air, pointing straight at her. "Defend yourself."

"What?"

The sword flew at her.

Gwen screamed.

ELEVEN

Gwen ran.

Tripped.

And ate the dirt like a goddamn champ.

She rolled onto her back, though she couldn't have told anybody why she wanted to see the giant sword that was about to murder her. Covering her head with her arms, she waited for the stabbing pain of being skewered by a floating sword.

When she wasn't pinned into the dirt by an enormous mythical blade, she lowered her arms. She saw the point of the weapon floating inches away from her face. With a squeak, she burst into flames.

Mordred laughed.

"It's not funny!" She glared at him as best as she could.

"It really rather is." The blade retreated.

Sitting up, she looked down at her arms that were ablaze and let out a heavy, annoyed sigh. "I'm a flaming pufferfish."

"A what?" He walked up to her.

"A tropical fish. It's covered in little flat spikes. When it gets scared, it puffs up into a pointy ball." She gestured with her hands to mime an object inflating. "To protect itself."

"I see." He extended his hand down to her. She took it, still impressed that he didn't stab her with the talons as he hefted her up to her feet. "I wished to see if your ability was currently fear-based. It seems it is."

"You could've just, I don't know, startled me." At least she wasn't cold anymore. She marveled at the sight of her hand. It would take her a while to get used to being made out of fire.

"Mmh. Could have. Not nearly as amusing as that, however." He chuckled again. "Question—did you honestly believe I was going to murder you, just now?"

"Kinda? I mean. It'd make sense if you just killed me, wouldn't it? You're trying to keep all the magic of the world trapped." She waved her hand in front of her, watching the fire trail through the air.

"Perhaps." He walked around her, circling her. She turned her head to watch him as he moved to stand behind her. He picked up a lock of her hair—which was also made out of fire, now—and curled it around his fingers. She watched as the iron of his armor began to glow, just a little.

"Does that hurt?" She frowned. "Your hand."

"No. You would have to burn much brighter than this to harm me." He rested his other hand on her shoulder, the points just barely resting on her skin. "Is that a relief or a disappointment, I wonder?"

"I don't want to hurt you."

"I am flattered." He stepped closer to her. She could feel him at her back, the armor just brushing up against her. "Hm. Your flame rises in temperature when you are nervous. Fascinating. You truly *are* a 'flaming pufferfish,' aren't you?" He chuckled. Placing his other hand on her shoulder, he now had one resting on either side of her neck. He tightened his grip just barely. Just enough to make his point.

Sure enough, she watched as her fire glowed brighter.

Maybe it wasn't nervousness that made it happen. She sure as hell wasn't going to tell him how conflicted she felt when he touched her. He was frightening—but it *did* things to her. Things she didn't know how to handle.

She had to remind herself why she was supposed to hate him. More importantly, remind herself why she was supposed to be trying to overthrow him. "Why did you imprison the elementals?"

He let out a heavy breath and walked away from her. "I will reward you with your answer when we are done training."

She watched as his armor flowed over the rest of him, not just his arms. It took over his body with its twisted, jagged, asymmetrical plates that were both graceful, beautiful, and strangely grotesque all at once. He was a work of art in his own right.

A helm overtook his face, and now he looked like a twisted knight from a nightmare. It resembled the skull of a dragon. He truly was a dread prince in rusted armor. Bizarre and awe-inspiring.

"Pick up your sword." He gestured to where it lay on the packed dirt.

"Are you kidding me?" She stared down at the sword and then up at him. "You're going to *clobber* me."

"I have trained children to fight. You cannot be so different." His smirk was audible even from behind the helm. Caliburn floated nearer to him, and he plucked it from the air. It was clearly supposed to be held with two hands, and the bastard could easily heft it with one.

"Hah, hah." She sighed. The sword felt like a foreign object in her hand. She'd never really tried to use one before. When the hell would she have had the chance? "How is this supposed to help me control my fire?"

"In short? I am not sure it will." He laughed. "But oh, it's going to be fun."

"For you." She glared at him half-heartedly, her stomach still in knots from the moments before.

"And?" He cracked his neck from one side to the other, his armor clanking. "You're standing all wrong."

"I don't know what I'm doing!"

"Like this." He changed his posture. When she mimicked him, he nodded. "A good start. At least you take instruction well."

"Thanks? I think?"

He walked up to her, and nudged her shoulders into apparently where they were supposed to be, and lifted her elbow farther away from her side. "There is only one problem."

"Which is?"

"This." He promptly kicked her right leg out, sending her toppling to the dirt.

"Ow." She grunted and pushed up onto her elbow. "What the hell, man?"

"You put too much weight on your right leg. I should be able to strike at either leg, and you should stay upright." He offered her a hand up. When she took it, he hefted her back onto her feet. "Again."

Grumbling, she took the stance he had shown her. She fixed her shoulders and then her elbow.

When he kicked out her right foot and she didn't fall over, he hummed in approval. He did it for the left foot, and she still stayed upright, even if it kind of hurt to have a guy with metal boots swiping out her bare feet. She'd have bruises later.

"Now, focus. Think of yourself as the roots of a tree." He shoved her in the shoulder.

The movement sent her staggering away, nearly falling over again. "Hey!"

"Does a tree allow itself to be moved? No. It does not. Again."

"You're, like, twelve times my size, asshole." But she sighed and planted her feet again.

"I am not trying, trust me." He shoved her again, and that time she only staggered a foot or two before she managed to recover. "Better. Still bad. But better."

"You suck."

"I take it that is an insult?"

"Yep."

"Insult me all you like. I think I rather enjoy it from you. You look so adorably perturbed when you say them." He pushed her a little harder, sending her staggering again. "A tree who does not yield to the forces around it is brittle and will snap. Steel is stronger because it bends." He shoved her again. That time, she tilted over but managed to stay where she was. "Good. Very good."

She let herself smile at that, just a little.

"Now, lift your sword."

With a whine, she did so. "Please don't—"

He swung his sword into hers without warning.

It was so jarring that she nearly threw her own blade out of her hands. "Ow!" She waved her hands in the air. "Jesus *fuck*."

"How profane. Utterly blasphemous." He sounded amused. "I love it."

She waved her hand again. It was still on fire. Which was super weird. "Can you teach me how to turn this shit off, by the way?"

"That is precisely what I am doing." He gestured to her sword on the ground.

"No, you're beating me up." She picked up the blade obediently and, with a grumble, set her stance again.

"I can be doing both." He nudged her sword higher with the tip of his own blade. "Now, when I strike your sword, you have a choice. You can either move with the blow, or you can attempt to withstand the force. Which do you think is a better choice?"

"I know which one hurts."

"Then I suggest you try the other one." He swung his sword into hers. She let him knock the blade away. When she didn't move the sword back in front of her fast enough, he rested the tip of his blade underneath her chin. It yet again sent her stomach twisting into knots. "You are small. Speed will be your advantage in a fight like this. You must anticipate my strikes and be planning on how you will recover from them before they land. Not after." He lowered his sword. "Again."

It took her ten more tries before she finally managed to get what he was saying. He was big, and it made his movements predictable when he wound up for a swing. The next time he swept his blade for hers, she moved it out of the way before they connected, and it let her place her sword back in front of her before he completed his swing.

"There you are. That is it. Very good." He honestly sounded pleased.

A little bit of pride welled up in her chest. It offset the pain in her hands and the bruises she knew were forming from being shoved and knocked around by a giant man in armor. But she was used to hard work on the farm, and there was something a little rewarding about this. Like overworking at the gym.

"Still don't know what this has to do with the fire thing."

"Then I will show you what it has to do with the 'fire thing.' Lower your blade." He walked up to her as she did as he asked. "You can either resist the force that is within you, or you can move with it. Which do you choose to do?"

"I can't…"

He placed the point of a claw beneath her chin and used it to tilt her head up to look at him. "You can. You just did. Feel its movement. Predict it. Anticipate. Move with it." He lowered his hand back to his side. "It is a part of you—this raging battle. But do not think of it as an opponent. Think of it as a partner you are sparring with. An ally."

Letting out a breath, she shut her eyes. Because of her anxiety, she always felt like she was living in a barn with a family of rabid hyperactive squirrels. They were always jabbering and chittering, running amok and causing problems. But now that she had some weird elemental force inside of her, the squirrels had turned into giant badgers. And not the cute British ones either. The nasty American ones. And they were on fire. The mental image of flaming badgers made her snicker.

"Focus, girl."

"Yeah, yeah." She took another deep breath, held it, and let it out in a rush. The power felt like an itch in her, a strange sensation that she hadn't had the chance to notice the last time she had burst into flame. It was like the need to run—the need to be free or to do. "It makes me antsy."

"You are a fire elemental. You wish to burn. Of course it makes you restless. Control it."

"Easier said than done…"

"I believe you have yet to try. So far, you've only complained."

She wanted to say something snippy back at him, but figured it was a waste of time. And he was probably right, anyway. She studied the feeling again. And she did exactly as he'd been teaching her to do the past hour or so. She saw it for what it was. Saw it move.

And instead of fighting it…she moved with it.

She shivered as suddenly she was cold again. Blinking her eyes open, she looked down at herself, and saw her skin was now normal. Laughing in disbelief, she examined her hands. "Hey! Look at that!"

"Yes, it is almost as though I know what I am talking about." His armor dissolved into him, leaving him in his black linen shirt and black pants. He was smiling down at her.

Acting out of impulse, she hugged him. Her arms barely reached around his waist. The dude was a damn tank. "Thank you."

He froze. Locked solid for a split second. After a moment, he rested a hand—a normal hand, without the claws for once—atop her head. "You are welcome, firefly."

Stepping away from him, she winced. Now the adrenaline was fading, every ache was making itself known. "I hurt. A lot."

Mordred paid her a small, soft smile. "I never said this would be easy."

Shivering, she went back to the table where her normal, warmer clothes were resting. She gestured for him to turn around, and he did as she requested. Changing back, she was glad to have the extra layer of fabric on. Especially with how he watched her when she was wearing just the chainmail. "Done."

There was tenderness in his expression, but it was mixed with a hunger she didn't know what to do with. The two at once made her feel both excited and nervous. So, she was very eager to tie up her sandals if it meant she could avoid eye contact for a few seconds.

"We will train again tomorrow. You may have learned to extinguish yourself, but that is only the beginning."

"Oh, great." She stood, feeling her back twinge in revolt from the movement. "At least I'll get in shape while I'm here."

"I suspect you shall." He walked up to her, and she froze like a deer in the headlights.

Mordred placed the metal necklace back around her neck, and she felt it click shut. "I do hope you forgive the precaution."

"Here I was thinking you just like me wearing this stupid thing to mess with me." It was a bad attempt at teasing him. She needed to lighten the mood and dispel the tension.

"It is convenient, I will admit." To prove his point, he hooked a finger into the front of it and tugged her closer to him. For a moment, he looked as though he was going to kiss her.

And she wanted him to.

With another faint smile, he walked away. "Come. Gather your things. I believe I owe you a stiff drink and a long story." And just like that, he was gone.

Pressing the heels of her palms into her cheekbones, she let out an exasperated groan and followed him. She was getting herself in too deep. But the disappointment when he hadn't kissed her had been almost visceral.

But the idea of finally having answers spurred her into action, jogging after him to catch up. The bastard had long legs.

At least soon enough she'd know why everybody hated him so much.

Because except for the foreboding appearance and being a little *severe*, she couldn't figure out why he had such a lousy reputation.

Or why he was single.

Stupid, Gwen. Stupid, stupid, stupid Gwen.

TWELVE

Mordred had led her to an enormous room with a massive metal table in the center of it. It was circular, with elaborate chairs placed around the edge. Each chair was made of a different kind of metal—iron, gold, silver, copper, tin, and what looked like cobalt and nickel. Seven in total.

A seat for Mordred and each of his knights, it was clear. She let out a breath. This was as close to being at the round table as she would ever get, she expected.

In the center of the table, some eight feet in diameter, was inlaid a map of what must be Avalon. It was an island, dominated by a single mountain peak in the middle.

She couldn't help but picture Neverland—she wondered if this place had managed to inspire *Peter Pan* in any way. It seemed like it would track. It certainly had a scary man with metal weapons for hands, that was for damn sure.

"Tell me your story, Gwendolyn Wright."

Gwen blinked. She hadn't been expecting that. She glanced over to him. Mordred was pouring her what looked like whiskey into a glass. She wasn't usually one for straight alcohol, but *man* she was sore from their so-called training. When he approached her with it, she smiled and muttered a quiet thank-you.

Taking a sip, she coughed. "Damn." She took another sip, feeling much less of a burn that time.

He chuckled, clearly deeply amused. "Well, go on."

"Why do you want to know? I'm not the interesting one." She looked back down at the map. There were little figurines placed around on the surface like a war map from some medieval movie. They all looked extremely dusty—as though they hadn't been touched in, well, centuries. "And I thought I was here to learn your story?"

"You are. But as I suspect yours is much shorter, we should start with that."

Rolling her eyes, she took another sip of the whiskey. He had a point, she supposed. "There isn't much to tell. I grew up on a farm, raising animals and growing corn. I went to school and did great. I wanted to go to college to become a historian or a veterinarian—an animal doctor—because animals are, like, my favorite thing in the world. But that wasn't in the cards."

"Why not?" He walked around the edge of the table to stand by the iron chair, his gaze fixed on the map in front of him.

"I . . . well, you've seen it. I have panic attacks." She shrugged. "I've had them ever since I was little. I can't breathe and, more often than not, I pass out. My parents didn't think sending me away to a big city was safe. We also couldn't afford it. So I . . . stayed behind."

"You clearly do not agree with their decision."

"It is what it is." She sipped the whiskey. It was tasty now that she'd got over the burning. "I just wish—" No. There was no point in going down that road.

"What, Gwendolyn?"

"You can call me Gwen, by the way. It's easier. I only get called Gwendolyn when I'm in trouble." She smiled faintly at him. "And I just wish I could have gone with all my friends to the city. I didn't want to be trapped in Kansas on the farm my whole life. Maybe if I could have gone, my boyfriend wouldn't have cheated on me."

That caught his attention. Rust-colored eyes flicked up to her. "I am sorry. Betrayal is never an easy thing to overcome." His expression darkened. "I empathize. Trust me."

"That sounds like a whole-ass can of worms."

He shook his head. "Another tale for another time. You will know it soon enough, I am sure. Continue—how did you come to Avalon?"

She didn't want to lie to Mordred, but she also had no reason to trust him. And until she knew what he was planning on doing to her, she wasn't going to stick her finger into the proverbial live socket. She might not like Merlin, but she also didn't have any reason to believe that Mordred wouldn't chuck her into the Iron Crystal the moment he learned that the asshole cat had brought her there.

"I was having a bad day. I had just learned that Mick was cheating on me, and we broke up. I ordered a pizza, lit a candle, and settled in to watch a movie." Now came the lie. She stared down into her alcohol, hoping it helped hide her fib. "The candle must have gotten knocked over. The house caught fire. In a panic, I ran upstairs. There was a—I don't know how to describe it—a portal? Hole in space? Whatever. I jumped through, figuring it was better than burning to death. I woke up in a crater in the woods, naked, and found my way to the village. You know the rest from there."

"I see." It was clear he didn't quite believe her story. But he also didn't seem like he wanted to call her out on it. He swirled the alcohol in his own glass before taking a sip of it.

He was staring down at the map of Avalon with a dourness she'd yet to see from him. She wanted to examine the map

closer—she had a million questions, including about the portion of the map by the center mountain which read *Ruins of
Camelot.*

But now wasn't the time.

"Tell me, Gwen—what would you sacrifice to protect your
world, even from itself?"

"I . . . honestly don't know. It's never come up." She tried to
make a joke, but it fell as flat as a lead balloon.

"Sadly, it has for me. And in the end, I sacrificed everything—
and everyone—to protect Avalon from its own arrogance and
destruction." He shut his eyes for a moment. "But I am getting
too far ahead of myself. Time was once that Avalon's population
was a million strong, perhaps more," Mordred began. "Now we
are twenty thousand, if that. The rest are imprisoned within
the Iron Crystal. And there, they must remain, lest Avalon be
pitched once more into war and chaos."

Reaching down to the table, he picked up a small figurine. It
was made from iron—which wasn't surprising. He tossed it to
her. Catching it, she studied the little thing. It was in the shape
of a monster—or a demon. A strange creature with the posture
of a gorilla but resembling a lion more. It had one broken, jagged horn and one that curled away from its head like a gazelle.
Its face was caught in a rage-filled roar.

"We elementals are fueled by the magic of Avalon—and are
just as unpredictable. The island chooses who to 'gift' with its
power. It is not given to those who *deserve* or *earn* it. No, sometimes I think indeed the island has a sick sense of humor in
who it chooses and who it does not." He sneered. It was clear
he had strong feelings on the subject.

Gwen stayed quiet, listening to him talk.

"When the demon Grinn, the so-called and self-titled

Ash King, decided to wage war upon the whole of Avalon, I rose to stand in opposition. I would not let the monster go unchecked—for he wished to reduce all life to cinders, to turn it into his own personal Hell."

"Did you kill the demon?"

"No. To kill another elemental is against the law of Avalon, save by unanimous vote of the others." He laughed, a dark and unhappy sound. "They could not even agree upon *that*. A war against the demon that ended in imprisonment was the only answer. But I foolishly sought the aid of the elementals to assist me in my fight. And for a time...they did."

"For a time?" She frowned.

"And therein is the rub. There lies the reason why I did what I had to do. For those *bastards* cannot be trusted." He grimaced. "They saw me as a threat, due to iron serving as a foil for all the rest of them. Afraid of my strength, they waited until I had defeated the demon to strike against me. Insisting that I should not exist, they sought my head on a pike. In that, they stood united."

She swallowed a lump in her throat. "Clearly, you won."

"Indeed." He huffed a laugh. "Their alliances could not last long enough to see them put an end to me. They turned their bickering inwards. If they had managed to simply unite against me, I would not be standing here today. And Avalon would likely be nothing but char and coal."

"But you could have killed them all. I mean, laws are laws, but clearly, you're now the guy in charge."

"Yes. But if we do not hold ourselves to our own standards, what do we have in the end?" He downed the rest of his glass of alcohol. "Nothing." He walked away to stand by the fire burning in the hearth by the wall, gazing into the flames. If the world was always this gray and dreary, she imagined they went through a *lot* of firewood.

"How many other elementals are—were—there?"

"Twenty, thirty perhaps. I am unsure. We could not be trusted in one place all at the same time without a brawl breaking loose." He sneered down into the fire. "The factions shifted and changed as chaotically as the power that wielded it. Betrayals were more common than friendships."

He paused for a long moment, clearly debating whether or not to ask his next question. "Would you rather live in a world that is stagnant, or a world gripped by constant war?"

"I don't know." And that was true. She really didn't. She looked out the window at the dreary gray sky beyond. "Does the sun ever shine here?"

"No. Nor do the seasons change."

Wincing, she sighed. "Then I really don't know."

"Thank you for your honesty, Gwen." He shut his eyes and leaned his forehead on his wrist. "So many once sought to placate me—they fed me lies, promising that they were on *my* side. That they would embrace this cold, sterile order, if it meant they could remain free of the Crystal. Each time I was betrayed."

Trust issues. Check. That explained a lot. She sighed. "I promise I won't ever tell you something untrue." She paused. "I just can't promise to tell you everything." Like about the stupid cat and his stupid plot.

He smiled wearily. "That is the kindest gift you could give me, firefly. Thank you."

"Doesn't it get lonely, though? With nobody else around?"

"Immensely." Mordred tilted his head to the right. She heard it pop loudly. He repeated the action to the left, and it came along with another loud pop.

"At least you have your knights."

He laughed darkly again, as if she had said something extremely funny without realizing what it was. "I believe I prefer the company of my hounds."

Oh! Right! Maewenn had mentioned that he had dogs. Her mood instantly brightened. "Can we go see them?"

He turned to look at her a little quizzically, as if surprised.

She smiled a little sheepishly. "I really love animals."

"Yes. Right. So you said." He shrugged. "Very well. I could use a distraction. It will give you something to do with those meat pies."

She hopped up and down, thrilled at the notion. She could use some time with some pets to brighten her day. It had been a little rough, all things considered. Although the whiskey was helping. She emptied the rest of her glass, coughed, and grinned at the prince. "Let's go!"

He chuckled, amused, and walked from the room, leading her down the hallway. "You are a strange one, firefly."

"Says the guy with knives for hands." She jogged to walk beside him.

There was still a darkness in his eyes, but his smile seemed legitimate if weak. "I suppose that is very fair."

What a sad, lonely, terrifying man. Now she knew the truth of why he had imprisoned the elementals. And maybe he wasn't so wrong in his reasoning. *Maybe Merlin is wrong. Maybe Avalon is better this way.*

Or maybe she was making a terrible mistake.

Mordred managed to make it into and out of the kitchen with Maewenn none the wiser. The cook meant well, but he simply did not have the energy or emotional fortitude in the moment to put up with the woman's complaints, valid as they might be.

He had too much on his mind that day.

Namely—Gwendolyn Wright. *Gwen.*

As he walked with Gwendolyn through the castle, he pointed out anything he thought she might find interesting. She listened, taking in every detail. They walked out of the main building into the yard that was separated from the field beyond by a large stone rampart. He could already hear the hounds excitedly barking upon seeing him approach.

"So are your dogs, like, actual dogs? Not . . . metal dogs?" Her curiosity was as endearing as it was unflinching.

"I do not need to feed metal creations."

"I'm just surprised, is all." She shrugged, looking down at the two meat pies he had stolen from the kitchen.

"Dogs do not betray their masters."

Her expression fell. "Oh."

Well done, Mordred. Well done, indeed. He sighed. "Forgive me, Gwendolyn. I am not accustomed to visitors."

"It's fine. I honestly wouldn't blame you, not if you've spent your entire time here getting betrayed by other elementals." She frowned. "It sucks to have your trust broken."

"You do not yet know the half of it." He sighed. "But enough of such dour topics." He pushed open the door to the kennel next to the stables and watched as her face lit up at the sight of the four enormous hounds jumping up and down in excitement to see him.

And her, he supposed. She was carrying meat pies, after all.

"Oh shit, they're *huge.*" She laughed as she walked in. The four dogs were kept separate from the entrance by a low gate. They had all they could need, including openings to the outside where they could enjoy what meager sunlight Avalon received. "Wolfhounds? Mastiffs?"

"They are native to Avalon. I could not say if there is a name for their breed." He clicked his tongue at one of the dogs who was scrambling at the fence, overexcited in her need to say hello. "Easy, Luri." He reached out and ruffled the dog's curly fur and long ears.

"Do you always keep them outside?" Gwen was peeling off a piece of the pastry and feeding one of the dogs that was now obediently sitting, tongue hanging out of his mouth, eagerly awaiting the treat.

"No. They are often allowed in the keep. But I have long since learned that once a mutt is allowed in a bed, they will only ever abandon it when time comes for them." He smiled, if a bit mournfully. "And my life is much longer than theirs. I fear I was uninterested in suffering that kind of loss again."

"Losing pets can be hard." She was feeding chunks to the second hound now. Luri had abandoned him to wait her turn for some meat. "But the love they give us in the meanwhile more than makes up for it."

"Perhaps you are right."

"I wouldn't mind sharing a bed with this big doofus," she said through a chuckle, as she petted one of the hounds. "I bet you take up the whole dang thing, don'tcha? Yeah, you do, huh doggo? Yeah, you do."

He had to laugh at the tone of voice she took when talking to the animals. They seemed to enjoy it, however undignified it was. "You are good with them."

"I'm holding greasy meat." But the young woman was

beaming. And it was clear the dogs instantly recognized her affection for them and sought to return it.

"Well, regardless, you are welcome to come and enjoy their company as often as you wish. You may even let them out and take them inside if the dreary chill becomes too much for you." He wasn't certain why he was giving her such free rein in his home.

Hope, he supposed. What a treacherous thing, that.

After the two pies were gone, eagerly gobbled up by the dogs, she even let one of them hop up and lick her face. She did seem to adore them. And Mordred could tell that it was easily and instantly requited. Although, he should not be so surprised. There were precious few creatures of flesh and blood that called his keep their home.

The animals did not take kindly to his armored creations.

"Thank you." She smiled at him again. "For not keeping me locked up in a cell, or...torturing me, or putting me in the Crystal."

"Do not thank me. You simply have not yet had reason to suffer the weight of my cruelty." He kicked himself mentally as he watched her expression fade again to one of nervousness. "For the moment, I have no reason to be unkind to you. I do not believe you have come here to Avalon of your own volition." He reached out and petted one of his hounds. "I believe you know more than you are telling me, however."

"I—um—"

"No." He lifted his clawed hand to silence her. "Do not lie to me. Do not make excuses. You are protecting yourself and your own safety. I cannot fault you for it."

She smiled at him. It broke something in him he had not

known was left to shatter. "You don't seem like the asshole everybody makes you out to be."

"Thank you. I suppose." He studied her for a long moment, the hope that perhaps he could trust someone, finally, after all the centuries, clawing at him again, scratching at the door to his soul like an impatient animal.

He was a fool. A total, utter, complete idiot. With a breath, he shut his eyes and gave up. Opening the gate to the kennel, he let the four dogs free to run about the courtyard. One of them, the bigger male named Eod, was dancing around Gwen. He was smitten with the young woman.

With a slowly building sense of impending dread, Mordred wondered if the dog was alone in that or not.

He needed some time to think. "I must leave you for the afternoon. I have business to attend. Will you join us for dinner?"

"Us?" She looked up at him curiously.

"My knights. Those who remain in the keep at the moment."

"Oh." She smiled. "Sure. I can spend an afternoon playing with *this big puppy*, huh?" She ruffled Eod's ears.

"His name is Eod." Mordred tried not to feel jealous of the dog's receipt of her attention. Though he did not much wish for her to speak to him like he was an infant. "And he is hardly a puppy."

"Nope. All dogs are puppies." She seemed quite sure of herself on that topic, and he did not have the heart to argue with her over it. "Some are just older than others."

By the Ancients, he needed to put distance between them before he threw her over his shoulder and brought her to his bed.

"Have a good afternoon, Gwen." Without another word, he walked away from her, desperate to get some air and to clear his head.

"Um—bye," she called after him.

Cursing himself, he marched to the keep, one question burning in his mind. *Damn it all to the pits, what am I to do now?*

Thirteen

My lady?"

Someone nudged Gwen in the shoulder. She hummed, lifting her head. She had launched into an epic game of stick with Eod before they had gone inside. After that, she had sat down on a sofa next to a fire, the dog curled up next to her, and that must've been enough for her to doze off. It had been an exhausting day so far, to be fair.

The dog in question was upside down, legs stuck up in the air at odd angles, next to her, snoring. She smiled.

A suit of armor was standing in front of her. He bowed his head. "The prince invites you to join him for supper."

Was it that late already? She rubbed her eyes with the back of her hand. "Yeah, sure. Sorry." Standing, she smoothed out her clothes and her cape, and then ruffled the dog's ears. "Hey, buddy. Dinnertime."

That got the dog awake in an instant. In a tangle of long limbs, he was up and shaking himself off. The armor bowed again, and turned to lead her to the great hall.

When she walked in, the dog let out a loud *boof* and ran into the room, nails scrabbling on the wood floor. It was only when she saw the direction the dog was going in that she realized there were more people in the room than she expected. *Oh, right. The other knights.*

Mordred sat at the head of the table, staring sourly at his goblet. There were three other men in the room, one of whom she recognized as Galahad. She had seen one of the others, the man in silver, the night she had been chained to the post in the village. But he had been in full armor and, to be fair, they hadn't really exactly met. The other was a stranger.

The man in silver had dark brown hair and glistening eyes that looked like the molten metal he represented. He looked young, with a friendly face and a bright smile. The word for him was *dashing*, there was no other option. He was the one that Eod had run over to greet, and he was now happily scratching the animal's head and letting the dog lick his cheek. "Hello, Eod! My lovely gentleman, who let you in, hm? I certainly won't complain. But you know how Mordred is about you being underfoot."

The man in copper was probably shorter than the rest, but looked twice as wide. He instantly kind of reminded her of a fantasy dwarf, if a dwarf shaved. He had a rigid, blocky chin and bold features. His expression was more wary than the others'. His hair was the color of polished copper.

"Um. Hi, guys." Gwen smiled nervously.

Upon seeing her, the man in silver shot up to his feet, almost tripping over himself to bow. "My lady, welcome. Forgive my rudeness."

She chuckled. "I'm not a lady. Trust me. But thanks." She walked up to him and held out her hand to shake his. "And thank you for the cloak the other night."

He took her hand but bent to kiss her knuckles. Right. That's what they did here. "It was my pleasure." He smiled at her, his cheeks dimpling like a cherub as he did. "I am Sir Lancelot, the Knight in Silver."

"Gwen." She smiled, trying not to feel like she was meeting a celebrity. "The idiot on fire."

Mordred snorted at that.

Lancelot chuckled and gestured at the other two men at the table. "This is Sir Percival, the Knight in Copper. I believe you have already met our dear Galahad."

"Hard to miss Lurch from the Addams Family over there." At Lancelot's confused stare, she sighed. "Sorry. I keep making references nobody is going to get. I just meant he, uh, stands out."

"That he does." Lancelot smiled. "Like a signpost in a marsh. Will you join us?"

Gwen looked to Mordred. He finally lifted his gaze from his goblet and gestured a clawed hand at the seat next to him. They had left her a spot between him and Lancelot. A second later, he grasped his goblet and downed the contents before pouring himself another glass of wine.

What's gotten into him? She furrowed her brow.

"Forgive him his moods," Lancelot murmured to her, barely audibly. "If you can."

"I heard you, knight." Now Mordred was glaring a dagger at the other man.

"I am hardly to blame for your poor company this evening." Lancelot shrugged and led Gwen to the chair. He pulled it out for her, and as she sat, he pushed it in. "Nor should she suffer for it."

She was fairly convinced that she was to blame, however. She just wasn't sure what she'd done to set him off. "It's all right. He's allowed."

"Do not give him excuses," Lancelot said with a small smile. "Though he never needs any."

"Enough." Mordred's gauntleted hand tightened to a fist on the table.

"Tell us of Earth, Lady Gwen." Percival interrupted the awkward exchange. He had a deep, gruff, but not unpleasant voice. "It has been many ages since we have seen it."

"I. Well." Now she really wished she had paid more attention in history class. "A lot has changed, but I guess a lot has stayed the same too. People are still people. But we have all sorts of technology now. Like planes. We can fly anywhere in the world."

"Fly?" Lancelot blinked. "Truly?"

"Yeah. In, like, large metal vehicles with big engines strapped to the side of them, and—none of that is making any sense, is it?" She laughed. Galahad, Lancelot, and Percival were all staring at her with wide eyes. Mordred was still busy glaring into his goblet.

And Eod was now lying on her feet under the table.

Avalon was weird. Not really that unpleasant, all things considered—but weird.

"Okay, so—" She picked up a fork, then put her knife perpendicularly across it like a pair of wings. "Picture a big metal bird. But the wings don't move. Instead, you have big…spinning blades that create enough force that it can go forward. God, I suck at this. I'm sorry."

"No, please go on." Lancelot was leaning on the table, hanging on her every word. "The spinning blades push it forward like wings?"

"Right. It pushes it along, and the curve of the wings means that once it gets up to speed, it can take off and fly." She mimed the action with her weird fork-knife plane. "And it can carry hundreds of people and cargo across the world. We can go from America to England in, like…five hours? Six?"

That wound up with her launching into a long conversation with the knights about Earth and what had changed. They knew about America—it had just been settled when Avalon had shut its gates—but they were fascinated by things like the internet, modern politics and warfare, travel, cars, and the rest. When she was done with her lecture, Gwen reached out and took a roll from the tray in front of her. Tearing off a bit of it, she slipped it under the table to Eod, who happily gobbled it up from her fingers.

"You'll spoil him, you know." Galahad smiled at her warmly. It was clear he didn't really mind.

"That's what pets are for. To be spoiled rotten." She smiled back at him. "Although, I should watch my mouth. I'm about half a step from being the new resident pet here." She snickered and gestured at the iron necklace that kept her from bursting into flames. "Being a prisoner, and all."

"Hardly a pet." Lancelot smiled at her playfully. "But if you were, you could be certain I would be spoiling you rotten."

Mordred was attempting to glare a hole into the silver knight.

Oh no. Now she had to deal with *two* of them flirting with her? She really hoped Galahad and Percival didn't make things worse and add to the problem.

She cleared her throat and downed her glass of wine. She coughed and reached for a refill before picking at the dinner on her plate. It was all very tasty, but it was hard not to be distracted by the tense conversation going on around her. "Thanks. I think."

"The thanks is mine to give you, believe me." Lancelot poured her the new glass of wine. "It has been quite some time since we have had such lovely and entertaining company. God knows we have been here by ourselves for far, far too long." He shot a glance at Galahad. "The gold one has started to look appealing."

"Do not try your luck, whelp." Galahad's smile revealed he was hardly upset. "I can still knock you about the ears if I must."

She chuckled. What a group of weirdos. But she found herself smiling more than not. Even if Mordred did look like he was about to explode. Or murder somebody. Or both. In no particular order.

"Tell me, Lady Gwendolyn," Lancelot began, picking up a grape from a platter of food in front of him. "Do you ride?"

"Horses? And just Gwen is fine. Seriously." She sipped her wine. "I love horses."

"Would you like to join me for a ride tomorrow morning at dawn? I often take the hounds out to the woods to hunt for rabbits. They need the exercise." Lancelot smiled.

Mordred growled quietly, his hand tightening into a fist.

Gwen glanced to the prince, then to the knight, and then back to the prince. "Am . . . I allowed?"

"Yes, my *liege,* is she allowed?" Lancelot sneered at Mordred.

Oh, shit. There was drama between those two. Drama she was clearly now smack in the middle of. She shrank back into her chair. "I don't want to start problems."

Mordred shut his eyes, obviously on the edge of losing his temper. "You may ride with Lancelot if you wish." Each word clearly took every ounce of patience he had.

Lancelot was smiling at her, his silver eyes bright with hope. It was clear he very, very much wanted her to go with him.

Riding out into the woods and seeing more of Avalon sounded exciting. Gwen loved horses, and it'd been a long time since she had a chance to ride. "Um . . . sure. That sounds great."

"Fantastic! It is settled. Do not worry, my prince, I will return her to you in one piece." Lancelot raised his glass to Mordred in a clearly sarcastic salute.

"Ensure that you do." Mordred pushed up from the table abruptly and stormed from the room. Everyone watched him leave with various reactions.

Galahad looked disappointed. Percival, wary. And Lancelot looked like the cat who had eaten the canary.

Gwen felt guilty all of a sudden. Mordred clearly was upset, and she didn't know why. "I'll see you all around. It was really nice to meet you all." Getting up, she headed out of the room without waiting for anyone to reply.

Feeling a chill breeze, she headed in its direction. There was a door open that led to a balcony overlooking the courtyard.

Mordred was standing by the railing, his clawed hands resting on the stone. The hood of his black cloak was up over his hair, and he looked like a proper nightmare, cut against the fading daylight and gray sky.

"Are you all right?" She approached but kept her distance. He reminded her of a semi-tamed jungle cat. Probably wasn't going to lash out, but it was a roll of the dice every time.

He turned his head slightly. "Come to scold me for my poor manners?"

"No. Just worried about you." She leaned against the wall by the door.

"You cannot possibly be concerned about me."

"Yeah, I can, because you don't seem okay." She knew she probably shouldn't care. But here she was, and she was an idiot when it came to things like this. She shrugged. "And maybe I shouldn't be worried, but I am."

After a moment of silence, he spoke up. "Be wary of Lancelot. He cannot be trusted." His claws tapped against the stone in succession. *Tap-tap-tap-tap.* It sent a shiver down her spine.

"Then . . . why do you keep him around?" She frowned.

He laughed mirthlessly. "I am certain he will tell you the tale tomorrow. I suppose it would be time for you to fully grasp the truth of who I am." He turned to her, and before she could retreat, he closed the distance between them. Hooking his claw through the front of her metal necklace, he yanked her roughly away from the wall, sending her staggering into him. She had to grab him to keep from planting straight into his chest.

Smirking down at her, he tightened his grasp. "You should fear me."

Searching his rust-colored eyes, she knew he was probably right. Sure, he was scary as hell, but she didn't think that was really the core of the problem. "Why do you want me to hate you?"

He flinched. But he didn't retreat. "Because it is inevitable."

"Maybe that's true." She met his molten gaze. "But I get to make my own choices. I'll decide whether or not I hate or fear you."

He wrapped an arm around her lower back and pulled her flush against him. He was wearing his armor that was part of him, but it felt no less firm than it should have. It was cold against her skin. "Who is the one who holds your leash, firefly? Who is the one who has sent you here? Give me his name."

She had promised not to lie to him. "I don't know. He won't tell me."

He hummed. "Then he is no fool." The claw that was hooked into her necklace released her to trace the sharp point up along her cheek. She shuddered, her arms breaking out in goose bumps at the sensation.

He rested his thumb against the hollow of her chin, the point of the talon pricking her lower lip. She couldn't move. She couldn't breathe. He smelled sharp and metallic, but also had the hint of sandalwood and spices about him.

Her head was spinning. "I..."

Just as quickly as he was there, he was gone. He took a step away from her and gestured for the exit. "Go on, firefly. Before you faint again."

Her heart was pounding in her ears. She didn't argue. Heading for the hallway as fast as she could, she made it a hundred feet before she fell against the wall, struggling to fill her lungs. Damn it. Damn it all.

But it hadn't just been fear that had been to blame for her racing heart or her hasty retreat.

It was the fact that he had looked like he was going to kiss her.

And she had wanted him to.

I am so screwed.

FOURTEEN

Gwen spent the next hour pacing the keep. Sure, she was exploring. But mostly she was just wandering. She didn't know what to do. Part of her wanted to storm up to Mordred and slap him for being such a shithead. Part of her wanted to kiss him. Or more accurately, have *him* kiss *her*.

The other part wanted to see if she could make a break for it and run for her life.

What she needed to be doing was earning the prince's trust so she could convince him to take the damn necklace off permanently. But could she win his confidence just to turn around and break it? Did she honestly have a choice?

If she didn't... he'd cram her in the Crystal with everyone else. Wouldn't he? He was just waiting to learn the secret of the jackass cat.

Her feet were starting to get sore when she gave up her incessant wandering and decided to flop down in a fluffy chair in a library. She wrapped a fur blanket around herself and glared at the cold, unlit fireplace.

Stupid Avalon being cold all the time. She shivered.

"Can you not light it?"

Jolting in surprise, she looked up. It was Lancelot. The silver knight smiled lopsidedly down at her. He, like all of Mordred's knights and the prince himself, was attractive. She wondered if all of Arthur's knights had been lookers. But Lancelot had that *dashing*, knight-in-shining-armor thing down to a T. She supposed he should, he likely invented the vibe.

"No." She tapped the necklace. "And even if I could try, I'd probably just succeed in burning the whole dumb building down instead."

Lancelot laughed. "I meant with a striker, you silly thing." He walked over to the fire and knelt.

"Oh." Now she really did feel like an idiot. "Yeah, I guess I could've tried that first."

He shook his head, still chuckling, as he lit the fire and puffed on it to get the cinders going. "Cold tends to cling to this place. And you will be more sensitive to it than most, given your nature."

"Yay, me."

He stood, brushing some dust from his knees, and nudged at one of the logs with a poker. It was already crackling. "I must apologize for Mordred's behavior. He is prone to fits of deep despair and violent anger. It has always been his way."

"I guess I'll take the despair over the anger, although neither are really that fun." She smiled at him. "Thanks for the warmth."

"Of course. May I join you?"

"Sure."

He sat in a chair opposite her and studied her for a minute. "I am sorry to see you trapped in this place with him. With all of us. We are no more cheerful than he is, I fear."

"You seem to hate him."

"I despise him."

"Then . . . why do you serve him?"

"I must." He grimaced in disgust. "I have no choice, my lady. And for more reasons than knightly honor."

"Like . . . what?"

He sighed. "The walls have armored ears. I will tell you the whole tale tomorrow. While Mordred knows the truth of it, same as I, he might take offense at my choice of words."

That sounded like a giant can of worms. Great. More drama. "Is he really as bad as everybody makes him out to be?"

"He does what he does in the belief he serves a noble cause. For that, I cannot fully condemn his terrible deeds. But each time I see a beautiful flower trodden beneath his boot in the name of this malignant peace of his, I weep for it." Lancelot stared into the fire, his expression tight.

She was glad he wasn't looking at her. She'd hate to see her blush at being called beautiful. Or at least, she assumed he was talking about her. "I just want to go home. I don't think I belong here."

"No one belongs here. Not anymore."

"What do you mean?"

He sighed. "Avalon is meant to be a wilderness—a chaotic tangle of magic and mystery. So, *what* if we were always gripped with shifting factions and war? We were alive. We had beauty and danger—love and loss. Now we merely stagnate in this . . . nonexistence." Lancelot shut his silver eyes and bowed his head. "Forgive me. I should not be troubling you with all this."

"No, every bit helps. I still don't know which end is up. I'm just a pawn in somebody else's game, so . . . it's nice to meet the other pieces on the board." Gwen smiled gently to reassure the knight that he was actually helping her. It wasn't a total lie. Her smile faded quickly, however. "I'm trying to figure out what I'm supposed to do—or even better, what I *want* to do. I need to understand everything before I figure out whether or not I should go home."

"Sadly, elementals like you are doomed to stay in Avalon, lest you fade and die. I fear you are trapped here."

"I guess." Well, that was if she were a real elemental. And not simply borrowing Merlin's powers because of their weird life-joining-thingy. Hopefully, the cat wasn't lying to her and it was reversible. Hopefully. But she didn't trust that cat as far as she could throw him. Although, honestly, it would be pretty easy to pick up that scrawny creature and chuck him off a balcony. Now that she knew he wasn't even really a cat, she probably wouldn't feel too bad about it either.

But it meant she had no one to trust. She wished she had someone to rely on. Well, someone that wasn't Eod the dog, anyway. Her thoughts trailed back to Mordred.

And it went from Mordred on to everything the Prince in Iron had done. To both the island *and* his knights. She sighed. "I'm sorry you're trapped here too."

"Weep not for me, my lady. I wrote my own fate long ago." He leaned back in his chair and cast her a weary smile. "Though if it still allows me to spend time with you, I suppose it cannot be all for naught."

She chuckled and glanced away. She didn't know how to handle being flirted with on a good day, let alone this kind of situation. "Oh, come on. I'm sure there's a lovely suit of armor around here for you to romance."

He joined her in her laugh. "I fear my tastes run differently. Call me predictable, if you will."

"You men are all the same. Wanting a lady who has, y'know,

flesh." She was enjoying teasing him, even if it was inching into dangerous territory. But who said she couldn't flirt with the handsome knight if she wanted to?

"I know. What rogues we are." He was grinning at her playfully. "Veritable demons." He leaned his elbows on his knees. The firelight made his silver eyes glint in a fascinating way. "I look forward to our ride tomorrow."

"I'd love to see more of Avalon."

"Sadly, there is not much to see these days. Not since the Crystal was made." He stood. Taking her hand, he bowed and kissed her knuckles. "I will take my leave. Sleep well, my lady. And if your room is cold when you go to bed...try lighting the fire."

Laughing, she rolled her eyes. "Yeah, *yeah*..."

Silver eyes twinkling in mischief, he left her there alone. The moment he was gone, she realized she had been enjoying his company. It had done wonders in filling the silence. And more importantly, it had drowned out her thoughts.

And her single, burning question.

What am I supposed to do?

Gwen woke up in the middle of the night to someone knocking quietly on the door. Well, she assumed it was the middle of the night. The fire that had been burning was now little more than coals. And she was in that groggy who-the-hell-am-I, what-year-is-it state of groggy as she sat up. "Yeah?"

"Someone is...eh...insisting on seeing you, my lady." It was one of the guards on the other side of the door. "I'm afraid he's going to ruin the woodwork. May I let him in?"

Furrowing her brow, she blinked away her sleepiness and sat

up. "Um. Sure?" If it was Mordred or Lancelot, she was going to have to—

The door clicked open. A scrabble of nails, and then a giant dog jumped onto the bed, tail swishing excitedly.

Laughing, she almost fell back over. "Oh, it's just you, buddy. Hi, Eod." She chuckled and ruffled the dog's ears. "All right, you can sleep up here." Honestly, she would be happy to have the extra warmth. And the company.

The door clicked shut as the guard closed it again.

Flopping back down on her side, she settled in. Eod seemed more than happy to curl up next to her and let out a long, exaggerated sigh as he did the same thing. Slinging an arm over his furry side, she shut her eyes. "You better not have fleas."

A few stray kicks to the side notwithstanding, she slept better that night than she had the previous one. And maybe Eod scared off Merlin, because she didn't wake up to getting lectured by the asshole cat. It's not like he'd have had any new instructions for her—the mission was still clear.

Get Mordred to take the necklace off permanently, so she could try to blow up the Crystal. She was assuming the second part. But she didn't know if she agreed with its destruction in the first place. What if Avalon really was better off this way?

She'd have to do some digging. Find out some more information about Avalon. Once she had all the information, she'd make up her mind for herself whether or not the Iron Crystal should exist or not—cat be damned.

Research. She liked doing research. It wasn't a good plan, but it was something.

With a sigh, she got dressed, brushed her hair, and decided that she was going to have to ask about having a bath. She knew people in Ye Olde Times didn't shower, but she was not going to be stinky if she could help it. Eod followed her downstairs, leading her to where breakfast was set out on the large table.

She figured she'd eat a quick meal—half of which would go to the dog—then go find Lancelot by the stables for their ride. Then, she'd—

"Good morning."

With a squeak, she whirled. For a guy who was as big as Mordred and was always wearing armor, he could move *silently* when he wanted to. "Damn it!" Her heart was instantly racing. "Don't startle me."

His expression was flat. "You cannot burst into flames. I see no harm in it. Though I suppose having you faint at the breakfast table would be quite rude."

"Look, it's not my fault I have anxiety." She took a deep breath and tried to settle herself, taking a step away from him. He could be so very intense. "I didn't choose to be like this." She went to grab herself a buttered fruit-and-something pastry— something that wasn't a muffin, an action that also served to put a few extra feet between her and Mordred. "I get panic attacks."

"So you have said. What does that mean, and what inspires them?"

"It means I get these moments where I, well, panic. Sometimes, for a good reason. Sometimes, for no reason at all. I can't breathe, everything gets too close. I feel smothered. I usually then pass out, yeah." She sighed. "They ruin my life. So please don't make fun of me for it. People've been doing that ever since I was a kid."

His expression smoothed, some of the hardness softening.

"Forgive me. I did not mean to offend. Have you never attempted to control them?"

"Oh, sure. But it's not as easy as it sounds. And my parents don't believe in medication for it, so if I'm living with them, I can't very well go around their backs." She shut her eyes.

He stepped back up to her, closing the distance between them. With the crook of a claw, he lifted her head up to look at him. "Do you miss your home?"

"A little." She felt caught in those molten rusty eyes of his. "Maybe. How'd you guess?"

"The look in your eye when you said it." His hand rested on her shoulder. It was clear the next words were a struggle for him to say. "Forgive me for my harsh moods yesterday."

"It's all right." She smiled faintly. "I guess being as old as you are is gonna come with some emotional baggage."

He huffed a laugh. "I suppose." He paused. "Perhaps, in time, Avalon could become your home. Perhaps this place could be what it was you sought in the city with your friends."

It was a lovely thought. And maybe it was something she could honestly have. "You'd get sick of me underfoot and pestering you with a thousand questions a minute."

"It has been silent here for a very long time. We could use a little chatter." After a moment's hesitation, he pulled his hand from her shoulder. "Please be careful this morning. Lancelot is a kind man, but I will remind you that he is not to be trusted."

"Can anybody be trusted around here?" She gestured at Eod. "Besides the dog."

"No one." He reached down and scratched the animal's head. "Besides the dog."

"Have you lied to me?"

"Well, for one, if I were to lie to you, why would I confess it now?" He walked over to the chair by the fireplace and sank into it. "And two, no. I have not. I have told you, perhaps too bluntly, the truth as I have it."

"Thank you for that. That's all I'd need."

"What, for the tyrant who is keeping you his prisoner of war to be feeding you lies as well? Yes, I do suppose that would make things more inconvenient." He snorted.

"You're making fun of me again."

"Not in the slightest." He smirked.

Silence stretched between them for a second. She let out a breath. "Can I ask you for a favor?"

"I may not grant it. But you may ask."

"Would it be possible to bathe later today?" She tore off a small piece of the food she was holding, making sure to avoid the fruit, and gave it to Eod. She was not above bribing an animal for affection. Not in the slightest.

"After we train this afternoon, I will see what I can do."

She winced. Great. More training. "Just promise not to kick my ass again."

"I will make no such promise. It is very easy to 'kick your ass.' I may do it unintentionally."

She glared at him.

"And you wanted me not to lie to you." He huffed. "How quickly their minds change." But he was clearly fighting a smile.

"Jerk." She also couldn't help but smile again. "C'mon, Eod. Let's go find Lancelot. Maybe they have squirrels in Avalon. You wanna go chase a magical fucked-up squirrel? Do you? I think you do!"

Judging by the way his ears perked up, yes, they did very much have squirrels in Avalon. Whether or not they were magical or fucked-up remained to be seen.

She heard Mordred quietly laughing as she left the room.

He was a confusing bag of problems. But she'd deal with things one at a time. And right now, she had a knight waiting for her and a dog eager to chase squirrels. She'd better not keep either of them waiting.

FIFTEEN

Gwen was smiling as she walked into the stables. She shouldn't be. She had been sucked into a magical world full of monsters and her life was in danger. But weirdly it didn't *feel* in danger. Honestly, that might be because everything still felt like she was stuck in a dream. She wasn't really surrounded by strange, magical suits of armor. Or men who had been alive since before the Middle Ages and who had fought with King Arthur. It was all a dream.

She'd wake up in the hospital, covered in burns—or maybe she was in a coma and she'd never wake up again. Or maybe this was her messed-up version of an afterlife. She didn't know. It just made it easier to ignore all the insanity if she refused to accept, deep down, that any of it was really happening.

She wasn't about to go on a nice little countryside ride on a horse with the actual, honest-to-God, one and only *Lancelot.* Nope. Just lying in a hospital bed somewhere, dying of severe burns. Which would explain the whole "lol, I'm made of fire" portion of her delusion.

Didn't it?

But, hey. She had an option. She could either devolve into fits of hysteria and screaming...or she could embrace the adventure. She finally had a chance at what she had always wanted—to go somewhere, to do something, to *mean* something. Even if that was right smack into the middle of some otherworldly drama, it was at least better than being stuck on a farm in Kansas.

And this morning there were horses. The stable was full. And most were even normal-looking horses. There was one in the back that she just *had* to assume was Mordred's. It was made entirely out of armor, and its eyes were glowing the same eerie opal-white as all the rest of the magic in the world.

And it was scary-looking as all hell. She chuckled as she saw it, shaking her head in disbelief. It was almost as tall as a Clydesdale, with jagged, pointed panels of armor. When it noticed her looking at it, it snorted and kicked its hoof against the wooden gate.

"Ignore him. He's...unfriendly." Lancelot was in one of the other stables, patting the neck of a normal-looking white stallion. "Much like his master."

"Maybe he just needs a hug." She smirked. *Much like his master,* she finished in her head. She opted to leave that bit out. That was all she needed—a lecture from Lancelot about her interest in Mordred.

Was it interest? There was certainly attraction. She didn't know. She needed more time to figure it out.

The knight chuckled. "Good luck and godspeed should you try." He motioned toward one of the other open stables. "Nina is all ready for you."

"Oh, hello there, sweetheart." She smiled at the horse in question. She was a beautiful black-and-white-spotted mare. Walking up to her, she reached out her hand to let the horse sniff her. When the animal nosed her, wondering if she had treats, she chuckled. "Maybe when we get back, I'll see if I can find a nice carrot for you, huh?"

"Do you spoil your lovers the same way you spoil animals?" Lancelot teased as he led his own horse out of the stable and into the center aisle. The four hounds were already running around the courtyard, barking and playing, sensing that they were about to go out and about.

"Animals deserve it." Gwen followed after him, holding the reins to Nina as she led the mare outside. Lancelot was a flirt. That tracked, she supposed. But she didn't take it seriously. It was probably just how he liked to talk.

"Well, I suppose I will just have to earn it then. My lady, do you need assistance with mounting your horse?"

"Nah, but thanks." She smiled. "This isn't the first time I've saddled up and ridden, though I admit I'm a little out of practice."

He put his foot in the stirrup and mounted his stallion. Lancelot grinned at her playfully over his shoulder. "You could saddle me and ride me off into the field if it would help."

She laughed and rolled her eyes at the same time. "That was the worst pickup line I've ever heard. And you wish." She hopped up onto the horse, having to gather up the fabric of her dress around her thighs to keep from flashing Lancelot in the worst way. It was awkward, riding a horse in a skirt. But she was not going to ride side-saddle even if it killed her.

Lancelot led the way as they rode out of the courtyard, heading toward the gate in the rampart that was already open for them. The field beyond was dry, the grass the pale yellow-white color of hay. It swayed and rustled in the wind.

Perpetual autumn. Right. This place hadn't had a spring, summer, or winter in...honestly, she didn't know. Three hundred years, ish? Maybe? Or sunlight, for that matter. She rode alongside him as they plodded out into the field. Eod and his other doggy friends were already running ahead of them toward the woods, chasing each other or stopping to sniff things in the tall grass.

There was a packed dirt road that led down a slope toward the woods. Turning, she looked back up at the keep. It was an impressive stone building, looking like every cartoon or cliché castle she could think of. It sat built into a cliff, surrounded by nothing on three sides, and the field on the fourth. It must make it really easy to defend.

But also really easy to get trapped inside, she figured.

Mordred has a dragon. He can fly off whenever he wants.

"Do places like this still exist on Earth?" Lancelot asked, noticing what she was staring at.

"Mostly as museums or ruins. There are still some that people live in, I guess. It's beautiful, if a bit severe." *Much like its master,* she added again in her head.

"It would not look so gloomy if the sun ever shone in Avalon." He sighed. "I am merely glad that the plants and animals receive enough light to survive. What a tragedy it would be if we were in a total wasteland."

"I'd get so depressed, never seeing the sun." She frowned. "I can't imagine how you all put up with it." Their horses walked side by side along the path as they approached the trees. They were tall, some with bare branches, others with brown leaves holding on. There were very few evergreens in the mix, but even those she saw were somehow forlorn and desaturated in the gray and dreary overcast light.

"We have no choice. We cannot die. We cannot live." Lancelot's features were set into a glower as he stared ahead at the woods. "But certainly, it is better to languish in such a terrible state of nonexistence when the alternative is chaos and war, yes?"

She almost laughed at how thick his sarcasm was. "I don't know, honestly. I'm still trying to figure that out. Do you really think it's my place to decide the fate of everybody on the island?" It was bizarre of her to think that they would put so much trust in her. They didn't know her. And she didn't know them. They must really be desperate.

"Yes! You must see that you are—" He sighed. "I am sorry. I do not mean to burden you with these troubles of ours. You have enough with which to contend without me heaping more atop the rest."

"No, I'd rather know. What do you mean?" The forest road turned a corner, taking them past a pond with an arrangement of rocks around the edges that didn't look natural. They were placed every few feet in a ring, almost like they were meant for people to sit on—or like a small stone henge. But judging by the moss and leaves covering them, whatever it was meant for hadn't been used in a long time.

"It would be best if I explained first why I am bound to service to Mordred. It might give you some insight into my feelings." Lancelot shut his eyes as if bracing himself for a long and painful story. "I was a loyal knight to King Arthur. The one and true ruler of Avalon. I came here with the others—including Mordred—when Arthur was mortally wounded in battle. We brought him here in hopes that his life could be saved by the magic of the isle. But in a crime against God and all fairness, it chose Mordred instead."

Gwen stayed quiet, listening. That lined up at least with the bit that Mordred had told her.

Lancelot continued. "On his deathbed, seeing that Mordred had been chosen over him, Arthur did the noble thing—passed his sword and his crown to his nephew."

His crown? Mordred was supposed to be king? "But he's still a prince." They rode past a giant tree that reached up high over them. It must have been ancient. She stared up at it, mouth agape, marveling at its enormity. She had gone to the West Coast a few times with her dad to visit family and go camping—the tree was easily the size of a redwood, though it looked more like an ash tree than anything else.

"The other elementals of Avalon refused to recognize him. And I agree with them." Lancelot sneered. "And my fervor to see the wrongs of this world made right began that day and has only increased since then. I rallied the loyal knights to stand against Mordred. I thought perhaps that if Mordred were dead, the gift of iron would go to Arthur as God intended."

"You tried to kill him?" *No wonder Mordred doesn't trust any of you. No wonder Mordred doesn't trust anyone.* She blinked. "Fuck. Clearly, it didn't work."

"No. He bested us all. And one by one, we fell to his blade." Lancelot's expression turned taut and strained. As if remembering something horrible. "He did not stop until he had slain us all."

As if remembering that time when he had died.

"You're…you're kidding me." She couldn't believe it. "You died? But—"

"How am I still here?" He laughed dryly. "Ah, therein is the other part of Mordred's *secret*. He was cursed long before he came here."

"I don't understand…"

"Arthur had a sister by the name of Morgana. *Half* sister, to be clear. The product of a mortal woman and a fae."

"Like Galahad."

"Indeed. Morgana was a powerful enchantress and fae in

her own right—that blood runs strong and oft outweighs the mortal half. And it was that curse that she passed on to her son, Mordred."

"Who was Mordred's father?"

Lancelot sneered. "If you are to believe some? Arthur himself."

She wrinkled her nose. "Ew."

"In short, no one knows for certain. I doubt Mordred even knows." He shrugged. "But, Morgana was power-hungry and ruthless. I would not put it past her to disguise herself with a glamor to seduce her own half brother if it meant her own off-spring would become King of the Britons. How proud she must be, watching us from her grave, the *bitch*."

They rode by an embankment next to a large field that stretched out to another wooded glade. Gwen could see the mountain at the center of Avalon off in the distance, the peak reaching up to the clouds and disappearing amongst them. Even faded and gray, it was beautiful here. "So, Mordred used fairy magic to bring you back?"

"In combination with his new gifts as an elemental, yes." He undid the tie of his cloak and unlaced the neck of his shirt. He pulled the hem to the side, revealing a strange, opalescent crystal embedded in his chest. The veins around it pulsed with the beat of his heart. "We are kept as we are—forced to serve him. We are not much more than his slaves."

She shivered at the idea. She understood why Mordred would be angry that they had turned on him...but this? Sixteen hundred years of slavery? She furrowed her brow. "But why? Why keep you like this?"

"To punish us, I expect. And that is why it is so important that you have come here, my lady. I hate to burden you with all our troubles, but you *must* understand how crucial you are to us." He laced his shirt back up.

She shook her head. "But why? Why can't you just try to sneak up on him again?"

"I cannot act against Mordred. He has removed that freedom of choice from his *most loyal* knights." He grimaced in rage. He might not be able to raise his hand against Mordred, but damn if it wasn't obvious that he wanted to. "We cannot stand against him. But you... you can."

"Is that why you wanted to take me out here? To ask me to betray Mordred?" She gestured at the field as they kept riding, following the road back into the woods.

"And to enjoy the countryside with a beautiful young woman, yes." His expression softened. He ran a hand back over his dark hair. "Am I not allowed to have two motives?"

"I don't know if you're going to be successful with either of them." She shook her head. "I can't fight Mordred. Look at me. I'm just some idiot from backwater Kansas. I'm his prisoner. You honestly think I could stand up to him?"

"I'm not suggesting you pick up a broadsword." He chuckled. "You have another avenue of attack. You can get close to him. He has ventured out of his chambers more in these past few days than he has in years. He seeks you out. He is clearly smitten with you."

"Okay, look. I really don't like the fact that you people keep asking me to sleep with him just to put a knife in his back." She made a face. "It's sexist and it's wrong."

"People? Who else has suggested this?" Lancelot swiveled in his saddle to face her. "Who else wishes to see him brought down?"

"The thing that brought me here. I don't know his name."

She wondered if she hadn't just made a terrible mistake. But wasn't she supposed to be on Lancelot and Merlin's side? Wasn't she supposed to want to bring down the evil tyrant?

Problem was, Mordred didn't *seem* evil. Wrong, maybe. But not evil. She looked away. But how could she condone what he had done to Lancelot and the others? Did they really deserve it? She...honestly didn't know. But she needed to figure it out. Letting out a breath, she shook her head. "The thing that brought me here wants me to do the same thing you're asking me to do."

"Then, that is what you should do. I understand that it might feel underhanded to use your—"

"If you say 'feminine wiles,' I swear to *fuck* I'm going to scream."

Lancelot stammered. "Well. Um." He paused. "The fact remains."

"I'll think about it. Is that good enough?"

"That is all I could ask."

"Great." She kicked Nina in the sides, and sent the horse trotting past him. She wanted to feel the wind. She wanted to feel the freedom of a gallop. She also wanted to get the hell away from the conversation. She urged the horse forward, and Nina was more than happy to oblige.

The dogs saw the galloping horse and immediately wanted to join in the fun, racing alongside her or running ahead.

For a moment, Gwen felt like she was flying. For a moment, she felt free. When she finally trotted back to a walk by the forest, she was also ready to cry. She had gone from wanting an adventure to having people heap all of this nonsense on her. It was too much all at once.

"You're quite the rider," Lancelot called out as he slowed down beside her. "I am impressed. You ride like a man."

"No, I ride like a woman who knows how to ride a horse." She rolled her eyes. She supposed she couldn't fault the man for being a bit blockheaded. He was from a different time. "It helps when you can sit on a horse the right way. And not side-saddle."

"I suppose that is quite true. I imagine that trousers would also be of assistance in such an affair." He shrugged. "We should have some made for you."

"That'd help. I hate to think about the chafing I'm going to have later." She cringed. The dress was really comfortable, all things considered.

"I could—"

She cut him off before he could say something lascivious. "Nope, nope. Stop right there."

Laughing, he kicked his stallion and rode along the path into the woods. "You know me so well already."

"Your kind aren't hard to predict." She followed him.

"I fear you are much more of a mystery to me."

"Not used to girls who speak their minds?"

"Hardly. I have known many a fierce woman in my day. Avalon was once filled with them. A few remain, here or there, scattered about—but like all the rest of what made this world beautiful, they are now a rarity." He looked mournful again. She wondered if he'd lost someone he valued into the Crystal.

She decided she had heard enough tragedy for one day. "I'm not fierce. Trust me."

"By comparison to those you know, perhaps. But do not mistake me, I much prefer an equal in all matters." He glanced over his shoulder at her. "I cannot abide meekness."

"Well, I guess you have one good thing going in your favor."

"Just one?"

"Just one."

"Damn."

Nudging Nina to walk beside Lancelot and his stallion, she turned her attention out into the woods. The dogs had all gone off to do dog things. It looked, for all intents and purposes, like a normal glade. Just...trees. Underbrush. Pine needles. The chirping of birds and the rustle of critters up in the branches. The only thing that made it interesting was how...bland it all was. The muted, gray, and faded shades of fall.

"I would have taken you to see the pixies. Or perhaps the merfolk who once lived in the bay. Or the harpies—how they would have *loved* to meet you. They would have pestered you with questions, eager to know about how the world outside had grown and changed. They adored technology in all its forms. But they are all gone." Lancelot's tone was heavy and mournful.

Gwen's shoulders slumped. "I know. But...was the world really being torn apart?"

"We suffered war. Chaos. Death. The demon Grinn who wished it all to end. That much is true. Mordred is not lying to you when he tells you of the strife that frequented this land. But it did not *consume* it. It did not cripple it. It did not leave it a shadow of its former self." He gestured a hand around them. "It should be spring. This should all be alive with strange, wild creatures. It should be beautiful. Not...this."

"I'm sorry."

"You can be more than sorry. You can be of help." He winced. "Forgive me. I do not mean to be so curt. It is just a rarity that I am given hope."

"I get it. It's all right. I'll think it over. I promise." That was her plan, at any rate.

He smiled at her. "Thank you, my lady."

"Legit, I'm not a lady." She chuckled. "You—" She stopped. One of the dogs was barking loudly in the woods. It wasn't a happy bark. It was angry and afraid. "Shit." She kicked Nina and headed off in the direction of the sound.

"Wait!"

But she didn't. Gwen kicked the horse harder as the dog kept barking. Jumping over a fallen tree, she stopped at the edge of the clearing. It was Eod. He had his head low, his tail down, and his hair was all standing up as he growled, snarled, and barked at a black bear at the other edge of the small circle of grass.

The bear was none too pleased about the dog either. Without waiting to see how things would play out, Gwen kicked Nina in the sides. The horse brayed, but obeyed and ran between the bear and the dog.

Pulling the reins and kicking her in the sides at the same time, she hoped the horse got the cue. She did. Nina reared up on her hind legs, her front hooves pawing at the air in front of the bear. The black bear, deciding it wanted nothing to do with a horse, a human, and a snarling dog, took off in the other direction at a jog.

Letting out a puff of air, Gwen patted Nina's neck. "Thanks, girl. You've definitely earned a few carrots for that."

The horse snorted and stomped annoyedly.

"Yeah, fine. Carrots and an apple." She slipped off the saddle, straightened her skirt, and headed over to Eod. "And what do you think you were doing? Oh, don't look so damn proud of yourself."

Eod was now sitting, his tail thumping happily on the ground, his tongue hanging out of the side of his mouth.

"You had nothing to do with that." She ruffled his ears. "You big idiot. Are you okay? You don't look hurt."

The dog hopped up to lick her face. No, he was perfectly fine.

"You're still an idiot and I'm still frustrated." She chuckled. "But I'm glad you're all right."

"Was that a bear?" Lancelot came to a stop at the edge of the clearing. "Did you just chase off a bear?"

"It was just a black bear on his own. They don't like to mix it up unless they've got cubs. It's fine." She shrugged. It really was no big deal. "We don't get them frequently at home, but they get into the barn looking for the goat food or bird seed occasionally."

Lancelot shook his head. "And you say you are not fierce. I am afraid of the modern women of Earth."

"Good. You should be. They'd kick your smarmy ass." She climbed back up onto Nina and clicked her tongue. "We should probably head back before this fluffy doofus gets himself into any more trouble. C'mon, Eod." She started back toward the path.

"Smarmy?" Lancelot rode behind her, letting her lead. "What does smarmy mean?"

"You. It means you. You're smarmy."

"Why do I get the distinct implication that it is not a good thing?"

She smiled, not letting him see it. She didn't want to encourage him. "Because you might be smarmy, but you aren't stupid."

"Be still my heart, the lady flatters me."

His deadpan sarcasm made her laugh. All right, maybe she could encourage him just a little.

Even if it did make things complicated.

More complicated than they already were, at any rate.

She sighed.

Even if she tried to defeat Mordred—how the hell was she supposed to try to pull that off? She didn't want to betray him. It seemed like he'd had enough of that in his life.

But what other choice did she really have?

Wait to be put into the Crystal?

Or lure Mordred in, only to put a knife in his heart?

It should be an obvious pick.

She'd heard Mordred's side and now Lancelot's side—and part of her couldn't help but sympathize more with the Knight in Silver. Especially now that she had seen just a fraction of the faded and dreary world of Avalon.

Two points to Team Destroy the Crystal. One point to Team Leave It Alone. Gwen sighed. The round wasn't over yet—and it was still anybody's game. She needed to dig deeper and brace herself for the real possibility of having to try to take a stand against Mordred and betray him.

But damn if it didn't feel *wrong*.

SIXTEEN

Mordred found himself restlessly pacing. It was not uncommon for him—he seemed to vacillate between staring into the middle distance for hours and his current action. When someone knocked on the door to his study, he found the distraction shockingly welcome. "Come in."

He was surprised to see Percival, as the Knight in Copper stepped into the room. "To what do I owe the pleasure, knight?" Mordred arched an eyebrow at the other man.

"I wish to speak to you of our new...guest." Percival was not usually one to speak with subtle choices of words.

It made Mordred instantly suspicious. He clasped his metal-clad hands behind his back, and waited. Percival had come to see him; Percival could lead the charge.

The Knight in Copper stared out the window for a moment. "Your actions regarding her are confounding. I came to seek clarification on your motivation."

That caught Mordred again by surprise. "And since when do I owe you an explanation for my actions?"

"You do not." Percival's fingers twitched at his side. "But I do not understand why you let her remain loose from the Crystal. You have been unflinching in your quest to ensure all rogue magic is contained. But you let her stay free? Why?"

"Someone is pulling her strings, Percival. I wish to know who it is so that I may stop them."

"But they need her to succeed at their goals. If she is imprisoned, they are blocked from progressing. You needn't identify them if you can stop them."

Mordred walked to the long table by the wall to pour himself and Percival a glass of wine. "And that gives them a path to try again. It may take them days, it may take them a thousand years—but if I foil their attempts now, they will seek another way." He handed Percival the glass and sipped his own.

"So you are...using her as bait?" Percival seemed unconvinced. "And you have no other motive in leaving her free?"

"I never said that I did not." Mordred shrugged. "She is harmless. A distraction from the mundanity."

"Lancelot seems to agree with you."

It took everything within Mordred to keep his expression still. "Yes. It seems so."

"You know he despises you."

"He makes it very clear."

"And now he is off riding with the girl who you *know* is plotting against you." Percival shook his head. "Unless you believe Lancelot is to blame for her arrival, I do not know what you are trying to do by allowing a malcontent to scheme with a conspirator."

"Lancelot does not have the power to grant someone the gift of flame." Mordred turned his back to Percival to stand by the window. He was waiting for the two horses to reappear from the woods with the riders in question. "While I have no doubt he is encouraging her actions against me as we speak, I am unthreatened by Lancelot. He may run his mouth as much as he wishes, but that is all he is capable of. You are well aware of that."

"Words can inspire. Words can cause harm."

"And so do actions, Percival. Until his words inspire action against me, I shall do nothing to stop him. I wish for Gwendolyn to see in me someone worthy of her trust. The path of least resistance forward from this nonsense is if she willingly surrenders to me the truth of her arrival."

"Is that all you wish for her to see in you?"

"Watch your tongue, knight." Mordred glared at the other man briefly. "Lest I remove it for you."

"It simply strikes me as odd that you would, after all these years, allow a threat to your reign to stay as your guest, when—"

"And what if your insinuations were true, Percival?" He turned to the other man, his anger boiling up. "What then?" He loomed over the Knight in Copper, using his height to intimidate the other man. It had always worked in the past, and today was no different. "She is my prisoner of war. It is my right to do with her as I wish. I will let her acclimatize to this world, to decide for herself what her fate might be. You want to fault me for this?"

"It is . . . simply out of character for you." Percival took a step back, dropping his gaze to the floor. "That is all."

"Ah! I see. Out of *character.* And what would be more so?" He sneered. "What would be more appropriate for your vision of me? Perhaps if I flayed her alive? Strung her up and ripped her skin from her bones? Tortured her until she told me all she knows?"

"N—no, I—"

"Then *what?*" Mordred fought the urge to sink his claws deep into the man's throat and rip it out. It would serve no purpose except to satiate his rage and bloodlust. He would regret it the moment it was done. "Tell me, Percival, what would you have me do?"

"I—well—" The Knight in Copper took another step back.

"You come in here seeking insight into my actions. You came even perhaps seeking to advise me. So do so. Tell me your wisdom, oh knight."

"I simply believe that if you wish to maintain your grasp on Avalon, then contending with this threat immediately would make the most logical sense. I am merely confused."

"Confused or hopeful? Believe me, Percival, I am not so naive as to think that Lancelot is the only one of you who runs his mouth behind my back." He snatched Percival by the front of his cloak and yanked him forward, almost knocking the stocky man off his feet. "State your true purpose, knight."

"I am not speaking falsely, I—"

Lifting his clawed hand, Mordred flexed his power. The crystal embedded into Percival's heart responded. The captive magic, kept suspended and trapped by the iron he imbued within it, flared. The knight screamed in pain.

"Do you wish to try again?"

"Please, my prince—" Percival's knees went out. Mordred let him fall roughly to the ground. The Knight in Copper clutched his chest.

Mordred eased off. "Why did you come to speak to me, Percival? What did you seek to learn?"

"I wished to see if you were—growing weak. If you were weary of this life and were using the girl as an opportunity to surrender." Percival coughed, his head lowered.

Mordred laughed. "Of course. The shark in the water coming to see if he smells blood. I hate to disappoint you. Do you wish to know my true motives? Hm?" He placed his boot over Percival's fingers and leaned his weight onto them. Not breaking the bones. Not yet. "The young woman has piqued my interest. I wish to amuse myself with her for as long as the game may last. Some warmth in an otherwise bleak and companionless existence. I suppose you might find it more *in character* if I were to chain her to my bedposts, hm?"

"I—I am sorry, my prince, I—" The knight broke off in a gag of pain as Mordred shifted more weight onto Percival's fingers.

"It may be hard for you to understand why I let her roam free and why I will instead tempt from her what I wish instead of simply having it. Why I, the bastard tyrant you believe me to be, will simply not *take* from her what you feel I have *taken* from all of you. Consider this, then, Percival, the Knight in Copper...that perhaps she does not deserve to suffer the same as traitors." He lifted his foot from the other man's hand.

Percival stayed on his knees, cradling his injured hand against his chest.

"Go." Mordred turned from Percival to resume gazing out the window. "And do not return to speak to me in such a foolish manner ever again."

"Y—yes, my prince." Percival nearly ran from the room, shutting the door behind him.

By the Ancients, Mordred wanted to scream. Shutting his eyes, he took a deep breath and let it out, trying to calm his raging temper. He wanted to rip someone to shreds. It was times like these that he would go and get into a brawl at the bar, or pester his uncle into training him. But there was no one around with whom he wished to spar.

The sound of dogs barking in the distance prompted him to open his eyes in time to see two horses riding from the woods back into the field. His gaze landed on the young woman with the shock of fiery hair atop a black and white mare. She rode

like a man—sure and capable. It made him smile, if just a little, through his anger.

She had asked him to train her to fight.

And while it would not be the violent outlet that he sought
for his rage, it would certainly serve as a distraction. And one
he now desperately needed.

Turning from the window, he went to prepare himself for
the afternoon. No, Gwendolyn did not deserve the same fate as
those around him.

Not yet.

Gwen was pretty sore when she got off the horse and helped
put Nina back into the stables. The armored servants were
already taking the saddle and bridle off, brushing her down
and tending to her when Gwen came back with two carrots
and an apple.

Promises were promises.

Lancelot was still there, and she wondered if he was waiting
for her. He was the kind of guy that would have made her mom
ecstatic if she'd brought him over for dinner. Tall and handsome with a warm smile. Hell, he was the kind of guy her mom
would probably make eyes at when Gwen wasn't looking.

She held up the second carrot as Nina contentedly chomped
away on it. "I always wanted a horse."

"You never owned one?" Lancelot hummed. "I am surprised."

"Nah, Dad was allergic. We had goats. It's much harder to
ride those." She snickered.

Lancelot joined her in a laugh. "Were your parents good
people?"

"Yeah." She smiled a little sadly. "I miss them. I wish I could tell them that I was okay." *For now.* She sighed. "I promise I'm not a child."

"I never said you were." He reached out and gently pulled her into an embrace. She went stiff for a second, but figured he was just trying to console her. She rested her head on his shoulder. "You have been thrust into a terrible, untenable situation. Your future is uncertain, and your past has, for lack of a better phrase, gone up in smoke. You love your family, and for that you should be commended. Anyone would be upset, my lady."

"Thanks." Gently pushing away from him, she did feel a little better.

"Let us regale the others with the tale of your bravery today." He smiled, his silver eyes shining.

"It really wasn't that big of a deal." Gwen fell in step beside him as he headed back into the keep. "It was just a stupid black bear." Eod, however, was acting like he was the new King of Avalon, and was running in front of her, prancing and proudly greeting everybody he saw.

"That mutt adores you now, you know." Lancelot lowered his voice. "He may not be the only stray dog in the castle who has taken a liking to you."

"Oh come on, you're hardly a stray," she teased.

"I wasn't referencing myself." He grinned wickedly. "I—"

"Ah. There you two are." Mordred was standing at the bottom of the stairs. Eod ran up to greet him, and the Prince in Iron scratched the dog's head with a gauntleted hand. "I was wondering if you would be gone all day and miss our appointment."

Lancelot bowed to the prince. "I have returned her to you, unscathed and on time, my liege."

Gwen wondered if she was supposed to curtsey or something.

She suddenly realized she had no fucking idea *how* to do that, even if she wanted to. So she just smiled shyly. "It was a nice time. Thank you, Lancelot."

"It has been my pleasure, my lady. But now, I shall take my leave." Lancelot bowed to her in turn and, with a bit of a playful smirk, left her and Mordred alone. Well, with the dog, but she doubted Eod counted.

"Do you need to rest before we begin?" Mordred walked up to her. Damn it if she didn't keep forgetting how *tall* he was. She had to crane her neck to look up at him.

"I was hoping to take a bath, if possible."

"Perhaps once we are finished. Lest I render the first one moot." His expression was cold. Something had upset him again.

"Come." He turned and walked away with no other pomp or circumstance.

Sighing, she followed after him, Eod walking beside her. She wasn't sure if he was a monster or a tyrant, but he certainly wasn't wrong about his moods.

Great. She was gonna be bruised to hell again once this was done, wasn't she? "Are you okay?"

"You should not feel the need to ask me such things." He didn't glance back at her while he led the way. "You are my prisoner, and I, your warden. My happiness should be the least of your concerns."

"Actually, your happiness probably has a great deal to do with whether or not I'm going to walk away from this afternoon limping." She chuckled half-heartedly. "Or stuck in the Crystal. I'd say it matters a lot to me."

"Fair point." It was clear he didn't get that she was teasing.

"I could see why it would be of a high concern to your own interests."

"That—I'm sorry, that isn't what I meant. I was just playing around." She frowned, and reached over to pet Eod's fur. At least she had the dog around.

Mordred's shoulders slumped slightly. "And I am not one who frequently jests. Nor am I in the mood to do so today."

That much was clear. "If you want to skip training today . . ."

"No." He brought her to the same courtyard as before. "We are nothing if we are not our discipline."

Letting out a wavering breath, she started wondering if seduction wouldn't have been the easier option. Certainly, less painful. Or at least, she'd hoped it would be.

But probably would wind up with the same amount of bruises.

She snickered.

"What is funny?"

"Nothing. Nothing." She tried to keep from laughing again. She was about to get beaten up in a so-called training session. She shouldn't be lusting after the guy she was supposed to be figuring out how to overthrow.

Well, at least she kept herself from laughing again. The rest? Too late.

SEVENTEEN

Pick your sword, and we shall begin." His armor molded over him like liquid metal. She caught herself staring at him again in awe as it overtook his body. Everything except the helmet. Caliburn shimmered into existence beside him, and he plucked it from the air.

"What about the necklace?"

"Today we will only work on your sword work and footing. Until you understand more of how to control your body, your strength will be unpredictable."

That didn't sound fun at all. "This is gonna be rough, isn't it?" The tone of her voice matched the dread she felt. She picked the same short sword off the rack.

"Yes. I suppose it will be." Damn it if he didn't sound like he was smiling. Sure, *now* he was smiling. "On guard."

For as bad as she was expecting it to be?

Yeah. It was worse than that.

"Ow!" Gwen shook off her hand as she backed away from Mordred. The bastard wasn't taking it easy on her at all. She felt that impact from his sword into hers all the way up to her shoulder. It was jarring, to put it lightly. "Ease up, you jerk."

"Your opponent will never ease up." He swung his sword again. That time, she managed to duck under his arm and run behind him, at least putting some distance between them. "And consider this training for when you decide to turn against me."

Oh.

That's why he was cranky.

"Mordred, I—" She squeaked and ducked another swing of his sword. "Can we just *talk* about this?"

"No." He used the opportunity while she was speaking to step forward and shoulder-check her, knocking her to the ground. She landed onto the packed dirt with a grunt, and before she could move, he had the point of his sword hovering over her neck, barely an inch away. "Talking on the battlefield will result in your death."

"Noted. But if you're upset with me—"

"You were off riding with Lancelot, were you not? The bastard likely told you all the details of his betrayal and why he now serves me by force." Mordred stepped back, letting her climb to her feet on her own. "Pick up your sword. We will go again."

Great. Damn it all. She picked up the blade and readied herself for him to strike. "He told me his side of things."

"There is no other side." Mordred swung, and she managed to dodge that time. She hadn't figured out how she was supposed to fight back, but she was at least learning how not to get knocked around like an idiot.

Though she suspected he wasn't trying. "What do you mean?"

"The knights betrayed me. They sought my head in hopes the elemental power bestowed upon me by Avalon would choose the dying Arthur. I murdered them all in my rage, and used my mother's craft to raise them from the grave to serve me. Is that not what he told you?" Mordred attacked her again, and she dodged—although this time he shoved her as she passed by him and sent her staggering forward.

"Yeah. That's what he said. I figured you had a softer explanation."

"No. I keep them in my service as a reminder to all of the cost for betraying the Prince in Iron. They were like my brothers—my *kin*." He snarled.

Shit. Shit, shit, shit. Now she was fighting an angry Mordred. She didn't like this. "Maybe we should stop—"

"No." He swung for her again, twice as hard.

She squeaked and ducked, hearing Caliburn cut through the air above her. That could've seriously killed her. She ran for the far side of the courtyard. "Mordred! Enough!"

"How long before you do the same, Gwendolyn? How long before you seek to bury a knife in my back, hm?" He stalked toward her. "First you scheme with this force that brought you here, and now with Lancelot."

"I'm not scheming!" Okay, maybe a little, but not like he was claiming. "I don't know what to do, and I haven't told any-body I'm going to *do* anything!" She dodged his next attack, but barely. She wasn't stupid enough to try to deflect his swings with her own sword. He was a giant, angry, rusty, fuming Mack truck on legs. She had a snowball's chance in hell.

"But they have asked you to." He was on her again. Damn him and his long legs. He swung, she ducked, and he used his other arm to knock her flat on her ass. Again.

She groaned in pain. "I give up. Stop. I'm done. Please. I'm not going to be your fucking punching bag."

"Then fight back, girl." He reached down and grabbed her by

the front of her chainmail top. She let out a yelp as he dragged her back up to her feet. "Pick up your sword and *fight me!*"

No. That was it. She chucked her sword, sending it clattering against the wall. She stormed up to him. He wasn't wearing his helmet. Which was good. Because then this was going to hurt more than it already was about to.

She rounded back and slapped him.

As hard as she possibly could.

His head turned with the blow, though she doubted she actually hurt him. And her hand stung like hell. But it was worth it.

Slowly, he turned his head back to her, those molten rusty eyes watching her with an unreadable expression. Maybe he'd rip her throat out. She waited for his rage. When it didn't come, she squared her shoulders. "Two things." She held up her hand and counted them off on her fingers. "One—don't take your shit out on me. And two—*don't ever call me girl again.*"

She stormed away from him. "C'mon, Eod. I need a fucking snack."

The dog got up from where he had been lying down by the wall to watch the exchange and jogged after her.

Lunch. And maybe a stiff drink.

That sounded like a damn good plan.

* * *

Mordred stood there in the center of the training area and . . . quite honestly did not know what to do with himself.

She had struck him. And not only that, she scolded him like a child. He should be furious. He should be *livid*. He should be taking her to task as he would any other insubordinate creature. If she had been a villager, he would have snapped her neck.

Yet it was not rage that he felt coursing through his veins.

It was something else entirely.

Clenching and relaxing his fists, he tried to grapple with the undeniable sensation that was overwhelming him.

Because quite simply...

He did not know if he had ever desired anyone so badly before in all his considerable years.

And while he was strict, he could not help but admit that she was right to reprimand him. He had been unreasonable with her. He knew, though he loathed to do it...that he should apologize.

"You poor thing! Sit down, sit down. What did that rusted bastard do to you?"

Gwen smiled faintly at the metal cook as she walked into the kitchen. Gwen was limping a little. One of the times she had met the dirt abruptly had jarred her hip. That, coupled with the ride through the woods, and she was ready to curl up and sleep for a week. "Training. I'll be fine."

"Pah!" Maewenn was already rummaging around to make her food. Gwen hated being waited on—she wasn't used to it—but she knew it gave the cook a sense of purpose to take care of people.

Eod certainly didn't mind. The hound was already sitting obediently beside the cook, tail thumping on the ground, ears perked up and waiting for treats. Maewenn reached down and patted the dog before handing him a slice of cheese.

"I suppose you're going to be spoiled rotten now, eh, pooch?"

The cook ruffled the dog's ears. "And I suppose you deserve it." Maewenn gestured to a stool. "Sit, dear, let me make you something for your empty stomach. And fetch the whiskey to help the rest."

"Thanks." Gwen sat down on the stool with a groan. "Yeah, okay, he was rough on me."

"Looks like he was sparring with you the same as he spars with the boys." Maewenn huffed. "Never mind the fact you're a fourth his size and a woman."

"It's more the fact that I've never picked up a sword before. Not a lot of need in modern-day America." She shrugged. "I kind of appreciate the fact that he doesn't go easy on me. I guess. But it definitely hurts." She chuckled.

"I suppose." Maewenn placed a plate of sausages, cheese, bread, and fruit in front of Gwen. It looked like heaven. "If you say so. Let me fetch that whiskey, eh?"

Gwen didn't waste any time digging into the food. Eod quickly learned that Gwen was now his easy mark, and was sitting at her feet, looking up at her both patiently and pleadingly in the way that only a dog can do.

"Maybe next time I should give you some of that bastard's sleeping powder to slip into his tea." Maewenn huffed a laugh.

"He has trouble sleeping?"

"Oh yes, long as anybody's known him. I mix him up a powder that makes it so that not even *he* can argue about it." Maewenn pulled a glass from a cabinet and dug out an old-fashioned-looking glass bottle. Onion bottle, maybe? Gwen thought she remembered having seen one way back when. The cook poured the amber liquid into the glass and slid the whiskey to Gwen.

She didn't know what was going to come out of her time

in Avalon, but it certainly was turning her into a drinker. She picked up the glass and sipped it. That time, at least she didn't cough like an idiot. "I think I remembered him mentioning that he has trouble sleeping."

"Aye. I think he has more of a guilty conscience than he likes to let on." Maewenn sighed. "Not like he'll admit to it or change his ways."

Gwen sipped the alcohol again, frowning down into her plate of food. Eod reached up a paw and plopped it on her leg, reminding her that he was waiting for more treats. Chuckling, she tore off a piece of one of the cured sausages and fed it to him. "At least *you're* happy, doggo."

"I am glad to see you making friends." Maewenn was cleaning a pot now, wiping it down with a dish towel. "I hope you settle in here. I hope..." She shook her head. "What'm I doing, sitting here hoping, when we all know what happens to hope in a place like this."

Gwen's heart broke again. "I'm sorry."

"Don't be. You've been a ray of sunshine in this dreary place. I'll take whatever glimpse of happiness I can get." Maewenn put the pot on a hanger that dangled from a heavy wood overhead beam, and picked up another one out of the pile. "I didn't mean to drag down your mood, dear."

"It was already pretty low. Don't worry about it." She folded up a piece of sliced cheese and ate it. After giving a piece to Eod, of course. "Lancelot told me about why they're forced to serve Mordred."

"A terrible story. But that idiot boy does himself no favors, let me tell you that. More keen to let his mouth lead the way instead of his brain. Don't let him get you into trouble."

"I'll do my best." Something told her she was already in

trouble. And Maewenn certainly wasn't wrong in any way, shape, or form. "How do you like it here?"

"Oh, well enough. I have my duty, and I'm happy to do it. I wish there was more life in this place—I wish there was more life in Avalon. But I know why Mordred felt the need to do what he's done." Maewenn finished with the second pot and picked up a third.

"What was it like before?"

"Honestly couldn't tell you. I don't think I existed before the Crystal. I don't think any of us armor folks did." She shrugged with a quiet clank. "But if it was the way I hear tell of it, it was constant chaos and death. Elementals were like warlords—rampaging and taking what they wanted, fighting with each other for power, caring nothing for the lives that got stuck in the crossfire."

That did sound terrible. But so did living in a blank, empty, lifeless, sunless world. "I don't know who's right and who's wrong. I've been trying to figure it out, but I keep changing my mind."

Maewenn let out a long, wistful sigh. "Deary, when you live to see a few hundred years pass, you learn something—nobody's ever truly right. Nobody's ever truly wrong. It's always a mix of the two."

Gwen nodded. That made perfect sense. She didn't disagree—she just didn't like it.

"Lady Gwendolyn?"

She looked up as another suit of armor walked into the room. A guard, judging by the spear he was carrying. "Yeah?"

"The prince has asked you come with me."

Her stomach fell. "Am . . . am I in trouble?" She cringed. She knew she shouldn't have slapped him.

"I only have my orders. Please follow me."

Downing the rest of her whiskey, she fed another piece of sausage to Eod. "Maewenn, would you watch Eod?"

"Of course, dear." The metal cook sounded as worried as Gwen felt. "Take care, please."

"I will." She smiled, trying not to be too scared. But her nerves were already on edge, and now she felt the prickle of her anxiety needling at the back of her head. "I'll do my best, anyway."

Gwen followed the suit of armor out of the room. She began twisting the fabric of the sleeves of her dress between her hands, trying to find somewhere to put her nervous energy that wasn't smack into a panic attack. That was all she needed.

At least then she'd be unconscious if Mordred shoved her in the damn Crystal.

Nah, he'd wait until I was awake. He seems like that kind of guy.

They descended several sets of stairs. When they reached a hallway that was warm and humid, she almost let out a breath of relief. The rest of the castle was so damn chilly all the time. The guard pushed open a metal door, and gestured for her to walk inside.

Was the Crystal kept down here? Or Mordred's torture chamber?

But when she did, her jaw dropped. "Whoa…"

A giant indoor, below-ground pool wasn't what she had been expecting. Steam rose from the water in curls, revealing that the opaque, greenish-white liquid was likely from a hot spring. Like that place in Iceland she'd seen photos of. The air smelled a little like sulfur.

The pool was about thirty feet wide and maybe twelve or so

across, surrounded on all sides by elegant S-shaped columns made out of iron. The heat and the moisture of the room had turned them every shade of rust. The curling, asymmetrical shape was detailed over every inch with depictions of a wild hunt—dogs chasing lions chasing dragons chasing deer chasing creatures she didn't even know the name of.

The floor was black marble, lined with white veins that spider-webbed out across the surface. And around the very edge of the pool was a mosaic of various metals and semiprecious stones in a bizarre pattern.

The walls were covered with faded murals of scenes of battle and mystical animals. Fires burned in brass bowls that were arranged along the edge of the walls, lighting the room and providing even more heat. The whole space took her breath away.

The excess water ran over the edges into grooves in the ground. Sitting on the edge of the pool was a tray with soap, a cloth, and a jar of something she didn't recognize. A towel was folded up beside that.

She had asked for a bath. She smiled faintly. "This is where the prince asked you to bring me?"

"Aye, my lady. I will be waiting outside if you need anything." The guard shut the door behind him, leaving her alone in the steamy room.

Was this Mordred trying to buy forgiveness? Too bad she was still ticked. Stripping out of her dress, she folded it and put it on a bench by the wall, before walking over to the edge of the water and dipping her in. It was hot. Wonderfully so.

Climbing in, she groaned as the hot water rushed over her. It felt so damn good. The water was opaque and, scooping up some in her hand, she could see the little particles of whatever sediment it was in the natural spring floating about in it. Cool.

She dunked her head in and picked up the soap to start scrubbing herself down. She didn't know how frequently she'd be allowed to do this.

She was halfway through soaping up her hair when the door clicked open. With a squeak, she lowered herself down to her neck in the water. "I—oh." She froze. It wasn't a guard.

Mordred walked in. "Mind if I join you?"

Gwen could only stammer uselessly. She was angry at him—but he had caught her entirely off guard.

"I will take that as a yes." He gathered up the hem of his shirt and pulled it off over his head.

And at that point in time, all useful thought in Gwen's head ceased. All except one thing, as she couldn't help but stare at him.

I am in so much trouble.

EIGHTEEN

Mordred walked into the room, half expecting to find Gwendolyn sitting in the corner, steadfastly refusing to get into the water. He was pleased to find her in his hot spring, even if she was up to her neck. He wasn't sure how her anger at him would change her ability to accept his gifts.

She was so wonderfully shy, even when she was glowering at him. It was so very much fun to watch her struggle with what he hoped was a mutual attraction between them, despite how annoyed she clearly was with him. The way she watched him as he stripped off his shirt gave him hope.

She sank an inch farther into the water. "Uh. Why're you here?"

"For the same reason as you, I expect." He smirked. "You know, I *have* already seen you naked."

"I know, but. Um." She sighed, defeated. "I know."

He shut his eyes and did that which he knew he needed to do. "I apologize for my behavior. I have not had to deal with those unaccustomed to my ways in a very long time. I fear I have rather become entrenched in my poor moods."

Gwen went silent for a long time before nodding slightly. "Just try to knock it off. It's hardly fair to me, seeing as I'm your prisoner."

"If you prefer it to be a more level playing ground, that can be done." He walked around to the side of the pool, delighting in how her eyes went wide at the sight of him.

"I—I mean—it's—it's fine—"

Laughing, he began to unlace his trousers. "Well, I plan on joining you anyway."

"Oh, God." She turned her back to him.

"No one has called me that before," he teased. She was so much fun to torment. And it seemed to be an effective way of lightening the mood. He stepped out of his shoes and trousers, and into the hot water, keeping his distance from her. For now. The pool was a few yards wide and twice that distance in length, so there was plenty of room for him without crowding her.

Though he very much wished to crowd her. And do far more to her than that. But he did not wish to find out what happened when a fire elemental ignited in a pool of water. He imagined it would go poorly for both the state of his spring and the elemental in question. He was once more glad for the necklace he had made her.

"You're not mad at me for hitting you?"

Sitting on the bench that ran around the outside lip, he groaned and tilted his head back, enjoying how the hot water loosened his tense muscles. And the Ancients knew he had enough knots in need of being worked out. "Men of my ilk can rarely be reasoned with in words." He chuckled. "My mood was not your fault, yet I sought in you an outlet to release my frustrations."

Gwen finally peeked over at him. Seeing him submerged, she turned back around. "What happened?"

"Percival sent me into something of a rage. You are right— it was wrong for me to take my 'shit' out on you." He rested his arms on the side of the pool, stretching out. "Will you forgive me?"

"Yeah. I get it. Things are complicated here." Gwendolyn was cleaning herself with the soap, having wedged herself in the far corner of the pool where the excess ran off the quickest. She was currently running some of it through her orange and crimson hair. "Complicated and miserable."

"Less so since you have arrived. Miserable, I mean. Certainly, no less complicated." Watching her was certainly distracting, for more than one part of him.

She smiled faintly. "No kidding." Her expression faded to sadness. "Why don't you let them go? Your knights, I mean?"

"And with whom should I replace them? No one is loyal to me, Gwen. No one. If I allowed my knights their final rest, all I would be left with would be my metal amalgams. How terrible that would be." He cringed at the notion of it. He was lonely enough as it was. "And that is before you consider how brilliant they are as fighters."

"I can't imagine what it's like, though, living every day worrying who is plotting against you." She dunked herself under the water for a moment, smoothing her wet hair back.

Distracting indeed.

"Such has been the nature of my life for as long as I can remember it. One becomes adjusted to a suspicious way of thinking. I will admit that it is not precisely what I would call an enjoyable way to live, but it is simply the way of it."

"Yeah, but... I don't know, don't you think it's a self-fulfilling prophecy at this point?" She ran the soap up over her arms.

He distinctly wanted to do that for her. But he would not. He also did not wish to scare her with how his body had reacted to her presence. She was like a young doe—curious but wary. He did not want to frighten her off.

"Are you implying that some part of my inherited personality or my actions have caused me to be in the predicament I am in?" He grinned. "Are you insulting me, firefly?"

"I—no, I mean. What I mean is—" She flinched.

Laughing, he stood to walk across the pool closer to her. The water reached his waist as he moved, saving her from any sort of *untoward* show. But that did not stop her eyes from going just a little wider. She sank another half inch into the water. "Oh, be still." He smiled at her, doing his best to be reassuring. But he knew there was likely a wicked twist to it that was not helping matters. "I simply do not wish to shout across the room." He sat on the bench opposite her.

"I didn't mean to insult you. I'm just saying that if you go looking for traitors everywhere, you'll find them one way or the other." She placed the soap on the tray. "That's all."

"You are not wrong." He shrugged and leaned his elbows on the side of the pool. "Sadly, I fear I am what I am. And when one is accustomed to constant plotting and scheming happening around you to your detriment, this bias you say I have is often proven right more often than not."

She watched him curiously for a moment. "Aren't you going to rust in here?"

Laughing, he shook his head. "No, dear. You needn't worry."

She ran her fingers through her hair, combing out the strands and picking at some tangles. "What do you do for fun?"

"Pardon?"

"I mean, you have to do *something* other than sitting around in a chair and brooding in front of a fireplace."

"Is waging war upon the nature of Avalon, ensuring that magic remains within my control, not a hobby enough for you?"

"That's not a hobby, that's a job. A tyrannical job." She laughed. By the Ancients, he loved the sound of her laughter. It reminded him of the rays of the sun in the early morning.

Not that he had seen the sun in Avalon in three hundred years. But that was neither here nor there. Or was it? Was that not the entire issue at hand?

"I find ways to pass the time."

"Like what?"

"I sculpt new creations." He shrugged.

"Your armor minions?" She looked intrigued. "You sculpt them personally?"

"Indeed." He was not sure why she was asking. But there was an eager kind of fascination in her expression—something that told him she wished to ask another question but was too timid to do so.

"I'd love to watch you work someday."

His expression fell. "Perhaps. You may wish to be careful—playing two men like fiddles at the same time is a dangerous game."

"What do you mean?" She blinked. "Oh! You mean Lancelot?"

"You did spend a great deal of time in the woods with him today."

"It's not—he just—" Her cheeks went pink.

He laughed. "Calm yourself. If you wish to cavort with Lancelot, that is your choice. It would not be *my* choice or recommendation, but you are free to do as you wish."

"Really?" She arched an eyebrow.

Sighing, he ran a hand over his hair to push it back away from his face. "While there is much about your situation that I cannot make equitable or reasonable, where I can, I do not wish to make you suffer unduly." As jealous as he was of Lancelot's easy way with women. And this one in particular, it seemed. "No matter how much of a monster he might make me out to be."

"I don't think you're a monster."

He huffed a laugh.

"It's true, I don't." She sank another inch into the water, as if trying to hide. "I don't think you're evil. I know why you've locked up all of the magic. But...it still seems wrong to me." She paused. "Can we talk about something else?"

"If you desire." He was also not keen on discussing the merits of his methods of rule. He debated his next topic. "Tell me what you wished for in life before you fell to Avalon. You mentioned you wished to help animals. What else?"

"I mean, that was what I wanted—but I wasn't going to get it." She shrugged. "I don't really know. I just didn't want to spend my life trapped in backwater Kansas."

"Well, I believe your wish was granted, if not entirely perhaps in the way that you would have wished." He smiled slightly. "You are here now. Far away from this 'backwater Kansas' of yours."

She snorted. "Yeah, until you shove me in the Crystal. I think I'd take Kansas over that."

He supposed that was fair. "There may be a way to avoid that fate." He could not even fathom why he was saying that out loud. Perhaps Percival was right. Perhaps he was growing weak.

"Oh?" The hope on her face felt like a knife in his gut.

It would be that much more painful when he eventually crushed it.

"If I were to trust you—to know that you could not betray me—then I would have no reason to lock you away."

"Somehow I feel like earning your trust isn't possible." She sighed. "Especially when you're also telling me that the only reason you're leaving me running around free is because I'm *not* telling you everything."

"I suppose the proposition I am putting to you is this—tell me all that you know, swear fealty to me, and I will allow you to remain free."

"What does swearing fealty involve?" She wrinkled her nose. "You're not going to put one of those weird crystals in my chest, are you?"

He chuckled. "Not unless you betray me." Which was, in his mind, inevitable. He could not decide which was more tragic—having her locked away with all the others . . . or forced to serve him like his knights.

He could be a brute. But enslaving a hopeful lover was a depth to which he would never sink.

It seemed she was having the same thought, judging by how she was looking away from him, her features mirroring his own uncertainty. "Can I think about it?"

"Of course."

"I believe what you're saying, I just . . ."

"Believe that I am also a self-fulfilling prophecy. That I will seek out reasons or inspire you to betray me, to prove somehow to myself that I am right in my own paranoia?" He smirked.

Sheepishly, she looked down at the water. "Kinda?"

"Well. At least you are honest." He huffed.

"You said it! Not me!" She splashed water at him.

He blinked, surprised at her playfulness. He grinned wickedly at her, and watched with no small amount of satisfaction as her eyes grew wide in a sudden recognition of her poor choice. "If you wished to spar again with me, all you had to do was ask..."

"N—no, I just—I—um." Her cheeks were turning pink with her rampant blush.

He stood, both glad and disappointed that the water reached his waist. He walked toward her slowly, enjoying how she shrank away from him nervously, but did not run. She could tell him to stop. She could tell him to stay away. But she did not.

He placed each of his hands on the edge of the pool beside her, caging her in, and leaned down closer to her. "Teasing me is a very dangerous game to play, Gwendolyn Wright. A very dangerous game indeed."

"I—I mean—I didn't—I didn't mean to." She was staring at his collarbone, refusing to make eye contact, wonderfully shy.

"I know." He crooked his finger beneath her chin and lifted her head up. "But your intentions do not matter in this regard." He studied her thoughtfully, letting out a quiet hum. "Unless you mean to tell me that I am not attractive to you?"

"No, I—" She cringed again. "It's not that. This is all just too much at once."

"If Lancelot were here in my stead, what then?"

"I—I don't know. I don't think he's...I think it's like you said, I don't think he's really interested in me. I think he's using me and is bored."

"What do you believe my intentions are?"

"I don't know that either. But...not that."

He had to admit he was intrigued by her reply. "Then what do you believe inspires my courting of you?"

She grumbled her answer. "Horniness."

He did not know what that word meant. But he could guess. He chuckled. "Has it been some time since I have had relations with a woman? Yes. It has. I will return your honesty in kind. But that is not the only reason you intrigue me, Gwen." He traced the pad of his thumb against her cheek.

"But you don't *know* me."

"Then I look forward to discovering you." He smirked as he leaned in, closing the distance between them. She held her breath, likely in anticipation of a kiss. And he was tempted— sorely tempted.

But he also enjoyed tormenting her. He wanted her to come to him. He placed a kiss on her cheek instead. "I will let you finish your soak in peace." Straightening up, he climbed out of the pool, using the steps next to her. He did not miss her covering her eyes and muttering something under her breath.

Grinning still, he pulled on his robe and tied the sash around his waist. "Will you join us for dinner tonight?"

"Um. Sure." She sounded a bit shaken and unsure of herself. Good. He liked to keep her off her footing, just a little.

"Fantastic. I will see you then. Enjoy your afternoon, firefly."

"Y—you too." She wasn't looking at him, still likely too shy to check to see if he was still naked or not. Walking about his halls in the nude was not something he was in the habit of doing, but he supposed she had no way of knowing that.

It was also likely for the best. He wanted her—and his body had no qualms about expressing that desire. He left her to soak out the rest of her bruises and sore muscles, and found himself just slightly frustrated that he had not added to her collection in a more intimate way.

But there would be time enough for such things.

Perhaps a great deal of time, if she took him up on his offer. Kneel to him—swear fealty—and secure her freedom.

His thoughts darkened as he walked back to his chambers. Yes. Secure her freedom. Until the time that she inevitably tried to stab him in the back.

History would always repeat itself.

He simply wished with all his might that this time it would be different.

NINETEEN

Gwen was a confused, conflicted mess as she walked into the great hall for dinner. She had gone with a dark red dress that she thought might look nice with her wacky multicolored hair. She wished she had a mirror so she could see what she looked like with orange-red-yellow hair. When she had thought about how her dad would have *freaked* at the sight of her, her heart had broken again. She missed her parents. She also worried about how distraught they must be.

But there wasn't anything she could do about it. *No. There is. I can try to destroy the Crystal like Merlin wants me to and then Merlin'll send me home.* In all the insanity of the day, she had almost forgotten about the cynical black cat. The only way to go home was to break the prison that was holding back all of Avalon's magic.

And to betray Mordred in the process.

She cared more about the latter than the former, honestly. She felt bad for Mordred, going through his world never being able to trust anyone. But even he seemed to understand that it might partially be his fault.

Never mind the fact that he was handsome, sexy, and clearly wanted to take her to bed.

She was still left with a choice, however. Betray him and go home—if she could even trust Merlin, either—or swear fealty to Mordred and stay in Avalon.

The knights were all gathered when she walked into the great hall. She smiled as she walked up to the table. Food was already served, with an enormous roast pig as the centerpiece. It was still hysterical to walk into what looked like a spread put out for a Renaissance fair, but hey. She figured she could probably teach Maewenn how to make hamburgers if she was really desperate for a taste of home. "Hi, guys."

Lancelot was already beaming at the sight of her. "And there is the huntress herself."

"I didn't hunt anything, Lancelot." She rolled her eyes, if a bit teasingly, as she sat down.

Mordred was watching the exchange with a guarded expression. He was resting his temple on his gauntleted knuckles.

"You did scare off a bear, at the very least." Lancelot raised a pewter mug to her. "Quite fearlessly, I might add."

Mordred arched an eyebrow at that. "Pardon?"

She sighed. "Look, there was a bear in the woods. Eod picked a fight with it, and I rode my horse at it to scare it off. It was just a little black bear, all by himself. It wasn't like it was dangerous."

"How is it that you are so very frightened of us, but not of a bear?" Galahad asked, honestly seeming to be confused.

She snorted. "Y'all showed up on *dragons*. Giant, freaky, evil, metal dragons. And I'd been told that the Prince in Iron was going to murder me. So, y'know, there was that."

"You have a fit when meeting me, yet you did not have one of these 'panic attacks' of yours, while facing down the bear?" Mordred asked.

Picking up a small bowl that was about the same size as a

salt shaker and, judging by the salt *in* it, seemed to serve the same purpose, she plunked it down in front of her. "Bear." She gestured at the dead pig. "Dragon."

Lancelot snickered.

"Besides," she continued. "I'm used to wildlife, having grown up on a farm. Bears are pretty rare, but trust me—American badgers are worse."

Galahad hummed. "Well. Here is to you, Gwendolyn Wright, protector of dogs." He lifted his mug to her.

Smiling, she picked up her own that was placed at her setting and raised it back to him. "Sure. Why not." Sipping the liquid in the mug, she blinked and stared down into it. "What's this?"

"Mead," Mordred answered. "Have you never had it before?"

"I think I've drank more here than I ever did at home."

Lancelot tilted his head to the side slightly. "Why is that?"

"Drinking age is technically twenty-one. I'm nineteen." She shrugged.

Lancelot let out a "huh" and shook his head. "Very odd, modern culture."

"It has its ups and downs. I think I prefer it to living in Ye Olde Times." She sipped the mead again. It was good. Sharp and tangy, and weirdly fruity. It wasn't as bitter as the wine was the night before. "I don't think I'd last very long in medieval England."

"Why not?" Lancelot smiled. "I think you would have made quite the lady."

"I like having rights. And pants." She paused. "And electricity."

"We would have the latter, if we were not closed off from the worlds around us." Lancelot shot a look at Mordred. "But who is to say about the former."

"Careful, Lancelot. You can still serve me as my knight without a tongue," Mordred warned the other man.

"Could we not?" Gwen shut her eyes. "It's been a long day and I don't think I want to listen to more fighting."

"Hear, hear," Percival interjected.

"I did put you through your paces today." Mordred's tone was coy, almost teasing. It was clear what he was insinuating. "You will wake up sore on the morrow, I imagine, if not as sore as I would wish."

Her cheeks went warm. Damn her stupid blushing. She took a sip of the mead. She liked it. A lot. She'd have to be careful with that. "Great."

"And you have another session of training tomorrow afternoon," he reminded her. "I would take your rest where you can. I recommend you not go riding with Lancelot again in the morning."

"The lady can do as she likes," Lancelot replied stiffly. "Unless you are commanding her to do otherwise."

"I am doing simply as I said—recommending." Mordred's reply was just as curt.

"Knock it off, both of you." She glared at each of them in turn. "I'm not going to be fought over like you're idiots in high school." She decided she was going to need more mead to survive the dinner, and, reaching for the jug of it, refilled her mug. She didn't miss Mordred's small smirk.

"As the lady wishes." Mordred paused for a second. "You do look lovely tonight. I suspected that dress might suit you nicely. I am pleased to see I was right."

"Thanks." It was weird to think that he had spent the time picking out clothing for her. "Did this come from storage, too?"

"No. I sent some servants to the city nearby. Well. To us, it is a city. To you, I am certain it would be rather disappointing." He shrugged idly between bites of food.

It still sounded interesting. "I mean . . . I'd still kind of like to see it." She smiled. "If that's all right."

Mordred considered it for a moment. "Very well. I will take you there on the morrow then. It may be good for the townsfolk to see that I have not sealed you away."

"Yet," Lancelot added. "And I thought she was meant to rest tomorrow?"

God, she wanted to scream. She drank more of the mead.

Mordred glared at the knight. "A trip to the city is quite different than riding into the wilderness."

"Nope. Both. Stop." She picked up a knife. "Or I'm gonna stab the both of you."

Lancelot lifted his hands in a show of playful surrender. "Mercy, my lady."

"I beg for quarter," Mordred added.

"Smarmy assholes, both of you," she muttered as she put the knife back down.

"Tell us more of Earth, Lady Gwen," Galahad interjected before either of the other two men could spark up the argument again.

Thankful for the distraction, she was more than happy to talk about how the world had changed. Technology, warfare, social changes. Discoveries, landing on the moon, and the like. She realized as she talked how little she actually *knew*. When they asked her to dig deeper, she often found herself struggling to remember details or not knowing them at all. She was nineteen, and even though she loved history, she found there were big parts that were missing from her understanding of things.

But she did her best, and they hung on her every word. Even

Percival, who looked like the grumpy asshole of the bunch, was listening intently as she talked. And ate. And drank.

And maybe drank too much.

By the time dinner was over, her head was a little fluffy and the world felt just a bit more *fun* than it had before. She didn't think she was drunk, but she was definitely buzzed. And Mordred seemed to see it, with his knowing little smile and the devious glint in his rust-colored eyes.

"I think I should probably go to bed," she said, rubbing a hand over her brow. "Note to self—I like mead."

Mordred chuckled. "That it seems you do. I shall escort you back to your room with your permission, my lady."

That had to rub Lancelot the wrong way. And with how the Knight in Silver was glowering at his prince, it did. She hadn't ever been in the center of a love triangle before, and she had to say she hated it. Besides, she didn't really trust either of them were being at all sincere.

Poor Lancelot. She felt for the guy and his impossible situation, all the same. "It's fine," she said quietly as she stood from the table. She was just a little wobbly. "I know where I'm going."

"Yes, but I wish to ensure you do not tumble over a railing or wind up sleeping in a potted plant." Mordred stood as well, clearly amused by her.

"I'm fine." She was! She wasn't *that* drunk. She was just a *little* drunk. People got drunk all the time, didn't they?

"And I am certain you are. But allow me the peace of mind to accompany you regardless, my lady? I would sleep easier knowing with certainty." He walked up to her, offering her his hand, palm up. The claws of his gauntlet were still terrifying—like rusty, broken knives. They reminded her a bit of the forgotten and ancient tools she'd find in the barn from time to time. Neglected, but still extremely dangerous.

"I'm glad I'm up to date on my tetanus shots." She put her hand in his.

"Pardon?"

His quizzical expression made him kind of adorable, she decided.

"Lockjaw? Y'know, when people get all twitchy and spasm and then die. From, like—cuts from infected things. Like somebody with *stabby knives for fuckin' hands*." Okay, fine, yeah, she was drunk.

Somebody snickered from behind her. She didn't know who it was. Probably Percival or Lancelot. They seemed like the snickering types over Galahad.

"Ah." Mordred seemed more amused than offended. He tucked her hand into his elbow and began to walk her from the room. She was suddenly a little glad for the support. "Let us get you to bed, my lady."

"G'night, guys," she called over her shoulder at the three knights still seated at the table. They all mumbled a reply, but she was too distracted keeping her feet under her to know who said what. She walked beside Mordred as he led her down the hallway. "Sorry I'm a lightweight."

"I should have warned you about the mead. It is easy to let it get away from you, with how sweet it tastes." He placed his other metal hand over the back of hers. "I was too entertained, however, to stop you."

"I see how it is," she teased. "Getting me drunk so you can pump me for information."

He huffed a laugh. "If that is a euphemism, I fear interrogating you would be the farthest thing from my mind."

"Augh!" Her cheeks felt so hot that she actually had to check her hand to make sure she hadn't burst into flames. "I didn't mean—"

"I know."

Sighing, she leaned on his arm as they walked. The feeling of her face against the armor wasn't as uncomfortable as she thought it would be.

"What is troubling you?"

"Do you want the list?" She started counting off on her fingers. "Sucked into a magical world after my house *bursts into flames*. Find out that I now have wacky fire powers that I can't control. Get abducted by the demigod tyrant of said world whose uncle was *fucking King Arthur*, who has no business being as hot as he is for a guy who has everybody shoved in a magical supermax prison. Lancelot—fucking *the* Lancelot—is hitting on me but probably is doing it just because he hates said hot demigod. And I'm probably gonna get shoved in the supermax prison because my asshole cat—" She stopped. Shit. Shit, shit, shit! Stupid mead!

"Your cat?" Mordred arched an eyebrow down at her.

"I—um—I think he's the one who knocked a candle over." That was true. That was totally true. "It might have been what started the fire. I don't really know." Also true. Not the most graceful recovery, but none of it was technically a lie.

"Hm." It was clear he didn't quite believe her. "And I am a 'hot' demigod tyrant, am I? Would you care to explain the insult to me? I would like to know precisely how you think I am deficient in this regard."

Insult? *Oh.* Oooh, he thought *hot* was an insult. She laughed. She couldn't help it. And as he looked down at her, clearly a little offended, she laughed even harder. Her laughter doubled down on his annoyance, and she doubled down on her giggling.

"I'm sorry—it's not—" She couldn't help it. Every time she tried to explain herself, his grumpiness made her start laughing again. She shut her eyes and took a deep breath, waving her hands to stop her giggle fit. "Calling you hot isn't an insult. It's a compliment."

"I . . . see." He didn't seem to believe her. "In what way?"

"I'm calling you attractive, that's—whoa!" She almost fell over with her eyes shut, the alcohol making her balance questionable at best. His arms snapped around her to keep her from toppling to the ground. She was laughing again, smiling up at him. Now he just looked bemused. But at least he wasn't angry anymore. "You have *no right* to be this handsome. It's really frustrating." She poked him in the middle of the chest—well, breastplate. Stupid armor.

"Is it? How so?" Now he was smiling, if vaguely.

"Because you're *the bad guy*. Right?" She sighed. "Stupid—stupid fuckin' Crystal thing. You should blow it up."

"I fear I will have to disagree. And you are quite drunk."

"No, I'm not." Yeah, she probably was. "And I know you want to disagree, but you're changing the subject and—*hey!*" Her world upended. The bastard had just slung her over his shoulder like she was a sack of potatoes. "Put me down!"

"No." They were moving now. One of his arms was around her knees, keeping her legs pinned to his chest.

It left her with nothing to do except smack at his back. Which was armored. So it did absolutely no good. With a disgruntled sigh, she decided being semi–upside down was also not great for her stomach. So she propped herself up on her elbows to keep her head the right way up. "If I puke on you, it's not my fault."

"Noted." He was chuckling, clearly enjoying this.

"You suck. And that's an insult."

"Also noted."

Luckily, they reached her chambers pretty quickly, and she yelped again as he dropped her rather unceremoniously on the bed. "Gah! You can't just—" She stopped as the point of one of his claws touched the end of her nose. That shut her up real fast.

"Oh, I can. I am the 'bad guy,' remember?" He smirked down at her. "Sleep. Stay in your room until the morrow. I will not have you wandering about like this."

"I'm fine." She lay her head down on the pillow. The room was wheeling around a little bit, but she didn't think it was bad enough to make her sick. "But what if I said you didn't have to go? Or that you didn't have to be the bad guy?"

His expression softened. He sat down on the edge of the bed beside her and, reaching out, ran his claws through her hair. The points scraping against her scalp felt amazing. "I am what I am, and what I shall always be, Gwendolyn Wright. Whether or not you still find me an amicable suitor when you understand that is beyond my ability to control."

She'd have to be way more sober to figure out what he meant by that. "But—"

"No." He smiled in that lopsided way that made her want to jump his bones. "However tempted as I may be, I am a knight, above all things. That said . . . perhaps I will allow us both this one indulgence."

He leaned down over her, hovering his lips an inch from

hers. His breath pooled against her skin, and she found herself shivering in anticipation. When she didn't say anything or make any move to stop him, he closed the distance between them.

Like a warped Prince Charming, he kissed her. It was firm but not forceful, passionate but not overwhelming. He tasted just a little metallic, and she found it didn't bother her at all. Far from it. Her eyes slipped shut, and she found herself clinging to the cape he wore over his armor.

When he broke away, he was smiling. "Sleep well, Gwen."

It took her a long time to find the words to reply. It was like all the air had been sucked out of her lungs. "You too, Mordred."

"For the first time in a very long time...I think I shall." He stood. Before she could gather her wits enough to say anything else, he left, shutting the door. She heard a lock click shut.

Bastard.

Rolling onto her side, she shut her eyes. A bastard that she really wished had stayed with her.

TWENTY

Gwen yelped as something bit her nose. Hard. Jerking her face back, she covered her nose with her hand. There, sitting on her pillow, was Merlin. Glaring at her like he always was. She didn't think it was possible he could look more annoyed than he usually did, but he had pulled it off.

"Why are you *such* an asshole?" She flopped onto her back, rubbing her nose and checking her fingers for blood. Luckily, he didn't seem to have broken the skin. "What do you want now?"

"To make sure you remember that we are here with a job to do. Not to get drunk at dinners and cavort with the enemy." Merlin swished his tail. "And the bite was for nearly ruining everything and telling him about me."

"I covered for that. It was fine."

He huffed in disbelief.

"And besides," she argued. "*You* told me to seduce him, didn't you? Isn't that what I'm doing?" She glared right back at him.

He snorted. "No. What you are doing is embarrassing." He walked down to the end of the bed, sitting and curling his tail around his front feet. "And painful to watch."

She rolled onto her side, facing away from him. It was still dark out, and she was tired. "He kissed me. I think I'm doing just fine."

"Which is more of an indication of his desperation and less of your ability."

"Yeah, yeah. Whatever. Go away. I'm tired." She shut her eyes and snuggled into the pillow. "I'll try to show more cleavage later or something."

"I think perhaps you're better off pursuing Lancelot as an ally. He also seems…desperate…and at least wants to ensure the downfall of Mordred." The disgust in Merlin's voice was palpable. "If you can manage not to make an ass of yourself with that one. Perhaps you could play the two against each other."

"I think they're already against each other." She pulled the blankets up over her shoulder. "Please go away."

The cat climbed up onto her side, sinking his claws into the blanket and her skin. "You are not taking this seriously, girl. This is not a *vacation*. You have a job to do."

"I know, I know. Get the necklace off permanently. Blow up the Crystal. Send Avalon back into a state of complete chaos, and maybe you'll send me home. Or maybe you can't, and you're lying to me." She glared at him, and used her arm to push him off her. "Maybe Mordred is the only one telling me the truth around here."

"Do not tell me you are actually considering siding with him." Merlin let out that low angry cat warning sound that always reminded her of a tornado siren gearing up. "I knew you were a fool, but I couldn't imagine you were *this* stupid."

"Maybe if you weren't such an asshole to me all the time, and told me what was going on, I'd be a bit more trusting." She glared at him, giving up on falling back asleep while he was still intent on pestering her. "Fact of the matter is, one of you tells me the truth and the other one doesn't. One of you is nice to me, and the other one isn't."

"Typical human." The hair on his back rose and then flattened. "Only *me, me, me,* with no sense of the bigger picture. Do you want to know the truth? Very well. I have been trapped inside that damnable Crystal, suffering in a liminal state of being, hearing the millions of voices of the souls trapped with me, screaming and pleading for freedom and mercy. I have felt pieces of my power drain away, stolen by that bastard to be put into his trinkets and toys." He bared his teeth, single fang and all. "He is *destroying* us, Gwen. Little by little."

She sat up. "What?"

"How do you think he makes his armored servants, eh? Ask him yourself." The cat bared his single fang.

"I . . ."

"It is pieces of souls that he takes, pieces of our very essence that he robs to remake this world in his own damn image!" He kept his voice a low hiss to keep from alerting the guards. "I escaped and nearly died. And where do I wind up? With *you.* Trapped in this—this tiny, broken shape, with almost nothing of myself left. And my only hope for freedom—to be set free from this terrible suffering—is with *you.* A simpering, whining, idiot child who cannot stay focused for ten minutes!"

Gwen didn't know what to say. "I . . . I'm sorry."

"As you should be." He turned his back to her and walked across the bed toward the far end. "You are getting close to Mordred in order to betray him. Remember that." He jumped down, disappearing into a swirl of black smoke as he did, leaving her alone.

Lying back down with a hard exhale, something told her she wasn't going back to sleep. She tossed and turned for what felt like an hour before she got up, unable to take it anymore. Getting dressed and pulling a cloak around herself, she headed to the door. She pressed the latch and heard it click before she remembered that Mordred had locked it on his way out.

"Are you in need of something, my lady?" one of the guards called from outside.

"Yeah. I was hoping to go for a walk. I can't sleep." She sighed. "I promise I'm sober now."

The lock clicked, and the door swung open. One of the guards gestured toward the hallway. At least they were nice sentient suits of armor.

She smiled. "Thanks. I'll stay inside, I promise. I just need to clear my head."

Neither of them replied as she headed down the hallway. She realized she forgot to put shoes on the moment her feet touched the cold stone floors. But that was fine—it was a little bit of a relief, strangely. Something about it felt grounding.

Her wanderings brought her back to the balcony where she had found Mordred a day or so earlier—had it honestly been less than a week of this nonsense? *Cripes.* That didn't seem fair. Leaning against the stone railing, she shut her eyes and just let herself breathe in the chill night air. She could hear crickets chirping in the field. If she tried really hard—*really, really hard*—she could fool herself into thinking she was safe at home.

But this wasn't Kansas.

And she certainly wasn't safe.

"Can't sleep either?" someone said as they walked up to her.

Glancing over, she was surprised to see Lancelot. "No. Too much on my mind."

"I thought the mead might have knocked you out until morning." He smirked at her, clearly teasing her a little for her drunkenness.

"I wasn't *that* bad, was I?" She frowned.

"No. You were not. But I enjoy watching that little line appear between your brows when you are mildly concerned by something." He chuckled and poked her forehead lightly. "Like you're doing right now."

"Great." She smiled at his ribbing, and returned to leaning on the railing and looking out over the dark field and the woods beyond. "You'll see it a lot, I'm sure."

"I hope that is the case. Meaning"—he quickly tried to cover—"that I hope I have the opportunity to see you in the future, not that I hope you are concerned by things."

He wasn't nearly as intense as Mordred. But that wasn't a bad thing. He seemed...almost normal. Almost a person. Not some extremely "extra" demigod supervillain. Resting her elbow on the railing and her head on her hand, she stared out at the woods. "I don't know what to do, Lance."

"Lance?"

"Lancelot has too many syllables for a nickname. Need something short and easy." She smiled faintly.

"I see." He joined her in leaning on the railing. "As to what to do...I am sorry for the position you have been put in. Do you want to talk?"

Letting out a puff of air, she watched it turn to mist in the chilly air. "I don't know if I can betray Mordred. Literally and figuratively. I don't know if I can bring myself to do it, and I don't know if I'd even be successful if I tried."

"So you're siding with him?"

"No. I don't know." She shut her eyes. "It should be super clear, right? He's the bad guy. He's keeping everybody locked away and suffering. He's using the magic he's stolen to create his armor things. But I also don't know what it was like *before*.

How bad it really was with all the constant warring and death. I believe that he thinks he honestly is doing the right thing."

"And so have many tyrants and bastards in this world." Lancelot sighed. "No one is ever the villain of their own tale. They will warp the reality around them to make themselves the hero in their own eyes—no matter how much of a farce that may be."

"I know. I know."

"He is charismatic in his own way. He is kind to you. But that does not stop him from being a monster." Lancelot turned to face her. She didn't dare meet his gaze. She felt too guilty about everything as it was. "I know that asking you to champion our cause is not fair to you. And I am deeply sorry for it. But you are the only hope we have had in three centuries that his reign might be put to an end."

"I don't get why you can't do it yourself. I mean—he *knows* you hate him. It's not like you're subtle."

Lancelot pulled the collar of his shirt aside, and she was distracted by the glow of the crystal embedded in his chest over his heart. "It is part of this curse that he has placed upon us. Any action we take against him would cause our death before we could see the deed through."

"What about, like, I don't know...poison or something?"

He chuckled, sarcastic and derisive. "I tried that. I laced his soup with nightshade. The moment his lips touched the spoon I was lost into a fit of convulsions. The agony was unbearable. And he knew precisely what I had done."

Cringing, she couldn't help but be sympathetic. "I'm sorry."

"I do not know what was worse, the pain from the curse or what he did to me afterwards for my insolence." Lancelot turned his back to her, and she was confused for a moment before he pulled his shirt from his trousers and lifted it to show her his back.

It was laced with scars.

Crisscrossed lines arched across his back in intersecting diagonals. They looked too systematic to have been done with a whip. They almost looked like they had been done with a knife. Or...claws.

"Oh, God." She put her hands over her mouth.

"That was what I paid for my second attempt at mutiny. The first resulted in the curse itself. I have not made a third attempt. I know it would be my last." He tucked his shirt back into his trousers and returned to leaning on the railing beside her. "It is not without desperation that I ask you for your help."

"I know, I *know*. I just..." She put her hands over her face. "I'm just a dumb kid from Kansas, I don't know what to do. How am I supposed to take him on? He doesn't trust anybody. Certainly not me. I can't get him to just let his guard down."

"Perhaps you can. Perhaps you already have, to a certain extent." Lancelot hummed. "You are a fire elemental. And fire can melt iron when raised to a hot enough degree. If you can learn to control your powers...you could destroy the Crystal. You would simply need someone to distract Mordred long enough for you to do the deed. Once you decide to end this all, tell me, and I will ensure you have enough time to do so."

She didn't like this plan. It sounded terrible. She hadn't even settled the first question of whether or not Mordred was wrong—although the score was now probably three for his downfall, one against. She wanted more time to figure it out, but nobody seemed to want to give her any.

And that was before she tried to address the question of whether or not she could even successfully *do* anything to Mordred. Even when she had the necklace off, she could barely control her fire, let alone focus it to do any damage to the Iron Crystal.

"I guess I'll keep training with him." Something about it still felt wrong. "And we'll see how I feel when we get to the point where I could even try."

Lancelot smiled, his silver eyes glittering. "I think that sounds like a brilliant idea. The best we have had in centuries."

"That tells me you've only had really shitty plans until now."

Laughing, he reached out and pulled her into a hug. "You do not know the short of it, Gwen."

She hugged him back. It felt...nice. Less prickly than Mordred with all his armor and his pointy claws.

"I am disappointed we are not going for a ride tomorrow. Perhaps I can steal you away later in the afternoon?" He pulled back far enough to cup her cheek in his hand. His touch was warm. Strong, but tender. "I find that I enjoyed our time together not only because you are my hope for salvation."

"I'm sure you say that to all the ladies."

"I certainly do not." He huffed. "There are no ladies around." When she groaned and slapped his chest, he laughed and pulled her tighter into a hug. "Oh come now, that was amusing."

"Yeah, whatever." She was laughing, despite herself.

"Was our time so insufferable to you?"

"No." It was an honest reply. "It wasn't. I'm just...everything is a lot right now. Like, a whole lot." She shook her head. "And Mordred..."

"Wants you as well. I know. There is no small part of me that seethes with jealousy. But if you are to play his interest in you as an advantage against him, it would be wise." He tucked a strand of her hair behind her ear. "And I will suffer in as much silence as I can manage."

"You all need to get out more, that's all I'm saying." She smiled. It was flattering, maybe, that these two guys were interested in her. But she knew it wasn't because she was special. It was because she was *shiny and new.*

Or in Lancelot's case, his only path to freedom.

And in Mordred's case, his only hope for a friend that he could trust.

God, I fucking hate all of this.

"I should get back to bed in case Mordred checks in on me." She gently nudged his arms away from her as she took a step back. "I don't want him stabbing either of us because he finds us together."

"Hm. Good point. And you look tired. Get some rest, my lady." He took her hand and kissed the back of her knuckles. The gesture made her cheeks go warm. "And I will see you on the morrow."

"G'night," she replied, still faintly smiling at the chivalrous gesture. "Lance."

He huffed a laugh again. "Lance. I do not know if I like that or not."

Walking away, she called over her shoulder. "I could come up with worse, you know."

"I'd prefer you didn't." He stayed on the balcony as she left.

It was with a faint smile that she went back to bed. He might be a smarmy bastard, but he had successfully cheered her up.

She had a plan. A plan that would lead to destroying the Crystal. Right?

Which was what she wanted to do.

Right?

TWENTY–ONE

W e're riding *him* to town?" Gwen stared up at the enormous
metal dragon that was sitting outside the gates of Mordred's
castle. She had been excited to go into the "city" and see what
it was like—to see more of Avalon than just the little that she
had experienced.

But *dragon.*

The creature peered down at her with its glowing white eyes
and let out a weird, raspy *harrumph.*

"I—I mean—no offense, you're really majestic and all,
but—" She laughed nervously. "I just—horses would be fine."

"It would take half the day to ride there, and a half day to
ride back." Mordred smirked at her obvious fear. "This will
take less than an hour."

"I . . . but . . . um."

"It is quite astonishing to fly. This time, perhaps, you will be
awake for the journey." He was grinning now. He patted her on
the shoulder with his clawed gauntlet. "I will not let you fall."

"It's not that I don't believe you." She chewed her lip. The
last thing she wanted to do was have a panic attack while midair on a damn metal dragon. Again.

The point was simply—*dragon.*

"Go on, firefly. I promise this flight will not be nearly as terrifying as the last." He nudged her gently forward.

"Does he have a name?" She kept staring up at the dragon who was watching her right back.

"No."

"That's stupid." She folded her arms across her chest and shot Mordred a disapproving, if somewhat playful, glance. "He should have a name."

"Then name him." Mordred smiled faintly. "Simply nothing embarrassing, is all I ask."

Studying the dragon for another moment, she grinned. "Tiny. Your name is now Tiny."

"I said nothing embarrassing."

"It isn't! I think it's cute. What do you think?" she asked the dragon.

The metal lizard let out another metallic grumble.

"Oh, do not side with her." Mordred rolled his eyes.

"What did he say?"

"That any name is better than none."

"See? I told you." She started climbing up the dragon's metal plates to the saddle on its back. It was much easier to do in the gray light of midmorning than in the middle of the night when she was about to faint from being so afraid. But she still watched where she put her feet as she reached the dragon's back and sat. Mordred joined her a moment later, sitting behind her, his thighs to the outside of hers.

When he wrapped an arm around her and pulled her to his chest, she felt her cheeks go warm. Lancelot was sweet and kind. Mordred was *not*. And damn it all if the Prince in Iron pushed her buttons in a way that Lancelot didn't.

His hand rested against her thigh, and she could feel his breath against her ear.

Damn it. Damn it all. She shut her eyes. "Is this the wrong time to tell you that I'm afraid of heights?"

"I would say that I suspect you are lying to me."

"I'm afraid of everything here."

He hummed. "The value of the soul can be summed in the fears it has learned to overcome."

"Way to call a girl cheap, thanks."

He chuckled before clicking his tongue. It sent the dragon into motion, lifting up from where it had been lying down for them to climb on board.

She squeaked and grabbed onto Mordred and clung for dear life. "Oooh shit—" Nope, it was still as terrifying the second time.

Her reaction sent Mordred into a deep laugh that rumbled at her back. He held her snugly. "You will not fall, firefly."

"Yeah, but I'll—" She screamed.

With a push from its powerful legs, the creature leapt into the air. She really wasn't sure how a giant metal dragon could actually fly, but she wasn't going to start arguing physics while midair.

She struggled to catch her breath. This was going to be a lousy time to have a panic attack. Again.

"Calm. I have you." Mordred leaned his head in close to her ear, his voice audible even through the rush of the air. "I will not let you fall. You are safe."

Safe. Right. On the back of a dragon. With an evil tyrant. Sure. Totally. Squeezing her eyes shut, she tried to focus on deep breaths. But it didn't work. She felt everything closing in around her. Her fingers began to tingle.

She was going to faint. Damn it. *Damn it!*

A clawed finger turned her head. She barely even noticed it. Everything was starting to sink away. She—

Lips pressed to hers. Her eyes flew back open. Mordred was cradling her head in his gauntlet, his metal nails just barely touching her scalp. He kissed her, firm and sure, insistent but not cruel. She felt like the air was sucked out of her lungs for a different reason, but at least the world was no longer going numb around her. Anything but.

When her heart was no longer racing a million miles an hour, and she felt as though her head wasn't spinning anymore, she rested her fingers on his cheek. He had just the barest amount of stubble. It was a little prickly, but she decided it was pleasant.

He broke away, those molten, rust-colored eyes finding hers. He smiled. "Welcome back, firefly."

That was a hell of a way to get her out of a panic attack. But hey. It worked. "Thanks. Cheater."

"If it works, I will not complain. And that was not entirely for your benefit." His smile twisted into that lopsided, almost roguish expression that he used so readily. "But you are welcome."

She went back to holding on to his arm to feel secure, but no longer felt like she was about to drop to her death. "I wasn't kidding when I said I was afraid of heights." She couldn't help it. She looked down. Squeaking, she leaned back against him and wished she could hide from what was happening.

"So I see." He laughed, and wrapped his paneled cloak around her, further insulating her from the wind whipping past them. "If I must distract you from another panic attack, I suppose I can be convinced to make that sacrifice."

Her cheeks went warm. "I—I think I'm okay now."

"Damn."

The dragon beat his wings from time to time with a loud *whoomf*, the action lurching them slightly as the animal kept them high above the treetops. When Gwen finally had the nerve to look around her, what she saw was astonishing. Waterfalls cascaded down the side of a cliff to their left. She could see the mountain that dominated the center of the island off in the distance, its top disappearing into the ever-present clouds. Forests stretched in all directions, dotted with clearings and the tiny structures of villages. Smoke curled up from several of the chimneys. Winding dirt roads snaked in and out of the woods.

It all looked so quaint.

So quaint but...bleak. All the colors were faded, even the orangey-reds of the fall leaves that dominated the trees. It was like late fall, when everything was starting to turn brown just before winter.

It was a terrible reminder of what the man behind her had done to the world in the name of saving it. He had taken all the vibrancy away.

They approached what she supposed passed for a city in Avalon. It wasn't huge, but certainly bigger than the villages or little collections of houses they had flown over. She clung to Mordred as the dragon circled the town before finding a place to land on the outskirts of the city center. The buildings in the city were built from stone, but still had the same strange, warped, and twisted appearance as everything else she had seen. Nothing seemed like it had been built in a straight line.

She cringed as the dragon landed with a hard *ka-thud*, the trees near the little town square creaking from the wind from the creature's wings. But Gwen was more than happy to be on the ground again.

"I will warn you, firefly—visiting the city with me may not go as you had hoped." Mordred unwrapped his arm from around her waist and dismounted from the saddle. "I am not loved." He climbed down, landing gracefully on the packed dirt, his paneled cloak pooling around his feet.

She knew he meant that in more ways than one. He meant he wasn't loved, not just by the villagers—but *at all*. That twisted a knife in her stomach. She knew he saw in her some kind of hope for companionship.

Damn it.

Damn it all.

Dismounting from the saddle—careful to make sure her skirt didn't ride up *too* far—she carefully climbed down the side of the dragon. The creature was watching her again with its white, glowing eyes.

"Thanks for the smooth ride." She smiled up at it. "Tiny."

It let out a *harrumph* and laid its head down, clearly intending on taking a nap while they went to do their business. The animal took up most of the area between the buildings, and she couldn't imagine how terrifying it must be for the people who lived there to suddenly have it snoozing out in front of their homes. Especially because it was clear the dragon could nuke the whole place if it wanted to.

"He thinks you are adorable for thanking him for doing what he was ordered to do." Mordred chuckled.

"It never hurts to be polite. Especially with something that can eat you." She pulled her own cloak tighter around her shoulders. She wondered if Avalon had been this chilly before the magic of the world had been locked away. She sincerely hoped not.

"That is a very wise point." He gestured for her to follow

him as he walked down the cobblestone street toward what she assumed was the center of town. She fell in step beside him, and tried to take in the details of everything around them.

What she noticed was how...quiet the city was. There was barely anybody else out and about. And those who were took one look at Mordred and either began walking twice as fast or ducked back into their homes and shut the doors.

He hadn't been kidding.

"Lancelot told me about how you make your armored people." She frowned. "And the dragon, too, I guess."

"I suppose he would seek any reason to turn you against me." Mordred's expression was fixed into a stern but otherwise unreadable one.

They walked in silence for another long minute. Gwen wrapped her arms around herself under the cloak.

Mordred let out a breath. "Magic leaks and coalesces from the Crystal. I have to keep careful watch, for it often cracks and threatens to shatter. It forms shards that, if left unchecked, combine and could form some manner of terrible amalgam. I opt to put it to better use."

"Do...they remember what or who they used to be?" Poor Maewenn. Poor guards. Poor Tiny.

"No. I assure you, they do not suffer." Mordred's voice was cold and matter of fact. "I fear you must decide whether or not I am the villain others make me."

He pulled the hood of his cloak over his head, obscuring his features. He looked for all the world like the Grim Reaper in rusted armor.

"Maybe if you didn't look so scary, people wouldn't be, y'know, so scared." It was a stupid suggestion, she knew, but she didn't know what else to say. When he turned his head to her, clearly shooting her a look, she shrugged. "What? I mean. You are."

"If I cannot command respect, I shall command fear."

"And, again, you wonder why nobody likes you."

"I do not wonder, firefly." He lifted one of his clawed gauntlets, scraping the thumb and forefinger together with a quiet *screeech*. "I am well aware."

"Then maybe you should stop being so moody about it," she mumbled under her breath.

"Pardon?"

"Nothing." She smiled.

"Hm." It was clear he didn't believe her. But he also didn't seem too upset. "Am I going to be the victim of your loose tongue, now that you are no longer concerned I will rip your heart from your chest?"

"I mean, probably." She wished she owned pockets. She liked to tuck her hands into things. "And are you?"

"I am still not planning on murdering you."

"Then, there we go." She smiled. It didn't stop the fact that the man looked like something out of a nightmare. But at least she wasn't having a panic attack just by standing near him.

He continued after a pause. "But I never said anything about torture."

That made her come to a full stop. "Wait—what?"

He turned to face her. "Come now." He placed the tip of his clawed pointer finger underneath her chin, and used it to lift her head up toward him. "Can you not tell when I am teasing you?"

That isn't the problem. Her cheeks went warm.

She didn't know what to do. But he took pity on her and

dropped his hand from her chin. "Come." He began walking again. "We are nearly to the city square."

She fell in step beside him again. They were just starting to get to the center of the city. There were shops huddled close together, the windows advertising everything from hardware to cheese, furniture, dresses, fabric, fruit, and more. Rolling carts were set up down the middle of the cobblestone road, the sellers hawking their wares to passersby. Until they saw Mordred. Then, they all quickly fell silent.

It took her a second to realize that they weren't just staring at him—they were also staring at her. She looked down at herself, trying to figure out why. And then it hit her. Right. She was an elemental—a thing that hadn't been free in Avalon for three hundred something years.

And she was wearing an iron necklace.

She couldn't even imagine what they were all thinking. Or, rather, she really could. Her face went hot, and she felt so damn ashamed of herself, she found herself staring at her feet to keep from meeting their wide-eyed stares.

"What is wrong?" Mordred paused, before clearly putting it together himself as well. "Ah. Yes. *Well*." He huffed. "I suppose this will do little to improve my reputation, now will it?"

"You don't have to sound so damn happy about it," she grumbled. "This is so embarrassing. I must look like your damn pet."

"You are not leashed." He really did sound amused. "Although...that is not to say that I am not tempted."

"Augh!" She covered her face with her hands. "Stop it, I swear to fuck if I could burst into flames right now, I would."

He chuckled. "Then, I am doubly glad for the necklace." His claw crooked under her chin again, this time using the side instead of the point. "Remember that these are peasants—they know nothing of you or your circumstances. Nor would they pay much mind if you told them."

"You don't think much of your people, huh?"

"No." He lowered his hand to his side. "Nor have they given me reason to change that opinion. Now...you wished to see more of Avalon, did you not?" He gestured out at the street. "Enjoy. And do not linger. I dislike it here."

No kidding. With a breath, she suddenly felt exceedingly self-conscious about just marching around the square. It wasn't like she had any money to buy anything with—hell, she didn't even know what they used for money in Avalon.

The city was fascinating, with shops of every kind packed close together in tight little windowed rows. Cheese, bread, cakes—it felt like something out of a Dickens novel. She stopped to marvel at a store that sold hand-made wooden toys and puppets painted to look like all the fanciful creatures of Avalon. There were figurines of knights in a row, and she recognized Galahad and Lancelot. There was a man in a golden crown who must be Arthur. There was even one of a man with a gray beard and a dark robe who she was sure *had* to be Merlin.

But no Mordred.

Frowning, she moved on to the next store. It was a clothing shop. Next to it was a milliner and a cobbler. She could spend all day here, she was certain of it, going from shop to shop poking at all the amazing collections.

"Mind if I pop in here?" She gestured at one of the storefronts. It had caught her attention, not because it sold any one particular thing, but because it seemed to be selling *everything*.

It was piled floor to ceiling with *stuff*. Baskets, chairs, signs, pots, pans, keys, doorknobs, everything she could imagine.

Mordred shrugged. "Do as you like."

Smiling, she opened the door and pushed it open, the little bell overhead chiming to announce her arrival.

"Eh?" The shopkeeper looked up. He was an old man with a pair of tiny glasses perched on the end of his bumpy nose. "Oh. You're new. And a—oh." He squinted. "Ah. Well. Can't say I'm surprised about the necklace. At least you aren't in that damnable Crystal with everyone else."

The man's judgmental tone was both irritating and embarrassing.

Everyone was going to jump to the worst conclusions, weren't they? That she was screwing Mordred for the sake of her freedom? There wasn't anything she could do to stop that, she supposed. Rumors were rumors. And it was a pretty logical conclusion to jump to, she had to admit. "I. Um." She frowned. "I'm new, yeah. I just ... I'm just browsing."

"Suit yourself, girl." He waved a grizzled hand at her dismissively. "Just don't break or steal anything."

"I'll do my best." She walked down a narrow aisle. Drawers from some long-gone cabinet were stacked in a pile, each one overflowing with letters that looked like they were from a printing press. She picked up a few, turning them over curiously before putting them back. She was glad to have a moment to herself.

It lasted exactly two seconds.

"*Psst*—hey, kid!" someone whispered harshly.

Blinking, she turned around. No one was there. Furrowing her brow, she shrugged and went back to what she had been doing.

"Hey, hey up here—"

"What the fuck?" She stopped, and did as the voice said. She looked up. There, sitting on the shelf, was a metal, fake carved pumpkin. It looked made out of copper, as it had patinated into greens and blues. It had a face carved into it—or rather, cast, or whatever. Two circular eyes that were mismatched in size and a grinning, toothy smile.

As she watched, two small, amber dots appeared in the eye sockets, as if it had opened them. Not white—but amber.

"Get me down from here," the pumpkin whispered. "My body is another aisle over. I need your help. I'd do it m'self, but I'm pretty sure that arse of a shopkeeper would notice me shuffling around."

"Why would I help you?" she whispered back. "And who are you, anyway?"

"You're gonna help me, because the day has come. It's time to rally the forces and start the revolution. You're—I mean, you're an elemental, aren't you? That means you want magic to be free again. Right?" The little lights went off then on again. The pumpkin had blinked. "Name's Bertin. What's your name?"

"Gwen." His name was *Bert*. Something about that made her want to laugh. But she let it go. "What revolution?"

"*The* revolution, of course. The one to take power away from Mordred and the elementals and give it back to the people."

"Yeah, okay, but if you're against elementals, why would I help you?" She put her hands on her hips. "That makes no sense."

"Because something tells me you don't want to go into that Crystal. You must be our chance." He blinked. She supposed it was all he could really do as a talking pumpkin head. "You're here to save us all."

"I really don't think so." She frowned. "I can't even save myself right now."

"Fact remains. You're here, which means he's distracted, which means it's time to strike." His accent was thick and reminded her of something like Cockney, although it wasn't quite the same. Maybe an older version of it? Whatever. "Unless you *do* want to go into the Crystal."

"No, I don't."

"That means you're on my side, and then I can help you. I see that necklace. Mordred's got you, huh? Can't even imagine what you're payin' him with to keep you free."

She rolled her eyes and crossed her arms over her chest. "It isn't like that."

"Sure, kid. Sure. I'm not judging you. If I had a real mouth, I'd have long since dropped to my knees and—"

"Ew, ew. Stop. Stop." She made a face. "Fine, I'll help you and your stupid revolution. Whatever. Just stop talking."

"Deal."

Going on her tiptoes to grab the pumpkin from the shelf, she pulled it down and brushed some of the dust off his head. He'd been up there for a long, long time. She was careful to keep him at arm's length as she went to the end of the aisle. The antique store was such a confusing maze of weird nooks and crannies, it took her a few seconds to find what Bertin was talking about.

There, up against the wall, was a scarecrow without a head. Its body was stuffed with sticks, hay, and even bits of random furniture. He had an old, busted piece of a table for a leg. It made him kind of resemble a pirate.

Instead of a head, a piece of a broom handle stuck up where she figured his head was supposed to go.

"What's your plan?" she whispered down at the metal pumpkin head.

"See if I can't find some old friends who went into hiding too. Then...we lie low until it's time. Then, we'll strike against Mordred."

She shot him a look. "An army of guys made out of straw," she whispered back. "Against him."

"I never said it was a *good* plan." Bert huffed.

She heard the little bell go off over the door. The old man at the counter spoke to whomever it was who had entered in frightened, short phrases. It must have been Mordred, coming in to see what was taking her so long.

With a sigh, she put the metal head on the stick. "I'll make sure they're both distracted. Go out the back."

The scarecrow stood up. It was exactly at that moment she realized she had put his head on *backwards*, and the body had actually been sitting with its legs going the wrong way around. She figured when you didn't have bones, it didn't really matter.

Bertin stood, waved his hands around for a second, before grabbing his head and twisting it back around straight. Taking a step, he staggered and fell into a bookshelf. She yelped and scrambled to catch some books before they hit the ground.

"I told you not to break anything!" The shopkeep didn't sound pleased.

"I will pay for whatever she has damaged." Mordred. A very unamused Mordred. "Gwendolyn, are you quite all right?"

"I'm—I'm fine, just tripped. I'm good." She laughed nervously. "You know me, just a klutz."

"What's a klutz?" Bertin whispered. He smelled like the family barn around the time of the fall harvest. Slightly mildewy from the dampness, but thick with the smell of hay.

"Doesn't matter. Get out of here." She shoved the scarecrow toward the back door she could see down a narrow, tilted hallway. The place looked like it was being held up entirely from the support of all the furniture and piles of things inside of it. "Before you get me into trouble."

"Thanks, kid." He patted her head with a stuffed glove. His other hand was a gardening fork, so she was much happier with the glove. "I'll be seein' you." Bert quickly made his way toward the back of the shop. "Gotta spread the good word—that there's hope. That it's time to take a stand against tyranny."

"Gwendolyn?" Mordred called.

"Here, sorry." She shook her head as she headed back toward the front. She figured she'd never see the scarecrow again.

Mordred arched an eyebrow at her. "Did you get lost?" He brushed some dust off of her shoulder.

"No. Found some cool old things, got distracted." It wasn't a lie. Just not the whole truth.

"Come. Let us return home. You can explore the city again at another time." Mordred held open the door for her. His patience had clearly run out. That was fine by her. She suddenly wasn't in the mood to go prowling around more stores filled with unfriendly judgmental people and weird talking severed pumpkin heads.

She didn't bother saying goodbye to the rude-ass store owner as she left. Walking alongside Mordred, she folded her arms over her chest. "Why do you do it, Mordred?"

"Do what?"

"Protect them. It's clear everybody hates you. I guess I don't get why you bother to help people that despise you."

He stayed silent and didn't respond to her statement. That was fine. She didn't know what else to say and was now too lost in her thoughts to keep up a conversation.

Lancelot, Merlin, and now Bert had all called her their "hope."

And Mordred hoped she'd be something else.

She didn't like being people's *hope.* She was just a dumb kid from Kansas. She didn't have any business trying to save a whole world.

But it didn't seem like she was going to have much say in the matter.

TWENTY-TWO

"Where're we going?" Gwen looked down at the ground beneath them as Tiny soared over the landscape. Because of the huge mountain in the center of the island, she was pretty sure the keep was to the northwest. And they were headed southeast, straight toward the mountain in question.

"I wish to show you something."

It was kind of wonderful, flying—once she wasn't afraid she was about to fall to her death. The view below them was stunning. Faded as it was, cloudy as it was, it was still a beautiful place. They flew over an enormous waterfall that poured into a lake that emptied into the ocean, dotted with rocks that jutted above the surface. She could almost imagine mermaids playing there.

It looked as though there was every kind of terrain in Avalon—she could see what seemed like a damn lava flow to the south, surrounded by dusty desert and bouldery terrain. She figured that elementals liked to live in their own, well, element. It would make sense.

But most of Avalon was a thick forest, interspersed with dirt roads that wound between sporadic villages, farms, and cities like the one they had just left. The island was bigger than she had imagined it to be from the maps. But she supposed everything looked smaller on paper.

As they approached the mountain in the center, she spied a ruined castle at the base of it. It was a strange place to put a castle—half in a valley, half on the rocks. It was as if it had just been dropped there randomly, not placed with any kind of thought or care.

Weird.

Wait.

"Is that?"

"You'll see soon enough." Mordred clicked his tongue. It wasn't nearly loud enough in the wind for the dragon to hear him, but the beast seemed to know what to do regardless. Tiny began to slowly swoop lower, circling before landing with a *ka-thud* out in front of the castle.

A castle that had seen much better days.

Parts of the walls and roof had crumbled away. If there were originally windows, they were long gone. The enormous wooden front doors were open, leaves piled up in front of them. It was clear they had not moved in a very long time.

Mordred let Gwen climb off the dragon first. When he joined her, he walked into the castle without a word. She assumed she was supposed to follow him. She couldn't help but stare at the building as they walked along the crumbling ruins deeper into the structure. Ripped and tattered tapestries hung lopsidedly on the walls, too stained and faded from time for her to make out what they once showed.

He looked like a nightmare, with his black hood over his head and his jagged claws. It was something she'd never get used to—and part of her never wanted to. He was, as he kept saying, who he was. She followed close behind him, careful to avoid the portions of the wooden floor that looked as though they were about to give out, or already had.

Finally, he brought her to a central chamber.

And then she knew for certain where she was.

The center of the room was dominated by a large, circular, wooden table. It resembled the one Mordred had in his own keep, though this one was in far worse shape. Chairs, mostly fallen apart or reduced to rubble, sat around it.

Surrounding the room were statues, each sculpted out of their own kind of metal. Each one was a work of art—slightly stylized, but unmistakable for what they were. Beneath each was a placard that read out their name and their title. Galahad, the Knight in Gold. Lancelot, the Knight in Silver. Percival, the Knight in Copper. Tristan, the Knight in Tin. Gawain, the Knight in Cobalt. And Bors, the Knight in Nickel.

And Mordred, the Prince in Iron. Looking as fearsome and terrifying as ever.

But standing at the head of the room was an enormous statue sculpted from an alloy of something that Gwen couldn't recognize. It was of a regal figure, his hands clasping the hilt of an enormous blade that she recognized—though it was in much better condition in the statue than it was now. Caliburn.

Atop the man's head sat a crown of gold, decorated with each of the other metals that surrounded her. She didn't need to read the plaque to know who it was meant to represent.

That was King Arthur.

She walked up to the statue, marveling at it. He looked stern, but with gentle eyes. This place felt like a . . . tomb, for lack of a better word. "Is he buried here?"

"Yes."

That would do it. She turned to Mordred, and found him glowering up at his own likeness. "I thought Camelot was on Earth."

"It was. Arthur was too wounded to travel. So that lunatic Merlin decided to move him, the castle, and all the rest of us at once." He let out a half-hearted laugh.

"What was he like, Merlin?"

"Obscenely powerful and always the smartest man in the room. Which is of course to say, he was a complete arse." He smiled and, while it was sad, it seemed real.

"What happened to him?"

"When Avalon chose me, he simply wandered off and disappeared. He is long dead by now, I expect. He was a powerful wizard, but he was a mortal man in the end." Mordred shook his head. "I was a disappointment to him. And to all the others."

She glanced back up at the statue of Arthur. "Was he really your dad?"

Mordred barked a laugh. "Lancelot told you that, did he?"

"Yeah."

"In short, firefly? I do not know. My mother never shared the truth of my parentage with me. And in the end, it did not matter." He walked to the remains of the wooden table in the center, and picked idly at the back of one of the destroyed and weathered chairs. "Though perhaps that is why he chose me as his successor, not Lancelot."

For some reason, she couldn't imagine Lancelot being in charge of anything. She wrinkled her nose. "I get the feeling he isn't responsible enough to handle a crown. I mean, I know he's old, and probably a great fighter. He's perfectly nice. But he... kind of reminds me of the guys I knew at school."

"Then you are wise beyond your years. If you believe he is impulsive and immature now, you should have seen him all those years ago when we were but humans." He shut his eyes and let out a dreary sigh.

"I still don't understand why people hate you so much, if the elementals were as bad as you say."

"You saw the world we flew over. What did you think of it?"

"I . . . don't know."

"No. You do. Do not spare my feelings. Tell me, what did you think of Avalon?" He walked up to her slowly, stopping only a foot or two away.

"I could tell how beautiful it must have been once, when the sun shone and there was magic." She hugged her arms to herself. It was chilly and damp in the old battered-down place, and she was almost always cold now to begin with.

"Precisely. Most of those who live on Avalon are of normal lifespans. They have lived and died for centuries without seeing the sun. Without knowing the horrors of rampaging, marauding elementals who believed themselves to be above all others." He reached out a hand and ran the back of his metal knuckles over her cheek. "Memories are short."

"You said you did all this to protect them. But *why*, if they hate you? You didn't answer me before."

He looked up at the statue of Arthur. "Because I was trusted to do so. Because, despite what all the others may think of my uncle's choice, I made a vow to be as rational and good a king as I could be."

King Arthur was a hell of an act to follow, she had to give him that. Something in the tone of his voice broke her heart. It was suddenly clear to her—Mordred had lived in that man's shadow all his life. And he was still haunted by him now.

"Hey. Ditch the armor."

"Pardon?" He arched an eyebrow down at her.

"Just ditch the armor."

With a slight shrug, he did as she asked. "I do not see what you—"

She hugged him. Wrapped her arms around him—though her hands didn't touch in the back—and rested her cheek to his chest.

She felt the air rush out of him. Finally, after a long pause, he returned the gesture and rested his chin atop her head. They stood there like that, silently, for a long time. Simply holding each other.

"I get it now." She shut her eyes. "And I'm sorry."

"Pity me not, dear firefly. Do not forget what I have done to my knights. Do not forget how I create my armored servants. You know how harsh my reign can be."

"Yeah. I guess. I'm still sorry."

He tilted her head up to look at him with the crook of a claw beneath her chin. He lowered his head to hers, and caught her lips in a kiss. It was slow. It was gentle. And it was a thank-you.

When he finally broke away, her knees felt weak. He took her hand in his, and led her silently from the abandoned castle. When they were back on Tiny, and he wrapped his arms around her, she rested her head back against him.

She had to choose a side.

And God help her, she didn't want to.

But she knew she wouldn't have that option.

⁕ ⁙ ⁖ ⁑

Mordred stepped into his study, his mind wheeling and his heart in a lurch. Gwen. Oh, Gwen. What was he to do with her? How sweet she tasted against his lips—cinnamon and woodsmoke, like the smell of a warm summer fire, like laughter and companionship.

He wanted her. He wanted her very badly. But there was something else in him that called out besides his hunger to have her in his bed. It was how she held him when she fully understood the reason behind his actions.

It was not for *his* sake that he ruled Avalon like a tyrant.

It was for those his uncle had sworn to protect.

It was for the sake of duty.

He wanted to trust her. Damn it, he needed to trust her. He had not had anyone by his side in... he could not remember how long. He'd had relations with women now and then, but nothing more than a passing fancy.

But Gwen felt different to him. How those fire-colored eyes had shone with sympathetic tears on his behalf. He was halfway through pouring himself a drink when he heard footsteps enter the room behind him. He did not need to turn to know who it was.

He braced himself. "What do you want, Lancelot?"

"How was the trip into the city? Did she enjoy it?"

"It was fine." He walked to his fire and kept from looking at the Knight in Silver. It might send him into a rage. The knight liked to goad him. As he could not lift a hand in violence, he would use his words instead. It was his way.

"I would like to train her this afternoon. I think it would be useful for her to have more than one tutor."

Mordred rolled his eyes and finally faced the other man. "You wish to simply drive a wedge further between her and me." He sipped his alcohol. He had the sense he was going to need it.

"I wish to give her another opinion to hear. You have kept

her enough to yourself." Lancelot headed to the bar to help himself to a drink. "I think we should give the girl the choice between us, no?"

"A word to the wise—do not call her girl." Mordred smirked. "On second thought, please do. I wish to see her rattle your brain in your head."

Lancelot scoffed. "She and I are fast friends, fast allies, and we would be faster lovers if you would not abscond with her so frequently."

"What is your game, Lancelot? Why would you seek to overburden her with such a facetious choice between us? Why not simply let the young lady choose on her own time?"

"I will tell you why. Because I despise how you are treating her. Because the longer she spends in your presence, the more danger she is in." Lancelot downed a glass of whiskey and poured himself another. "Why must you put her through such violent training? I see the bruises she wears. She has done nothing to you. Why do you push her about? Do you derive some sort of sick pleasure from it? I knew you were an evil bastard, but—"

"Mind yourself, Lancelot," Mordred warned.

"Why do you seek to hurt the girl, if not because you enjoy it. Hm?" Lancelot sneered at him. "Do not tell me she enjoys your manner of attention."

"I am teaching her how to control her power. That is all."

"And *that* is how you choose to do it?"

"Yes." He fought the urge to bash his fist into the wall and shatter the stone.

"Why train her in the first place? Do you want a challenge before you put her in the Crystal with all the rest?" Lancelot downed his second glass and put the empty container back on the bar with a heavy *thunk*.

"Because she has asked me to teach her." And because he was desperate to spend time with her. But he kept those words to himself. He needn't fuel Lancelot's anger with the truth. Mordred held his ground as Lancelot stormed up to him.

"You amuse yourself with her—you seek to sleep with her. You only allow her so much freedom so that you might trick her into your bed. For shame, *prince*. To take advantage of her in such a way." Lancelot's lip curled in disgust. "You are no knight of Arthur."

Snarling, Mordred took hold of Lancelot's throat with his claws, just barely puncturing the skin, and dragged the man closer. "Watch your tongue, knight. Gwendolyn stands upon a crossroads where she may choose with whom to place her trust."

"Then let's make it a fair competition, eh? Let me train her this afternoon instead and show her some kindness." Lancelot grinned through the pain. "Or are you too set on pleasuring yourself to the sound of her agony?"

Mordred slammed his other fist into the man's head. Lancelot staggered and fell to the ground, groaning. Mordred cracked his knuckles and readied himself for a brawl. *"Enough."*

"Then deny it. Deny you do not hurt her for your own gratification."

"Her pain brings me no pleasure." Mordred clenched his fists at his sides.

"Then why would you seek her out so frequently, if—oh. *Oh.*" Lancelot lifted a hand to show surrender. "It is more than lust." He sat back on his heels before climbing to his feet. "By God, Mordred—do not tell me you *love* her." He laughed.

"Do not be a fool." Mordred turned his back on Lancelot, having enough of the mockery. The knight was no threat to him, save to his mood. "Begone. I am done with you."

Lancelot was already heading to the exit. "I do not know who I pity more then. Her, for being bound for the Crystal—or you, when you finally lose someone you love to your own tyranny."

Mordred tightened his hands into fists. With a snarl, he picked up his empty glass and hurled it against the wall, watching it rain down to the ground as shards and specks.

Damn that forsaken knight. Damn the prince who ruled him. *Damn them all to the hells where they belonged.*

TWENTY-THREE

Gwen was almost happy for the distraction of "training" with Mordred. She really thought of it more as getting beaten up, but she supposed it was the same thing in his mind. And she wasn't the only one who was grumpy after their trip to the city and the ruins of Camelot. Walking into the circular court-yard, wearing her metal clothing, she pulled up short.

Uh-oh.

Mordred was in a *mood* again. She could tell by the way he was holding himself. And that was going to be very bad for her. Taking a sword from the rack by the wall, he threw it at her feet. "We will start by reviewing yesterday's lessons."

"More like yesterday's bruises," she grumbled, as she picked up the weapon. "You okay?"

He ignored her question. "If you do not wish to be battered about so much, then I suggest you learn faster." His clothing shifted to his full armor, and she shivered at the sight of him without meaning to. God, he was so damn tall. Tall and *pointy*. Caliburn appeared in the air beside him, and he grasped the hilt that she knew was meant to be handled with two hands, though he could wield it with one.

When he came at her, she did the only logical thing she could think of—she kept dodging out of the way. He was swinging the blade with a vengeance. He probably thought he was going easy on her. To her, it looked like he was legit trying to slice her in half.

She squeaked as his blade sliced the air beside her, close enough that she could feel it. "Hey!"

"Defend yourself, Gwendolyn."

"I'm trying!"

"Try harder."

When she stumbled, he used the opportunity to get in close and, using his elbow, knocked her to the ground. Her sword landed in the sand beside her as she landed hard on her ass with an *unf*. She only managed to push herself up onto her elbows before his blade was resting against her throat. She shivered again. "We've been through this. I can't beat you, Mordred."

"You say that, but I do not think you believe it. You cannot defeat me, Gwendolyn Wright. Not with a blade and not with your fire. Do you understand?" That was the Mordred people were used to dealing with. The Prince in Iron.

She wished she could crawl into the ground and stay there. She felt so small. "I . . . I do."

"Then tell me what kind of schemes you have been working behind my back." He stepped over her, his feet on either side of her thighs. "Tell me what you have been hiding from me."

She hesitated. Telling him the truth was going to get everyone in a lot of trouble. Including herself. Mostly herself, if she were being honest.

At her silence, he snarled. He moved the blade away from her throat only to replace it with his gauntlet. He reached down and grasped her by the iron around her neck and hefted her roughly to her feet. When he pushed her away, he held the necklace in his fist. He tossed it aside. "Then I will teach you this lesson again. Now you are free to use your flame. Do so. Fight me."

"I—but—" She yelped as he swung his sword at her. She staggered back, catching on fire as she did. Panic was starting to well in her chest, more proof that she was actually useless and everybody's hope in her was sorely misplaced. "Please, I—"

Any thought in her head that he wasn't really going to hurt her was gone the moment he swung for her with seemingly redoubled efforts. She dodged, but his sword nicked her arm. She hissed in pain, placing her hand to the burning surface. What came away in her palm looked like molten lava. It hissed when it touched the ground. "Mordred, please wait—"

"No." He didn't even give her a second to deal with the cut before going at her again. She staggered out of the way, struggling to stay out of the reach of his enormous sword.

Without thinking—without really understanding what she was doing—she pushed her hands toward him, just needing him to *fucking stop*. A roar of fire filled the air as a huge blast of flame left her hands and hit him head-on like it had come from a flamethrower. For a moment, Mordred was obscured by dark smoke.

Gwen blinked. "Whoa."

But she didn't have time to appreciate what she had just done. He stepped from the smoke like a nightmare, fire still curling from his iron armor where it glowed orangey-red. He looked for all the world like a demon stepping out of the gates of hell.

So she did the only thing she could think of.

She blasted him with fire again. She needed him to stop. She needed him to get away from her. But nothing she did to him seemed to even slow him down. He kept stalking her around the courtyard, his steps now methodical.

Didn't fire melt iron? Wasn't that the whole plan? No matter what she did, how many times she hit him with a *fireball*—it didn't even make him flinch.

"No magic can harm me." Mordred kept advancing on her, making her retreat each time. "You cannot cause me damage. No one can. I am an aberration in this world—I am the elemental that should never have been. Melt this castle down around my head, and it will do nothing to stop me. Destroy the Crystal? I shall simply make another and begin again. Do you understand? I am *inevitable*."

"What the fuck did I do? Why're you so mad?" She was crying. Little bits of lava were hitting the ground where they dripped from her cheeks and the cut on her arm. He was right. Dear God, he was right. What was she supposed to do against him? How was she supposed to win? She couldn't. Every bit of footing she had in Avalon was because Mordred had let her have it. Not because she had earned it.

Maybe she could run away. The necklace was off. That meant she could get out of here, and escape into the woods, or some shit. She turned, planning on doing just that—fuck the castle and if she set it on fire on the way out.

She made it halfway to the door before he caught up with her. A clawed fist snatched her by the hair, and a second later she was pressed up against the stone wall of the courtyard. He was at her back, his hand still fisted in her hair, keeping her cheek pinned to the cooler surface.

"Where do you think you are going? Where do you think you can hide from me, Gwendolyn? Out in the wilds of Avalon? I would hunt you down...believe you me, I would *relish* the opportunity."

"Mordred, please—" She pushed on the stone wall, trying to

get some space between them. But he was right there, caging her in. She couldn't budge him. It was like trying to move a car.

He shushed her, crouching to lower his head closer to hers. He dropped his voice. "I have treated you as my guest for your benefit and yours alone. I let you whisper in corridors with strangers, I let you scheme with my own knights against me. I let you keep your secrets in the hope that you will *choose* the right path. But do not think for one second that I do not know what you are doing."

His thigh pressed between her legs, further pinning her there. He ran his metal hand slowly down her arm. She was shaking like a leaf—for more reasons than one.

He's threatening my life. He's threatening my safety. Now is not *the time, you fucking idiot*—she yelled at herself silently in her head, squeezing her eyes closed and trying to shut up that part of her that suddenly, and entirely inexplicably, decided that this was super hot.

No pun intended.

"Necklace or not. Fire or not. You cannot fight me. Do you understand?" His voice was now close to her ear, sounding metallic and a little hollow from inside his helm.

She swallowed the rock in her throat. It didn't want to go down.

"Do you understand?" he snarled, his hand in her hair tightening. It pulled on her scalp, stinging her just a little. It hurt. And it didn't. The mix of sensations did nothing to help her confusion.

"Y—yes."

"What do you understand?"

Of course he was going to make her say it. "I can't beat you. No matter what I do."

"And?" Now his voice was a low growl, dangerous and sensual at the same moment. "What else?"

"That I—I can't escape." She cringed. "That I—"

He whirled her around. Before she could even blink, he grabbed her by the waist and hefted her up the wall. He stepped between her legs, the plates of his armor digging into her thighs as she wrapped her legs around him. His helm disappeared, melding into the rest of him, and his lips descended on hers with a vengeance.

His kisses before had been firm, but kind.

This was different.

This was very different.

This was a conquering warlord. This was bruising and harsh. Even though her lips were made of fire, it didn't seem to hurt him in the slightest. When she pushed on his chest, trying to catch some air, he grasped her wrists and pinned them to the wall beside her head, deepening his kiss as he did.

Did she just moan?

Oh God.

She did.

But she'd never felt anything like that before. Never once in her life. Her boyfriend had always been sweet and gentle, not...not like this. Not a literal force of nature. Mordred snarled in his throat at the sound she made, his tongue flicking at her lips.

She parted them. She let him in. She let him devour her. His hands released her wrists to let her drape her arms over his shoulders, no longer trying to push him away.

When he pressed his hips to hers, miming what he clearly wished to do to her, she gasped.

He finally broke the kiss, his lips wandering to her ear. "I will not take you. I want you to climb into my bed by your own choice. I want your own need to consume you. But once you do, my sweet firefly... I want you to understand what will be waiting for you." He pressed his hips to her again, harder than before.

It drew another quiet, shy moan from her lips. Her eyes were shut, lost in the sensation of him. She wanted it—wanted him. Wanted the feeling of being entirely *destroyed* by someone of his size and strength. She didn't know what that said about her. Probably nothing good. It certainly was all new information to her.

He chuckled, and kissed her cheek close to her earlobe. He stepped away. Once he put her down and her feet were once more on the dirt, he turned and walked away, his armor melding back into his normal clothing.

Wait. He was just *leaving*? After all that?

"What about the—" She was still on fire, after all.

"I believe I have proven my point that the necklace is for your comfort, not mine." And he was gone.

She slid down to the ground, sitting against the stone wall. Her legs felt like jelly. Burny jelly, but still jelly. Struggling to slow down her heart and steady her breathing, she leaned her head against the wall and tried to process what had just happened.

It was another ten minutes before she managed to calm down long enough to put out her fire. It was probably another five before she could stand up. And holy *shit* she was bruised up again. She cringed and looked down at the cut on her arm. A line of blood had reached her elbow. It wasn't bad—it didn't need stitches—but it definitely should get bandaged up.

That gave her something to focus on that wasn't, well,

Mordred. And the fact that he was an enormous asshole. And the fact that if he had tried to go all the way with her right there, she'd have absolutely let him.

Nope. She was not going to think about that. She was not going to think about that at all. Nope, she was going to focus on the fact that she needed to find some rubbing alcohol—if they even had that kind of thing in Avalon—and a bandage.

She knew where she had to go to probably find both of those things. And with a long-suffering sigh, she knew what she had to do. She had to go to the kitchen. And deal with the fussing of Maewenn, the cook, for how battered up she was again.

Fuck my life.

Mordred had made a mistake. He knew he had. In fact, he knew he had made several. But it had not stopped him. Nor would it likely deter him from following this new path wherever it might lead.

He sat in his study, his elbows on his steel table, his head in his hands. This was all going to get him into a great deal of trouble. He was inviting the girl to betray him—to work with the others to destroy the Crystal and set the magic of Avalon free again.

He had opened the door for her and was leaving it up to her whether or not she walked through it. Why? *Why?* This had now become self-destructive to the verge of madness. Perhaps Percival was right. Perhaps he had decided to end it all at the hands of a young woman with power she was only scratching at the surface of.

But by the Ancients. Watching her scramble away from him. The fear in those blazing eyes. The feeling of her body against his, the heat of it—the taste of the fire as he had kissed her. As she had *surrendered* to him.

He had been helpless. Utterly helpless. She might be his prisoner, but he did not think she understood that he was the one on the leash, not she. What had started off as an attempt to teach the lady her place had ended with him nearly ready to rip off her chainmail skirt and show her precisely how little her fire could injure him.

Would he risk letting her destroy all that he had worked for, just for the chance for her to climb into his bed?

Yes.

It seemed he would.

And he wondered if she had not suddenly burned the brain from out of his head during their brawl. Why could he not bring himself to do what needed to be done? Why could he not just have his way with her—which would be willing, if her reticent and uncertain reactions to him were anything to judge—and be done with it? Or put her in the Crystal and leave her there with all the others?

Why?

Why was he being such a fool?

There was only one answer. Only one.

Standing with a shout of rage, he threw his steel table, sending the object hurtling through the air and crashing against the wall. The answer would spell his downfall. It would spell the downfall of all Avalon. It made no sense. It should not *be*. But there it was. Staring at him in the face.

The reason why he was making all these foolish mistakes. And the reason why he would now have to resort to something drastic to save all that he had worked for, for so long. There was only one way forward. One answer. One path. And it made him wish to rip someone's limbs off in his fury.

I must make her betray me. I must, so that I can put her in the Crystal and be done with her.

Lancelot was right. And nothing pained Mordred more than to admit it.

I must. Because I love her.

TWENTY-FOUR

W hat has that blasted pile of ego and arrogance done to you? Oh, honey! Come here, sit—sit."

Gwen smiled faintly at Maewenn as the cook hustled her into the room and plopped down onto a stool. Maewenn was already gathering up some cloth that was likely used to wrap cheese or bread and dunking it into a pot of boiling water on the stove. "Thanks. It's fine. We were training and things got out of hand."

"Out of hand. Again? Pah! He should know better." Maewenn huffed. Gwen studied the cook, finding herself caught up in the details of the strange creature. Her dress was made out of panels of armor, linked together in a haphazard and almost nonsensical way. The armor she wore looked like it was made out of kitchen items that had been flattened in a trash compactor or under a steamroller. One section of her leg looked exactly like what Gwen would imagine a perfectly squished teapot would look like.

Once, when Gwen was a kid, she had left a bag of gummy bears out in the hot car on a summer day. It had all run together into one gloopy pile of bears. Her dad had poured it out onto a cookie sheet to cool in the fridge. What came out was perfectly smooth, but still with the distinct colorations and outlines of the bears.

Maewenn looked like that. Only with kitchen pots and pans and anything else metal that must have been nearby. The cook hummed thoughtfully. "I can't abide him training with a little thing like you... No, I think he was just looking for an excuse, dear."

"An excuse for what?" Gwen huffed. "To beat me up?"

"That is how some boys show their affection. Some grow out of it." The cook pulled the cloth out of the boiling water and wrung it out over the sink. Clearly, the hot liquid didn't bother her metal hands. "That bastard clearly hasn't."

"I knew a kid like that in high school. Picked on this one girl so hard that I thought she was going to cry. Pulled her hair, threw balled-up pieces of paper at her. They've been dating for a few years now." Gwen looked down at the cut on her arm. It wasn't *that* bad. But a bandage would be helpful.

"Boys. Like I said." Maewenn dabbed at the cut carefully.

The fabric was extremely hot but not burning her. And she didn't even mind the heat. Gwen blinked. *Can I even burn now? Even from water? Huh.* It was something she didn't really want to test out. "Yeah, he's interested in me. So is Lancelot. But they're both just bored."

"Couldn't be that you're an attractive young woman. Not at all." Maewenn poked her in the nose before beginning to wrap the wound. "You seem like a sweet thing too. I see you out there with the hounds. But you're smart to be wary of 'em both. Each of them could have ulterior motives. There was this one time—"

Maewenn launched into some long-winded story about some goat trader and his wife, about how the goat trader only got married because of the woman's huge tracts of land. Honestly,

Gwen had stopped paying attention. Instead, she was dwelling on Mordred.

Lancelot was sweet and well meaning. He was trying to save his world.

Mordred was cruel and dangerous. He was *also* trying to save his world.

But there was something about the Prince in Iron that pushed Gwen's buttons. There was something about the darkness that ran deep through him that was alluring. Something like a whisper in the shadows that called her name and said *come and see.* She knew she shouldn't. She *knew* it was a terrible idea.

But she wanted to.

She really wanted to.

Maewenn finished bandaging up Gwen's arm and tucked the end of the fabric into itself to keep it secure. "There! Right as rain by the morning, I suspect. You elementals heal quickly."

"That's a nice bonus." She stood from the stool. "I think I'm going to go lie down for a while." She couldn't get her thoughts straight. There were too many things tumbling around inside her head. "Thanks. For the bandage. And for being a friend."

"If you're troubled, go find Galahad. That big old tree of a man is always good for talking through difficult topics." Maewenn went back to the stove, stirring a pot of something that smelled like a pot roast.

"That's good advice. Thanks again." Gwen headed for the door, glad for the bandage, but not feeling much better about anything else. Maybe Maewenn was right. Maybe Galahad would have some good insight. He knew both Lancelot and Mordred better than she did, after all.

Couldn't be too hard to find a guy that was as tall as a damn telephone pole.

Or so she thought.

She wandered around the castle for probably an hour. By the time she found him, she was starting to limp a little. Her hip hurt.

When she caught sight of Galahad in a small courtyard toward the back of the keep, she froze. He was standing with his back to her, facing a lion's head fountain that poured from the wall into a half circle of stones that formed the base of the pool.

But that wasn't why she stopped. That wasn't why she ducked next to a column, afraid to disturb the scene. It was what was emerging out of the water that took her breath away.

Rising from the water was the figure of a woman made from threads and flecks of shimmering gold. Galahad had his hand outstretched, reaching for her. She was quite easily the most beautiful woman Gwen had ever seen in her life, though it was clear she was only a shadow of what was real.

Her hair flowed around her as if caught in water, and so did a long, flowing gown that draped from her shoulders. The woman was barely an outline that shone like dew in the torchlight. There was something forlorn about the sight—as though she were a ghost.

When the figure unfurled a set of double, gossamer butterfly wings from her back that stretched out behind her, Gwen gasped.

Galahad tightened his hand.

The flecks of gold dissolved into the fountain.

Galahad turned his head to look at her, his expression drawn and pained. "Good evening, Lady Gwendolyn."

"I—I'm sorry. I didn't mean to interrupt." She chewed her lip, feeling ashamed for having ruined the moment.

"It is quite all right." He let out a weary sigh and turned back to the water. "You caught me reminiscing, that is all." The ache in his voice was almost palpable.

Walking up to him, she hugged him. She didn't know if the gesture was welcome—it probably wasn't—but she couldn't help it. Gwen expected him to go rigid, but he did not hesitate to put his arms around her and return the gesture.

She didn't know who the woman was. She didn't need to know. It was clearly someone who he had lost and had meant a great deal to him. Not all fairy tales had happy endings, after all. "I'm so sorry," she murmured to him. Her head barely came up to his mid-chest.

"It is not your burden. But thank you." He stroked a hand over her hair. "You have enough to bear yourself, I fear. Why are you limping?"

"Mordred."

"Ah." It seemed she didn't need to explain any more than that. He gently stepped away from her and sat on the edge of the fountain, patting the stone beside him. She joined him. "I see your necklace is gone."

"He's making a point." She glared down at her feet.

"Which is?"

"That it was for my benefit, not his. That he was just trying to keep me from bursting into flames because it was inconvenient, not because I'm any kind of threat to him." She picked at the edge of her chainmail skirt.

"And do you wish to be a threat to him?"

"I don't know. I can't stand that he's...bottled everybody

up. This all feels wrong. But even if I somehow succeeded in destroying the Crystal, he'd just start over again."

"Yes, he would." Galahad paused. "But I do not think he enjoys this stasis any more than the rest of us, if he were truthful with himself. He simply sees no other way about it."

She took his hand and leaned against his arm, enjoying the comfortable, almost fatherly vibe the older knight had. He tightened his grasp, comforting her. "I can't stop him."

"No one can. That is the trouble with him." He chuckled. "One must find a way to reason with him, and he is... stubborn."

She snickered. "No shit." Realizing that he probably didn't know what those two words meant together, she translated. "No kidding." No, that probably wasn't good enough. "I mean—"

"It is fine. I understand." He chuckled again, resting his other hand on her arm. "What is your opinion on our prince?"

"He's lonely. Doesn't trust his own shadow. And I feel bad for him."

"Is that all?"

She sighed. "No. I...think I *like* him. Even if he's an asshole, beats me up while trying to train me, and really needs to take himself less seriously. I like being around him."

"And what of Lancelot? I see how the Silver Knight gazes upon you."

"Oh, there's nothing wrong with him. He's clearly the good boy, y'know? Sweet. Funny. Kind. Everything Mordred isn't." She shut her eyes. She missed her mom.

"But?"

"But." She shrugged. "I don't feel the same when I'm around him as I do around Mordred. But I shouldn't like Mordred. I'm supposed to be his enemy."

"Who tells you this?"

She paused. "Like, everybody. But I get why Mordred is doing all this. I just don't think it's right."

"You are an empathetic creature, Gwen. Most would not be able to see the reasons behind his actions and feel sympathy for him. I suppose the trouble simply remains in what you wish to do about where you have found yourself."

"I guess."

When Galahad spoke again, his voice was soft and overflowing with emotion. "Her name is Zoe. An elemental of air. She was—is—the love of my life. She resides in the Crystal with all the rest. My heart is trapped within that cage of iron with her."

She thought her heart might shatter for him. Just crack completely in two.

"But do not mistake me." Galahad shut his eyes. "Even with my own grief and loss . . . I would not shatter the Crystal to free her."

"What?" She blinked.

"It has taken me nearly all three centuries to come to terms with what he has done. To truly see the simple rational actions behind that which caused us so much horrible pain. But you have not seen the damage that elementals have caused—the price of their constant wars. You have not ridden through villages that were reduced to nothing but rubble and corpses." He looked away, the creases at his eyes deepening.

It was clear he was seeing those things in his mind's eye as he spoke. "You have not seen the bodies of mothers fallen over their children, trying to spare their little lives even at the cost of their own. You have not seen those same babes, dead in their arms. The sacrifice useless in the end. The elementals, each one at the other's throats, spelled the end for so many more broken hearts than simply mine."

"But...I..." She didn't know what to say.

"How many cities would you see like that, how many lives would you see needlessly spent, before you said enough? Mordred sought to save those who could not save themselves. And who am I, what kind of knight would I be, if I did not seek to do the same?"

She couldn't take it anymore. She stood and hugged him. Since he was sitting, they were almost at the same level. He rested his head on her shoulder and held her tight. She didn't know if he was crying, but now she certainly was.

It reminded her of the time that one of their first family goats had grown old and passed away. Her dad had sat next to the old billy, stroking his fur and weeping.

Dad tears were the worst.

When Galahad let out a breath and stood, she wiped away her tears and tried to regain her composure. Leaning down, he kissed the top of her head, and silently left her standing there by the fountain, watching the flecks of gold at the bottom shimmer.

She knew the answer to what she should do. She finally knew.

Mordred was right.

Lancelot was wrong.

The Crystal had to stay. Letting out a wavering sigh, it felt kind of good to have an answer, finally. Even if it meant mayhem. She had to tell Mordred the truth.

Gwen set off to go find him. It was late now—she had missed dinner. But that was fine, she wasn't that hungry. The clock said it was nearly midnight. The prince might be asleep.

She found him sitting in one of the many libraries, sitting at a table by the fire, gazing down at a map of Avalon.

"Can't sleep?" She cautiously approached the table. When they had last seen each other in the afternoon, he'd been in a *mood*.

"That is not uncommon for me." His gauntlets were gone, for once, and he ran a hand down his face. "You?"

"Haven't tried yet." She paused. "Can I join you?"

He gestured at a chair beside him. "I see you have yet to burn the building down."

"Nobody's given me a panic attack yet." She smirked and grunted a little as she sat down. Her hip hurt. "My attacks seem to be getting slowly spaced farther apart, anyway. That's a nice plus."

"Indeed." He paused. "I was unkind to you again this afternoon." It wasn't an apology, just a statement. She figured it was going to be the best that she got out of him.

She shrugged. "You made your point."

He arched an eyebrow at her, those molten, rust-orange eyes of his watching her. "Did I?"

"Ten years ago, a grody old cat showed up on our property, nearly dead. It was old, and tattered, and missing teeth and most of an ear. We saved its life and took it in. I named him Merlin because to me he looked like an ancient wizard. And even back then, I loved the old legends." She sighed. "He was the one who set my house on fire and opened a portal here, and I had a choice—burn to death or jump through. I jumped through. He's been harassing me ever since. He's an elemental from here, and I'm borrowing his power."

Reaching out a hand, she touched the flame of a candle that was burning at the center of the table. When she pulled her finger back, the flame was now dancing at the end of her digit. "I'm not really an elemental. He is. I'm just what's keeping him alive. He said he can't die unless I do, and vice versa. I'm his only hope at freedom. He wants me to destroy the Crystal to set him free. He says if I do, he'll be able to send me home again."

"Do you believe him?"

"I guess so, but I don't really know." She put her finger back to the wick, transferring the fire to its original spot. She folded her arms again. "Everybody wants me to destroy the Crystal. Even some weird-ass scarecrow thing in the antique store wants me to."

"Ah. That was who you were speaking to."

"Yeah." She sighed. "Everybody wanted me to get the necklace off so I could go and...I don't know, melt the thing or some shit. Lancelot's plan was once I got you to take it off, he'd distract you long enough that I could melt the Crystal. I think he has a crush on me, but I also think he needs me to destroy that thing, so he's got both motives running."

"I see. Is that all?"

"Merlin's stupid plan was that if I seduced you, you'd remove it." She snickered. "No, apparently, I just had to piss you off. Not like I could seduce anybody worth shit, anyway."

"I would not be so certain of that." He trailed a knuckle down her cheek. It sent her face going warm again. "Either way, the necklace is now removed. What do you plan to do next?"

"I talked to Galahad. He told me what it was like with the elementals loose. I know I can't stand against you. And now, I don't think I want to anymore." Oh yeah, she was blushing something fierce, she knew it. Her face felt like it was on fire.

His hand threaded into her hair and turned her to look at

him. He kissed her—slow and firm. It was missing the violent passion from before, but it was no less searing. No less demanding. It stole her breath and sent her eyes slipping shut again.

When he parted from her, he leaned his forehead against hers. "Thank you for telling me the truth, Gwen. It is a gift I rarely receive. And one I treasure deeply." He stood and headed for the door. She watched as his armor molded over him, everything save his helm. "If you will excuse me for a moment."

"Where're you going?" Something close to dread twisted in her stomach.

"Hm?" He paused at the doorway for a moment. Her dread was solidified with his next words. He smirked at her, cruel and vicious. "To kill Lancelot, of course."

Twenty-Five

*W*hat?" Gwen exploded out of the chair—almost literally, she could feel her arms start to sizzle with fire—and ran into the hallway after Mordred. She jumped in front of him. "You can't!"

Mordred pulled up his steps abruptly as she cut him off. He eyed her with a raised brow. "I am the Prince in Iron. Believe me. I can."

"But you *shouldn't*." Her heart was racing a mile a minute. And when that happened, her mouth followed suit. "You can't kill him, I wasn't supposed to get him in trouble, and it's my fault any of this has happened, it isn't—"

"Calm yourself."

She could feel the walls starting to close in. This was going to give her a panic attack. Covering her eyes with her palms, she struggled to breathe. "You can't do this, Mordred. You can't. You can't kill him. Please. It's not fair."

He brushed past her as he continued his path down the hallway. "Nothing is fair in life, Gwendolyn."

"No!" She chased after him again. This time, when she cut him off, she erupted into flame. She couldn't help it. "Stop. Please. Leave Lancelot alone."

"He has been conspiring against me. You would ask me to let that stand unpunished?"

"It—it was just talk—that's all he did was just talk."

His smile was a thin, lopsided twist to his lips. "That is what a conspiracy is, Gwen."

Growling in frustration, she pushed him. He didn't budge. She might as well have been pushing a big rusty Buick. "You know what I mean!"

When she went to go shove him again, he caught her wrists in his gauntlets and pulled her close to him. Proving once more the fact that she being on fire was no danger to him. "I have tolerated Lancelot's hatred of me for long enough that his continued existence is a manner of punishment in and of itself. He despises being forced to serve me. For the past thousand and more years, his ire has been toothless. He has been powerless to act against me. But now...with you? All that has changed."

"But I told you—"

"Yes. And I believe you have told me all that you know. But what happens next? What happens when he whispers in your ear enough sad tales of the Avalon that once was, that you seek to try to destroy the Crystal regardless of the hopelessness in such an endeavor?" He let go of her. "I seek to keep you free of the Crystal. I do this to protect you."

Taking a step back, she rubbed her wrists. It made sense. Everything he said, from a cruel and rational perspective, made perfect logical sense. But it was wrong. "Can't you understand why I want you to spare him?"

"Yes. Because you have a tender heart. You have not spent a thousand years listening to him *whine*." He grinned. "If you had, you would understand why his extermination is a kindness to both him and me."

Shaking her head, she couldn't accept it. "What can I trade? What can I do? Please, Mordred—I can't stand knowing it'll be my fault he's dead."

"Your fault? No. Because of you, perhaps. But your presence here is the fault of this 'Merlin' character, not you." He rested a metal hand on her shoulder.

She had forgotten that she was on fire. She couldn't be doing good things to the floor. Taking a breath, she focused, and put out the flames that she had transformed into. "Please..."

"What would you have me do instead? Send him from the isle? He would wither and die, as all those from Avalon must do if gone for too long." Mordred took a step back close to her, his other hand tracing his sharpened claws through her hair, just barely grazing her scalp. It sent a shiver down her spine. "Would you have me torture him instead? Break his mind? I think not. A clean death is the more honorable end for him."

She sniffled, feeling tears stinging her eyes. Man, she hated crying.

"Very well." He left her then, walking down the hallway in the direction he had been going before she interrupted him twice. "If you will not see him dead, then perhaps there is another choice."

What was that supposed to mean?

Mordred stopped some thirty feet away and turned to look at her. "Well? Are you not coming?"

Shit, shit, shit.

With a beleaguered sigh, she followed him.

Shit.

Mordred was now certain that Percival was right. He was not acting like himself. He was instead acting like a complete fool. But it was not for the reasons the Knight in Copper believed.

Percival had accused him of growing weak and tired of his position of power.

It was not that.

It was because of her that he felt himself *bending.* And it was like watching an oncoming tidal wave. It was unstoppable. He was swept up in the pull of it, and was certain to drown.

He had never been in love before.

And he could not say that he enjoyed it in the slightest.

But when those fiery, flickering eyes looked up at him in sorrow, pleading with him to show mercy…what could he do, save to grant her wish?

Lancelot would survive—in a manner of speaking. But when Mordred had finished out his punishment, Gwendolyn might come to regret her choice to stand in opposition to him on the matter.

Perhaps it would work in his favor. His firefly had shown him great vulnerability in revealing all her secrets to him. But would she continue to stay loyal? This might be the perfect way to discover whether or not she could be trusted.

She might now be his new weakness, but the chain that bound him to her was still brittle enough to be broken. If he tested its links, it was likely to shatter. So, that was what he would do.

He did not know if he wished it to break or stay true.

He did not know if he wished to love her or not.

But he supposed he would find out before long.

Kicking in the door to Lancelot's chambers, he stormed in. The Knight in Silver leapt out of his bed. Tripping over his sheets, he toppled to the floor. That was fine. Mordred helped him to stand by grasping a fistful of the man's hair and began to drag him out of the room.

Gwendolyn was pressed up against the wall, her hands over her mouth. Those fiery eyes were wide in horror and fear. The young thing had likely never seen such violence as she had in his presence. A shame she was likely to experience much more of it in her days.

Some part of him regretted being the one to teach her what Avalon was truly capable of.

Lancelot was shouting, digging in his heels, trying to fight back. But it was useless. Balling up his fist, Mordred punched the man hard in the temple, knocking him unconscious. That would make this all much faster. He had a need to be done with this quickly.

Usually, he would have enjoyed taunting the man.

But not with Gwendolyn watching.

Throwing the Knight in Silver over his shoulder, Mordred carried him down the stairs into the abyss beneath the keep.

"Where are we going?" Gwen was following close behind him.

"You wished for me to spare his life."

"I—I do. That isn't an answer." She jogged to try to keep up with him.

"Lancelot will live. But he may not thank you for it." He kept his gaze straight ahead. He did not wish to see the pain on her features.

"You're still not telling me where we're going or what you're going to do."

He didn't answer her. Instead, he walked the winding paths down and down and down again until he came to the corridor that housed the two enormous iron doors that were so familiar to him. The glow of glimmering white and opalescent light from underneath illuminated the cracks and the seams in the stone floor. It shimmered in a thousand colors.

"Mordred?" Her voice was quieter. Smaller. Afraid. She was beginning to suspect. "What's behind those doors?"

He gestured his hand, and the giant iron doors swung open in total silence, revealing the terrible majesty of his life's work beyond it. "The Iron Crystal."

Gwen had never felt smaller than when watching a pair of twenty-foot-tall, two-foot-thick, elaborate iron doors swing open in *total silence.* They should have creaked. Or whined. Or anything. But they opened up in front of her like ghosts from a nightmare. The curling, twisting vines and figures she couldn't quite wrap her head around gave way to the chamber beyond. She had never once been to anywhere like the Ancient Greek temples, or even any of the grander churches of Europe. But she had to imagine this was what it must feel like to be someplace so grand, so enormous in its purpose alone—that it made her feel microscopic by comparison.

What she saw next didn't help her feel any better in the slightest.

The room on the other side was circular, some eighty feet or so in diameter. She couldn't see the far walls, not really—they were obscured in stark shadows cast by the combination of a thousand flickering candles and the overwhelming opalescent glow from a pool in the center, filled with what looked at first like liquid with an odd texture.

Ringing the pool were seven stone pillars. About twenty feet up each stone column was the carved stone head of a monster, each one grotesque in its own unique way. From their mouths ran thick metal chains that connected to the centerpiece of the room, suspending it over the glowing eerie pool.

The Iron Crystal.

It was at least twice her height and probably five feet across. It was jagged and crude, like raw shards of rock. The metal was oxidized into a brilliant array of colors. She watched in awe as a strange liquid condensed on the side of it like water on the side of a glass on a hot day. It glowed the same brilliant tone as the pool beneath it. The glowing opal liquid hardened and fell to the pool with a *tink*.

Then she understood why the pool looked so strange. It wasn't filled with liquid. It was filled with crystals. The same ones that powered Mordred's armored creations—the same that were keeping his knights alive.

"Behold my masterpiece." The Prince in Iron didn't sound at all proud or enthusiastic. He dropped Lancelot at the edge of the pool with zero grace or care. "Is it not beautiful?"

It was horrifying, was what it was. Sure, it was *pretty*, she guessed. But there was something about it that was making her blood run cold and her heart pound.

It was the whispers.

"Save us—please—mercy, my liege—please—free us—it is so cold—" On and on, a thousand voices whispered as one, crying out in muted tones.

Her stomach lurched with the sudden realization that the people within the Crystal *knew* they were there. Knew what was going on. And they were suffering. She covered her mouth with her hands in an attempt to keep her lunch where she had put it. She wanted to weep. She wanted to run. She wanted to scream.

Any thought in her head that she could keep going on after seeing that terrible thing was gone. No. It had to be destroyed.

It had to. She had no idea *how* she was going to do it—but now she knew she had no choice.

Mordred nudged Lancelot with his boot none too gently. "On your knees, traitor."

The Knight in Silver groaned, rolling onto his side.

For a moment, Gwen had forgotten why they had come down here in the first place. She had forgotten all about Lancelot and what was going to happen to him. She ran to Mordred and grabbed his arm. "Please—Oh God, no—"

Mordred laughed, quiet and tired. "It is this or the grave. Which do you choose, firefly?"

She was crying again. She didn't care. She shoved Mordred—or tried. Once more he didn't even budge. "Why do you have to be like this?"

His smile was tinged with sadness. "I am who I am, and as I have always been. If you truly grasped the cruelty that those within the Crystal have committed, you would not despise me so. But you will not understand. You are too young."

Lancelot was slowly coming around. It took him a few seconds of staring at the Crystal to realize where he was. He let out a terrified moan and tried to scramble away. But Mordred wasn't having it. Another metal boot to the side, and Lancelot was back on his knees.

"My liege, please—" Lancelot was staring at the Crystal, wide-eyed and horrified. "Please do not do this."

"It is for the lady to decide. She is the reason you are in this predicament. But make your case as you see fit, I do not care." Mordred huffed. "Would you prefer the grave, or the Crystal, Silver Knight?"

Lancelot didn't seem to know what to do with that. He was

shaking, his usually tan features pale and stricken. He didn't even look at them.

Gwen knelt beside him and hugged him, her tears redoubling their efforts to blur her vision. "I'm so sorry, Lancelot—I'm so sorry. I didn't know this would happen..."

That seemed to shake Lancelot out of it. He hugged her back. "Do with me what you will, but spare her, Mordred. Spare her, if you have even a speck of kindness left in that empty tomb where your heart should be."

"I have no intention of sending her to join you, unless she follows your path of betrayal." Mordred was watching them both impassively. As if this didn't bother him in the slightest. "To date, she has done nothing to warrant imprisonment."

The message was clear. She hadn't done anything—*yet*.

"I'm so sorry," she murmured, as she hugged Lancelot tighter.

"This is not your fault. I should have known." He kissed her cheek and lowered his voice to a whisper. "I have faith you will find a way to free me. To free us all." He nudged her away. "Go, Gwendolyn Wright. There is nothing you can do to save me from this."

Nodding weakly, she stood and half walked, half staggered away. She didn't know how she could watch what was about to happen—she didn't know how she couldn't.

Mordred held out his clawed hand, its palm facing Lancelot. He tightened it into a fist. There was a feeling in the room like a sudden pressure change. Gwen's ears popped.

What happened next was going to haunt her for the rest of her life. It was going to be burned into her memory, she knew, and would probably wake her up in the middle of the night for the rest of her days.

It was as though Lancelot's soul was being sucked out of his body. His very life. In the matter of only a few seconds, he went from being a handsome man to a . . . a corpse. His cheeks were sunken, his eyes became nothing more than empty cavities. His lips dried, split, and pulled away from his teeth. In only the span of a few heartbeats, Lancelot became a dried, desiccated mummy.

She watched as a strange, glowing mist flew from him to the Crystal, swirling around it before being sucked inside like water down a drain. His body followed suit a second later—breaking down into dust, joining the swirling mist.

It felt like an eternity.

But it had only been a moment.

Fire enveloped Gwen as her panic attack came on suddenly and with no warning. Her head reeled. She collapsed, unable to keep her legs underneath her. Hands, metal and firm, held her shoulders.

Someone was talking to her. Far away and small. Their voice joined with the sound of *screaming* that came from the Crystal. But it was all falling away from her—or she was falling away from it. She never knew which it was.

Her hands tingled.

The world went mercifully dark.

TWENTY–SIX

Mordred sighed as he lifted Gwen into his arms. The poor thing had not handled Lancelot's imprisonment well. He honestly could not say that he was surprised. She had burst into flames, forgotten how to breathe, and promptly passed out. Luckily, her fire extinguished itself as she did. Not that it would bother him, but her bed would likely suffer for it.

He carried her back up the stairs from the crypt where he kept the Crystal. Ignoring the stares from the guards, he brought the young woman to her room and laid her down under the covers. Sitting at the foot of her bed was Eod. The hound's ears were drooped, and he was watching them with large, concerned eyes.

"Comfort her. Protect her." He patted the dog.

The animal did not hesitate to jump onto the bed and curl into a ball next to Gwen, flopping his large head onto her legs. Eod was a bit obstinate when it came to following commands, but the creature loved strongly and loyally.

Which was more than could be said about himself. He loved Gwendolyn Wright—and look what he had done. Cringing, he left the room and shut the door behind him quietly. He planned to drink himself into a stupor. It was not Lancelot's removal that twisted in his heart. It was not even the pain it had caused Gwen.

It was what Mordred knew he still had to do before he could be certain of her loyalty. He had to test her. And in doing so...

After making himself a large drink, he slumped down into his chair by the fireplace, vanishing his armor as he did. He had one sip of his drink before there was a knock on the door-jamb.

"What?" he asked. He was in no mood.

"Word travels quickly, my liege." It was Galahad. Of course it was. Who else would be daring enough to confront him on Lancelot's fate? Certainly not Percival.

"He deserved it." Mordred pressed his fingers to his forehead, shutting his eyes. He was going to have a headache before all of this was said and done. "He was attempting to coerce Gwendolyn into betraying me."

"Ah." Galahad paused. "And is she...?"

"Resting in her bed. She did not take to the sight of Lancelot's imprisonment." He bristled at the suggestion that he would have sent Gwendolyn to the Crystal as well, before realizing it was a perfectly logical conclusion.

"Ah," the knight repeated. "I am surprised that you did not simply execute him."

"That was my first intention. The young lady objected."

Galahad approached the fireplace, holding out his hands to warm himself. The fae was a tall and gangly thing, and always cast odd shadows on the wall behind him. "It may inspire her to do something rash."

"Yes. I suppose it may."

The Knight in Gold's expression fell as he pieced it all together. He turned to Mordred. "Tell me you jest. Why would you goad her into taking action against you? To what ends?"

"I wish to see what she will do. I wish to see if she is a true

ally, or simply another forced to serve me." He glared at Galahad. He had never truly forgiven his knights for their betrayal
so long ago. He was unsure as he ever would. But the closest
who had come to earning it was the one before him.

Galahad sighed and shut his eyes, shaking his head in
obvious disappointment. "You write the prophecy before you
and seek to fill it. If you are so bullheaded as to inspire those
around you to commit—"

"Commit what, knight? Treason? To attempt to kill me in
my sleep? I had loyal friends *once*, or so I believed them to be.
Until you lot proved me wrong." He grimaced. "Go. Begone.
I do not wish to speak to you any longer. My actions are my
own."

Galahad watched him for a moment before bowing his head
and leaving the room without another word.

Mordred downed the rest of his glass. He fetched the bottle
that time, and intended on finishing the rum before dawn. Perhaps then he might sleep.

But likely not.

Gwen woke up to someone licking her face. Luckily, it was a
dog. She gently nudged Eod away from her. "Easy—yes—hello,
good morning—" She couldn't help but laugh as the hound
belly-crawled closer and kept up his insistent licks and nudges.
"I get it, I get it, it's morning and you want out."

At the magic word that it seemed all dogs knew—*out*—Eod
was on his feet, wagging his tail and jumping off the bed to
stand eagerly by the door.

For one small second, the dog's antics made her forget about
Lancelot.

But it came back with a harsh vengeance.

The good thing about pets, however, was that they didn't give a shit about grief or sadness when they had a simple need. And Eod needed out. His tail thumped on the floor as he sat, staring at her impatiently.

"Yeah, yeah." She pulled on a cloak over the metallic clothing she was still wearing and put on a pair of simple boots. She must have incinerated her last pair, which...whatever. Mordred could deal. She opened the door, and watched as the dog ran happily down the hallway toward the door. She followed him, not knowing what else to do.

Not knowing where else to go. Or who to talk to.

She felt utterly helpless. Hopeless. And trapped.

Poor Lancelot.

She needed to save him—needed to break the Crystal. But *how?* Mordred would never let her anywhere near the thing. And if the guards alerted him that she was trying to sneak down there, he'd put her right inside with everybody else.

But she had to try anyway. She had to. But she needed a plan. She needed to somehow get Mordred out of the picture long enough to find the Crystal again and try to melt it with her fire. She either needed to find a way to get him indisposed or away from the keep.

Great. Cool. But the question still remained *how?*

She passed Mordred's study as she went toward the front of the building. She was surprised to see him sitting in his chair, staring at the fire, an empty glass bottle that looked like one of those antique onion-style ones sitting by his foot. He looked abjectly miserable.

Good.

He deserved to be miserable. He'd done a terrible thing.

"Can't sleep again?" she asked from the doorway.

He glanced over at her briefly. "No. You?"

"Dog wanted out."

He grunted in reply. At least they were *slightly* on speaking terms. Slightly. She watched him for a moment, studying the dire unhappiness on his features. Shaking her head, she resumed her path after Eod. She found the dog, likely having done his business, now happily romping around the courtyard saying hello to every single guard with a stick in his mouth, begging to play.

She smiled.

The world might be shit, but at least there was a cute dog. She whistled, and Eod bounded up to her at Mach one. Laughing, she grabbed the stick from him and after a brief wrestling match—that nearly wound up with her pulled to the ground—she hurled it through the air.

It was after about four rounds of stick-toss that she suddenly had an idea.

It was a terrible idea. It probably wouldn't work. But it just might. And it wasn't like she had any others lined up waiting to be tested.

Eod, however, wasn't done yet. But she knew what would distract the pup from the game of fetch. "Hey, let's go see Maewenn. Maybe she has some food for us."

Those ears perked up at the mention of *food*. Yep. Dogs were the best. He ran past her, stick forgotten, eager to go see the cook with a new singular goal in mind. But no matter how many times the dog made her smile, her happiness would always fade a second later.

Damn it.

Damn it all to hell.

By the time she made it to the kitchens, Eod was already

sitting at Maewenn's feet, tail thumping on the ground and doing his best adorable grin up at the metal woman. Maewenn was standing there with her hands on her hips, lecturing the dog in that tone of voice that said she wasn't really upset, and everyone knew it. Including Eod.

"Now, I don't need you comin' in here and licking all the hot pots and pans, you'll scald that big tongue of yours!"

Gwen smiled. "It's my fault. I mentioned food."

"That'd do it. Much like a man he is, with only one thing on his mind at a time and—oh." Maewenn let out a breath upon seeing her. "Darling, don't take this the wrong way, but you look terrible."

"I haven't slept." It was a lie. Well, okay, not really. She had passed out. That was kind of like sleeping. "I just...after what happened." She sat down on a stool at the large kitchen island. She felt the weight of everything press onto her shoulders. "It's all my fault."

"No, dear. It isn't. It's that damnable prince's fault. That man has more empty space in his head than I do, and I'm hollow." Maewenn chuckled, poured Gwen some tea, and placed that with some biscuits in front of her.

Eod decided—rightly—that Gwen was the easier mark, and was now sitting at her feet, begging for bits of the biscuit. And proving him right, she slipped him a few crumbs before even taking a bite of it herself.

"If I'd kept my mouth shut, Lancelot would still be free."

"If you kept your mouth shut, you'd likely be stuck in there with that old fool. Or you would all be dead. He never knew how to keep himself to himself. Always a bit of a death wish on that one, I'm afraid." Maewenn went back to making the breakfast that she was preparing.

And here came the next step in her plot. Gwen was glad the cook had her back turned to her, or else she might have seen Gwen cringe. "Do you have anything that can help me sleep? I figured you must, what with Mordred's insomnia."

"They have a word for it now? How wonderful." Maewenn pondered the question for a minute. "I do, but...well, I suppose since it's on his account you can't sleep, there's no harm in it." She reached up to a shelf and pulled down a small fabric pouch. "Ah, damn. He must have the rest of it. I'm afraid I only have a little. Just enough to make you drowsy."

"Is it dangerous?"

"Not really, but I wouldn't go around testing that theory." Maewenn handed it to her.

Gwen looked down at the bag and kept her frown to herself. It wasn't nearly enough to take out Mordred. She would have to find another way to get to it. It was probably in his room, kept with everything else, and sneaking in there was going to get her caught immediately by the guards.

Unless...

There was one way she could get into Mordred's room. It twisted a knot in her stomach in more ways than one. She tucked the little bag into her boot. "Thanks, Mae." She'd process the rest of her new plan when the thought of it wasn't going to make her blush bright red.

"Mae, is it? Friends are we now?" Mae hummed. "If so, I'd like that."

"I would too." Gwen smiled at the cook. She didn't know what would happen to Mordred's armored creations if she actually managed to blow up the Crystal. But she really *really* hoped they'd be all right.

Taking the biscuit to go, along with a second one, she headed back out of the kitchen and off to her next goal. The sleeping powder she had to get from Mordred's room was only one part of the equation.

She needed Mordred taken out for at least an hour, maybe more. So she would need to get the powder from the prince's room and have something she could slip it into for him to eat or drink. Hopefully, it wasn't too potent a taste.

Step one—getting the powder—was going to take her working up some serious nerve and the willingness to sink to a new low.

Step two—what she was putting the powder into—she could at least get a start on while she tried to figure out if she was capable of the first.

Because there was one guaranteed way into Mordred's room.

The memory of his lips against hers during their last training session made her stomach drop. Going into his room at night, climbing into his bed...their training sessions gave her a sense of what she would be getting herself into. Her stomach twisted in anticipation, not fear. It made her question her sanity for a hot second.

But it was clear to her how much she wanted him. How much she wanted to be with him. Even now, even after what he had done to Lancelot, Gwen cared about Mordred deeply. And she had no doubt that the attraction was very mutual. She had wanted to see if something more developed between them. And it almost had. But now, either she was Crystal-bound or she was going to melt it. There was no other way forward.

Sleeping with Mordred in order to steal his sleeping powder...it felt wrong. Underhanded. It felt more like a betrayal than the rest of her plan put together.

But what other option did she have?

Carrying the extra biscuit meant, of course, that Eod was right there next to her the entire time. When she walked back into Mordred's study, she wasn't exactly shocked to see that the man hadn't moved. Walking up to him, she offered him the uneaten biscuit. "To go with the booze. Before the headache sets in."

He glanced at her and, with a small huff that might have been a laugh, he took the food and obediently took a bite out of it. "I have had more to drink in a sitting than that, and been just fine."

"I'm sure you have." She sat down in a chair on the other side of the fire from him. She figured they needed to talk, no matter what happened next.

"Thank you for your concern." He paused. "I would have thought you would have no sympathy left for me."

"I have sympathy left for everybody." When he cringed, she shook her head. "That came out wrong. I know why you feel you needed to do it. I just...I disagree. And seeing that was—a lot." A lot, as in it would haunt her for the rest of her life probably, but hey. Whatever. What were a few nightmares between friends? Or whatever they were. Or whatever they were going to become.

Friends. Lovers. Enemies.

Mordred shut his eyes. "Thank you, Gwen."

He looked so tired, and not because he hadn't slept. But because she could almost see the weight of the world on him. He wasn't an old-looking man, even with his literal silver-gray hair. But now and then she could see it on his face that he was truly over a thousand years old.

She really did have sympathy for him.

But it only went so far.

"I have a favor to ask."

"Oh?"

She stood from the chair and headed to his desk for a piece of paper and a bit of charcoal. She began doodling out what she needed. "Since you can, y'know, make anything out of metal and all."

He walked up beside her, clearly too curious to wait. "What is that?"

"A muffin tray." She smiled. "Maewenn has some fresh blueberries and I have a craving for muffins." She finished drawing the simple, twelve-slot baking tray. "It should be about this big," she said, as she gestured with her hands.

"After what you have witnessed, you wish to cook?" He arched an eyebrow.

"It's how I deal with stress. And it's better than getting wasted." She gestured at the empty bottle still on the ground next to his chair.

He opened his mouth to argue, clearly decided he couldn't, and shrugged. "As you wish. Cast iron, I assume?"

"Yes, please." She'd have to season the metal before she could use it. Her grandma had owned a huge collection of cast iron goodies, and so Gwen was pretty familiar with their use and care. And she really did enjoy baking. She wasn't lying about that either.

He gestured his hands out in front of him, and she watched in awe as metal simply formed between his fingers. It was still amazing to her to see *magic*. Real magic. Sure, she could burst into flames—but she wasn't used to it yet. And she kind of hoped she never got bored of it.

In just a dozen seconds or more, he had a perfect muffin tray in his hands. He turned it over and shrugged. "I do not understand, but very well." He handed it to her.

"Thanks." She smiled. "I promise to bring you one when I'm done."

"I look forward to it." His smile back down at her was filled with such hope and tenderness that it broke her heart.

If he only knew.

Well...he was going to know pretty soon, if she actually got away with her scheme.

She headed out of the room without saying anything else, worried that her voice might crack if she did.

Now she needed the sleeping powder.

Which meant it was time to wait until nightfall.

Letting out a shuddering breath, she went back to her room, intending to sleep through as much of the day as she could manage. Eod stayed beside her, and honestly, he was the only company she was in the mood to deal with.

She hugged the dog as she buried her head in the pillow, and dozed off with one question repeating itself over and over in her mind.

Can I go through with this?

TWENTY-SEVEN

Gwen was pacing around her room, working up the nerve
to do what she knew she needed to do. It was past dinner, the
knights would all be asleep. And Mordred...well, if she was
lucky, he was in his chambers.

If she wasn't, she'd have to wait another night.

And she wasn't sure she'd have the resolve to go through
with it if she waited. This felt wrong. This felt evil. She felt like
she was using him. *But he needs to be stopped. This has gone
too far. The Crystal has to go.*

Maybe if she honestly didn't like him, it'd be easier. But the
problem was...she liked Mordred. She actually cared about
him. She felt for him. She wanted him, sure—but there was
more than that.

If things had gone another way, she could see them together.
The idea of her trying to take the grumpy rusty monolith on a
picnic made her smile despite herself. But that was a future
that wasn't going to happen now.

She had to betray him if she wanted to save Avalon. If she
wanted to save all those trapped inside the Crystal. Taking a
deep breath, she held it for a second before letting it out in
a long rush.

She put on the nicest dress she had in the wardrobe, ran a
comb through her hair, patted Eod on the head, and told him to

stay. The last thing she needed was the dog getting in the way during a . . . well, personal moment.

It was past midnight when she left her room and headed toward Mordred's. The knowledge of what was going to happen was twisting her stomach into knots. She felt as though she were crossing a point of no return.

One way or the other.

When she approached Mordred's room, she stopped. The guards that stood on either side of his door could have been mistaken for props in a museum if it weren't for the fact that their heads turned to watch her.

Standing in front of them, she did her best to hold her head up high, but she knew she was blushing. "Do I really need to explain it?"

The two guards looked to each other, then turned their heads back straight. It was clear they weren't going to stop her. Or ask what she was doing. Thank God.

Opening the door quietly, she stepped in, and shut it behind her with a click. The room was enormous—far larger than hers, although she shouldn't have been surprised. Two of the walls were filled with hand-painted murals of scenery, and several of the others had large, somewhat faded tapestries hanging from them, displaying battles and wars. An enormous canopy bed dominated one wall, and a fireplace the other.

It took her a second to find Mordred. He was in a large chair in front of the fire, his head propped up on his hand. He was staring emptily into the fire. He didn't react to her entrance.

She could have snuck around his room, searching for the powder, and then snuck back out. But the guards would tattle on her if she didn't spend . . . at least a little time in the room. Her cheeks went warm.

No, there was no way around it. It was already too late.

Taking off her boots, she put them by the bed. Barefoot, she walked up to the chair, taking a moment to marvel at the sight of him. Damn it if he wasn't perfect—chiseled out of stone. *More like sculpted out of metal.* His strong jaw. His broad shoulders. And even the damn claws made her more intrigued than frightened.

She wondered if he'd use them in bed.

She wondered how much she'd like them.

I'm learning so much about myself in Avalon.

His eyes flicked to her at her approach, but he said nothing. Reaching out, she ran her fingers through his hair, combing the strands, loving the feel of it in between her fingers.

His hand snapped around her wrist, the metal cinching tight as he squeezed.

She gasped.

Rusted, molten eyes met hers. What started off as anger, turned to confusion. She didn't pull back. She didn't fight. She simply stood there and watched him in return, in the flickering light of a fire that was too pale.

He didn't speak. She didn't either. She supposed neither of them needed to say a word. He let go of her hand, slowly, as if not believing she was really there. It was mutual.

Carefully, she moved closer, straddling his legs. She knelt on either side of him on the chair, and settled back to sit on his lap. Those burnished eyes of his flicked between hers, searchingly—wonderingly—almost in awe.

Running her hands through his hair again, she began to explore him. To touch him. God, he was so strong. The muscles of his shoulders as she stroked her hands over his chest felt like velvet over stone. She wasn't sure if she was ready to sleep with a man like him—but damn it if there wasn't only one way to find out.

Leaning in, she kissed him. Timid at first, unsure of herself, hoping he didn't lash out suddenly and gut her like a fish. He sat there, unmoving. And for a moment she worried she had made a mistake. That maybe she had been wrong.

But then he was cradling her head in his hand, pulling her in closer to him, deepening the kiss. What had started off as her naive exploration had turned suddenly passionate—suddenly *starving.*

She moaned against his lips, a little unsure of herself. Slowly, he broke away, and leaned his head back to put a few inches between them. He wanted her to see what he was doing as he began to unlace the bodice of her dress.

And God—plot or not, betrayal or not—she needed this so badly, she knew she couldn't stop now. She'd go mad.

She sat back a little and let him use both hands to unlace her dress. She had opted not to wear the bloomers they wore for underwear. And now she was very glad she hadn't. He pulled the dress and the chemise off over her head and tossed them aside, leaving her naked on his lap.

He exhaled as though she had punched him in the gut. She wanted to tease him, tell him that he'd already seen her naked—but the expression on his face left her silent. Something she didn't dare name. Something she didn't dare think about. Or else she knew she wouldn't have the heart to betray him.

Watching her, waiting for her reaction, he trailed his gauntleted hands up her sides, stroking her.

She shivered, her skin breaking out in goose bumps. She

shut her eyes, lost in the sensation of those pointed tips of his claws as they grazed over her.

He placed one hand against her back, supporting her weight as he leaned her back far enough that he could capture one of her nipples in his mouth. She bit back another moan, louder that time, as he teased the tender flesh.

Her hand tangled in his hair, she held on to him, needing to feel him. When he bit down on her—just enough to sting—she swallowed back a cry.

Chuckling, he kissed his way back up to her collarbone, along her throat, and then to her ear.

His hands fell to her waist and pulled her hips to his. That time, there was no holding back the noise she made as she felt the extent of his desire for her. Oh, no. Oh, hell.

He kissed her throat, running his tongue along her skin, before nibbling at the flesh there as he ran his hands over her back, up and down, caressing her ass and squeezing it before returning to wandering over her. "This will be gentle."

She shifted, unable to take her mind off what she felt pressing against her with only his pants between them. "What if I don't want it to be?"

This wasn't like her. This wasn't what a good girl from Kansas did. And she honestly couldn't care less. With him, even as his prisoner . . . she felt free.

Mordred growled. Her words were enough to seemingly send him over the edge. He stood, picking her up, and carried her in his arms to his bed. He placed her down on the sheets before pulling his shirt off over his head.

She watched, feeling nervous excitement twisting in her stomach as he kicked off his boots. When he stepped out of his pants, she knew she was in for it. The man was proportional. And way more than she had ever tangled with, in more ways than one. She pushed up onto her hands as he climbed onto the bed over her, seeking his lips with hers.

He kissed her like a starving man would devour a feast, his claws tangling in her hair as he suddenly fisted the strands and yanked her head back, stinging her scalp. When she gasped, he invaded her mouth with his tongue, conquering her.

He was a prince. He was a warlord.

No. She didn't want it to be gentle.

She wanted to *feel* this.

She wanted to feel him.

He nudged her legs apart, and before she could even register that they had moved, he was sitting on his heels and she was once more straddling his lap, his desire pressing against her.

Tentatively, almost worried that she was doing something wrong, she slipped her hand between them and wrapped it around him. She groaned at the feeling of the heat of him in her palm. He snarled against her lips, kissing her harder as she began to slowly stroke him.

All thoughts of right and wrong were tossed out of her mind. She wanted him. She needed him. When he broke the kiss finally, she could barely breathe. But she managed to whisper two words. "Mordred, please..."

He threw her back to the sheets, a clawed gauntlet resting over her throat, pinning her there. Not enough to hurt—not enough to even restrict her air. But enough that she knew that he could. And that was enough for her. She whimpered, writhing beneath him. He hooked one leg over his other arm and leaned forward.

He was there, pressing against her. Waiting. Waiting for her to protest. To change her mind. His gaze, lidded and dark with his own need, caught hers.

She nodded once.

He thrust his hips forward with a snap.

And her mind went white from pleasure. It might have been painful, the way he stretched her—filled her—pushed her past what she thought her limits should have been as he drove into her with an unflinching drive, fulfilling her request that he not take pity on her.

This was what she had wanted during their last training session. And what he had wanted too. To leave her bruised. But this time, she knew they would both be satisfied.

He continued to press forward until he was buried in her to the hilt, pressing his weight on her as if to dig even deeper. She turned her head to the side and let out a cry, arching her back, wanting to feel his hand around her throat press harder.

"Oh, firefly..." He moaned against her as he pulled back slowly, almost until nothing was left, before pressing forward with the same slow, unstoppable momentum.

He felt like a machine. Methodical and unwavering. Filling her to the point where the stretch was a wonderful deep ache before nearly abandoning her in full. It made her head reel.

It felt so damn good she thought she might implode.

Hopefully, I don't burst into flames.

But it wasn't enough. "Please—" she whispered to him, her hands resting on his arms.

He shifted his weight onto his knees, towering over her, one hand still wrapped around her throat, the other holding on to her waist as he obeyed her unfinished plea.

Then she met the warlord. The dread tyrant. The Prince in Iron. He drove into her, again and again, tempo and pressure never relenting, only growing, as he unleashed himself on her. And time after time, her mind went white-hot with pleasure as her body could only struggle to catch up with the onslaught of sensation that ripped through her in waves.

She could barely cling to him, hold on for dear life, as he growled deep in his chest over her. How long it went on, she had no idea. She only came back to reality when his thrusts became harder and more erratic. He let go of her throat to grasp her waist with both hands, picking her up and driving her onto him as he slammed his hips to hers, joining her in a crescendo of ecstasy that left her gasping.

He collapsed over her, his forehead against the pillow beside her, his body twitching in the aftermath of what they had done. "Gwen—"

She turned his head to hers and kissed him. She could taste the salt of his sweat against her lips. Running a hand through his hair again, she decided she loved the feel of it. The feel of him.

Come what may, she'd cherish this moment.

Wordlessly, he rolled onto his side next to her, and draped an arm over her, holding her close. She knew he had a hard time sleeping—but she hoped he slept deep. Lying there beside him, she let her breathing grow long, and slow. Let him think she was sleeping.

And she waited.

Waited to betray him.

A tear slipped from the corner of her eye.

And she wondered if she'd ever forgive herself.

Twenty-Eight

Gwen waited hours—seriously hours—lying there in bed waiting, before Mordred, who was clearly a light sleeper, rolled onto his back and she felt like she could move without disturbing him. She slipped carefully from the sheets and began searching the room as quietly as she could.

She could probably try to get to the Crystal and destroy it while he was sleeping, but she honestly didn't know if trying to melt something he had made would wake him up. She knew she'd probably need a decent amount of time to destroy it—time that hopefully the potion would give her.

They had made love. And oh man, her legs were *sore*. Mordred hadn't gone easy on her. And it had been incredible. But the weight of what she had to do next might crush her.

Swallowing down her guilt, she dug through his dressers, careful not to make too much noise. She finally found what she was looking for—a little leather pouch that looked identical to the one Maewenn had given her. Fetching her own bag out of her boot, she opened up Mordred's and inspected it. Both bags had a powder that was closer to the consistency of sugar than flour. And both were a slight, faint blue. It had to be the same stuff. Dumping most of his bag into hers, she cinched her bag back up and tucked it into the toe of her boot before returning his to his drawer.

She slipped back into the sheets with him. He murmured as she did, wrapping an arm around her and pulling her tight to his side. He felt like a wall of a man. Nuzzling in close, she tucked her head against his neck and shut her eyes.

Despite her whirling thoughts, she fell asleep in his arms.

And knew that, after the next day, she would never get the chance to do it again.

Mordred woke up with a beautiful woman asleep in his arms. Her fiery hair was pooled on the pillow in tendrils of red, yellow, and even some deep bluish purple. Her back was to him, her body nestled so wonderfully against his. Warm. Impossibly so. *Fire elemental.* He wondered if he hadn't dreamt the moment—her sneaking into his room unannounced, kissing him. Asking him to love her.

And oh, he loved her.

He did not know what inspired her to do it, but he certainly would not complain. He was certain she would likely be sore this morning, though he had not done even a quarter of the things he wished to do to her. But all that would follow in time. Best to wade into the deep waters—not simply throw her in and hope she did not drown.

His body tightened at the idea of it. And he found he could not help but let his hands roam her body, squeezing her breasts, her arse, whatever he could reach. When she moaned, her eyes fluttering open, she began to speak his name when he swallowed it in a kiss.

He pressed up onto his elbow, hooking her leg over his hip, and he filled her once more with a sudden stroke, loving how she writhed and squirmed when he took her. To the morning light, he loved her the way he wished he had the discipline to the night before—patient. Not gentle—but *slow*. Feeling every inch of her as she took every inch of him.

She was like a volcano around him. He could not take it for long—the bliss of her was too much. He brought them both to a peak of ecstasy together as she cried out against his lips.

When they could both breathe again, she had an arm thrown over her eyes, her chest still heaving with exertion.

"Breakfast?" she asked.

He grunted in reply, lying flat on his back.

She climbed out of bed, a little wobbly—which he took great pride in—and got dressed. She slipped on her boots. "I'll be back with muffins. Might take me a while."

He grunted again.

Chuckling, she left the room.

And he lay there with a distinctly sated smile on his face. Perhaps the future would not be so bad for them, after all.

Gwen went to work, but there was a fun fact that she learned pretty quickly—a fun and frustrating fact.

Baking soda and baking powder did not exist in the medieval era. Or colonial. Or whenever the last time people from Avalon had been allowed to travel and crib people's inventions.

It took one more batch after that before she finally got the trick of it without normal ingredients. Her final batch—one of the muffins loaded with the sleeping powder—looked *almost* normal. The texture was still a tiny bit off, but to someone who had never had a muffin before, they'd be fine.

Putting the finished ones into a basket, she made sure to put the one for Mordred in a special place. That said, she kept glancing at it nervously, wanting to make sure she didn't lose track of it. That's all she needed—having someone eat the wrong one and either her or one of the knights winding up face-planted on the carpet.

Her stomach was twisting in knots. She didn't want to do this. She didn't want to *have* to do it. They had just had sex—twice—and it was clear there was something blooming between them.

And besides, there were so many ways her terrible plan could go wrong. And so many ways it probably would. But she kept replaying the sight of Lancelot as he was being sucked into the Crystal over and over in her head, and it gave her the nerve to keep going.

Once everything was ready to go, she headed up to find Mordred. He was sitting in a different one of his studies at a desk, poring over papers and tapping the feathery end of a quill pen against his temple.

The lighting cut sharp angles across his features. She was once more struck by how damn handsome he was. Sure, foreboding and *evil*-looking, but... alluring all the same. Plucking up the special muffin from the basket—making triple sure it was the right one—she placed it down on the desk next to him. "They're best when they're fresh."

His smile was one that told her he didn't get gifts very often. It only served to twist the knife deeper in her side. She was preparing speeches in her head for when he said he wasn't hungry, or didn't like blueberries, or any of the other possible ways it could go wrong.

He picked it up and studied it thoughtfully. "I see the reason for the oddly shaped pan now."

"Yep." She picked up one of the muffins herself. Her hand

was shaking. She really hoped he didn't notice how nervous she was. "Usually, we have, like…little paper liners for them, but the cast iron works great once it's oiled up and seasoned."

He took a bite from the muffin.

Gwen held her breath.

And suddenly realized she had *no clue* how long the powder might take to start working. And she was damn sure she gave him the right one. But there was always the chance she had screwed it up.

He hummed, apparently enjoying the flavor, and took another big bite from it. "This is phenomenal, Gwendolyn. Do you enjoy cooking?"

"I do. Maybe I should give Mae a night or two off a week. I can make us some spaghetti or something." She was talking too fast. She needed to calm the fuck down. But how the hell was she supposed to do that? She ate a chunk of the muffin, playing over the hysterical mental image of her passing out on the ground instead of him.

"I have no idea what spaghetti is, but I find myself eager to find out." He finished off the muffin, brushing his hands together. "That was quite wonderful, thank you."

"You're flattering me."

"Hardly." He wrapped an arm around her waist to pull her close. "If I were flattering you, I would be far more ostentatious than to compliment your baking. I—" He paused and blinked, rubbing his hand over his eyes.

Well, that gave her the answer to how fast it would start working. She took a step away from him. "You look exhausted. Maybe you should go back to bed."

"I—" He grunted and shut his eyes. It didn't take him long to put two and two together. He was paranoid. She didn't figure he'd be left wondering for long. "Gwendolyn...what have you done?"

"I'm so sorry." She took another step away from him. "I'm really so sorry."

He stood, and his knees gave out. He collapsed, half catching himself on the table. She expected him to be angry. But instead, he laughed. "Sleeping powder. Clever, Gwendolyn. Very clever. From my bedstand table. Well played. I did not think you would"—he groaned—"act to betray me so quickly. But perhaps I am glad that you did. I do hate having my hopes shattered."

Cringing, she took another step back as he tried to move toward her, but nearly fell over and had to grab onto a chair to keep himself upright. It was clear he could barely keep his eyes open.

"I didn't want to. I really didn't want to. I just don't...I can't. I'm sorry."

"I—" Mordred never finished what he was saying. He collapsed to the ground with a heavy *thud*. He was entirely unconscious.

Chewing her lip, she felt terrible leaving him there. Gathering up a few pillows and a blanket from the nearby furniture, she tucked the pillows under his head and draped the blanket over him. "I'm so sorry," she murmured. Not like he could hear her. Not like he would care if he could.

She went to move away.

A hand snapped around her ankle.

She screamed, and whirled, just in time to see Mordred's eyes roll back into his head as he passed back out. Her heart was racing, and she jumped back away from him like he was a zombie in a haunted house.

"Shit!" She waited to see if he'd move again. But this time he seemed out for the count.

"I guess I should compliment you."

Gwen shrieked again and whirled. But it was Merlin. The cat was perched on the edge of a table, staring at Mordred, swishing his tail angrily.

"Damn it, stop scaring me. I've had a bad few days." She let out a puff, focusing on breathing normally. The last thing she needed was to fuck everything up with a panic attack. "But I'm glad you're here. Let's go."

"Thought you'd never manage to get this far." He hopped down from the table and headed out into the hallway. "We might have a problem with the guards. If they try to stop you, are you ready to fight?"

"I . . . I mean . . . I'd rather not? I don't want to melt people."

"They aren't people. They're abominations." He glanced over his shoulder at her.

"They seem like people to me." She frowned, thinking of poor Mae and who knew how many other well-meaning suits of armor who were clunking around the keep. "Can we sneak instead?"

The cat sighed. "Fine. But we will not be able to do that forever."

She followed him, ducking around corners and hiding from the guards as best as she could, until she came to the door that led to the stairs of the basement.

Standing there, doing their job, were two suits of armor. They turned to look at her.

"I . . . um . . . I'm going downstairs." Good. That was a great explanation. She nailed it on that one, didn't she? She winced. She was not cut out for this kind of B.S.

Like a cartoon, they lowered their lances to cross them in front of the door, blocking their way. Merlin was standing next to her and, when she glanced down at the cat, she figured she wasn't going to get any help from him.

Taking a breath, she held it for a moment before letting it out. "I'm going to go melt the Crystal. Mordred is passed out asleep on his study floor. I drugged him. He won't blame you, he'll blame me. I don't want to hurt you—I don't know if I can." She held up her hand and let it catch fire. "But I really don't want to try."

They glanced at each other, then turned their attention back to her. After a pause, they uncrossed their lances. Either they wanted the Crystal gone, or they had a sense of self-preservation. She didn't want to know which.

"Thanks." Extinguishing her hand, she headed past them. The mangy black cat ran ahead and down the stairs, clearly eager to be free. Hope, small and fleeting but there all the same, began to spark in her heart. Maybe she could pull this off! Maybe she could really go home!

She jogged after the cat. He took the twisting turns and corners like he knew the way by heart. Which was fine by her. She didn't want to linger longer than she needed to. Who knew how long the drugs would last on Mordred? She really didn't want to find out the hard way.

It wasn't long before the cat slowed down as he reached a hallway she recognized. The ones with the massive iron doors. She walked up to them and let out a breath. No handles. Mordred had just sort of . . . gestured at them, and they had opened. Which made sense. Finding a spot to tug on, she tried to budge them—no dice.

"You'll have to melt them, idiot." Merlin was sitting some fifteen feet away, tail curled around himself.

"I know, but I figured it was worth a try, and—" She sighed. "Never mind. Why are you always so mean to me?"

"I am mean in general. Deal with it."

"Hopefully, I won't have to for much longer." She shrugged off her cloak and kicked off her boots. She didn't want to burn them up. Standing in front of the door, she shook out her limbs like she was about to run a marathon. "You're gonna keep your promise, right? That you'll send me home once this is done?"

"Yes."

She glared at him.

"I said yes, what more do you want?" He huffed. "Just do it already, will you?"

Grumbling, she cracked her neck from one side to the other, and shut her eyes. She ignited herself, feeling the fire crawl over her like a warm blanket. She snickered. That was still so cool. Picking up her hands, she studied them as they blazed with fire—no, blazed and *were* fire. Focusing, she turned her palms toward the door and let loose the same jets of flame that she had when she had been fighting with Mordred.

The fire hit the doors and curled along the metal surface.

"Hotter, Gwendolyn." Merlin sounded just a little nervous. "You have to burn hotter."

"I don't know—*ow!*" She yelped and jumped to one side. The little fucker had bitten her ankle! "Don't make me kick you, you—"

"Look."

Her fire was no longer reddish-orange, but a bright yellow. Huh. It had worked. "I still hate you." She turned back to the doors. She didn't want to waste the moment. This time, when she blasted the doors, she saw the metal start to heat up. She focused, trying to burn hotter. She made herself remember everything that she had gone through. Falling. Waking up in a crater, naked. Merlin's assholery. Lancelot's suffering. Mick cheating on her.

The color shifted again, growing brighter until it was a greenish tone. The doors began to liquify, slowly oozing into puddles of burning goop on the ground.

She didn't know how long it had taken, but by the time the doors were melted enough for them to get through, her ears were ringing and she was exhausted. She let out a long breath and doubled over, resting her arms on her thighs. "Shit."

"I hope you're up to this. That was nothing compared to what's next." Merlin was already going ahead, jumping over the puddles of molten iron and into the eerily glowing room.

"Look, I know you're not wrong, but do you have to be such a dick about it?" She followed after him once she felt like she could breathe without passing out.

"Yes." He was sitting at the edge of the pool of magical shards, staring up at the massive Crystal. "Get to work, Gwendolyn. I do not think we will have much time."

Standing at the edge of the pool, she rolled her shoulders. It was just like that time she had to run the marathon in track class. She hated track class. And she had failed at running the marathon. But that wasn't the point.

Cracking her knuckles, she held out her palms toward the Crystal and let loose. She tried to focus all her energy. Tried to burn hotter. Harder. She had to melt the Crystal.

She had to.

She had to.

The other option was failure. And failure was death or imprisonment. Success meant freedom for everyone trapped inside. For Lancelot. For the return of beauty and magic to

Avalon. Her eyes were stinging. Her breathing felt short and shallow. She couldn't suck enough air into her lungs.

But she couldn't fail!

Merlin was yelling at her. She couldn't hear him over the ringing in her head that was drowning everything out. Even the rush of the fire that was erupting from her hands.

The world pitched around her.

No, no, no!

She pushed everything she had into the flame. Tried as hard as she could. Shutting her eyes, she screamed as she forced all of her might into destroying the Crystal.

Her knees buckled. She fell to the ground hard, pressing her palms into the cold stone. Her fire had gone out.

Merlin was silent.

She pressed back until she was kneeling, sitting on her ankles, and looked up. Maybe she had succeeded, and—

The Crystal hung in place.

Undamaged.

Tears stung her eyes. "I just need a second to try again. Let me catch my breath. I'll—"

Someone behind her was applauding. Slowly. Mockingly.

Her heart sank into her stomach.

"I fear it was not enough, firefly."

Twenty-Nine

Gwen shot up to her feet so fast she nearly fell back over again. Mordred was standing in the jamb, leaning heavily on the molten remains of one of the doors. The heat from the still-cooling metal didn't bother him. He didn't look great, but he was awake.

And awake meant trouble.

Shit, shit, shit!

Merlin was nowhere to be seen. The coward must have hidden. She squared her shoulders and faced her inevitable fate. "Mordred, I—"

"No. No excuses. No lies. You wished to free Lancelot and all the rest. You have deemed my rule too harsh to continue." He laughed quietly, a tired and cynical sound. He rubbed his hand over his face. He still looked half-drugged. "If you only understood what you seek to unleash on this world."

"It doesn't matter." She was shaking. Absolutely trembling like a leaf. "I failed. And now you'll kill me or shove me in there with all the rest, won't you?"

He grimaced in disgust. "I should. By all the Ancients in the eternal void, I should." Rage seemed to overcome him, and his armor appeared over his body as he rammed his fist into the remains of the iron door, denting it. "Why would you not *listen*?" he roared. "Why would you not heed my words!"

She squeaked and took a step back as he came at her with more speed than she expected him to. She almost slipped and tumbled into the pool of glowing shards behind her. As she glanced down to make sure she didn't misstep, Mordred had plenty of time to snatch her by the shoulders and yank her forward.

This was when she died. This was when it all ended.

Tears stung her eyes, and she didn't bother to wipe them away as they ran down her cheeks.

"You could have been... *we* could have been..." He snarled. "Tell me, was it all a lie? Did you feel nothing?"

"No! I just—it—I'm sorry." She cringed. "I—I'm sorry I hurt you. I didn't want to betray you. I just... I couldn't. I couldn't not try. This is wrong." Letting out a shaking breath, she braced herself for the inevitable. "Just do it." She shut her eyes. "I'm so sorry. Just please make it quick."

"You wish to see what Avalon once was? Very well, Gwendolyn Wright. I shall grant your wish." Mordred's tone was cold and cruel.

Looking up to him, she furrowed her brow, not understanding.

He sneered down at her, looking for all the world like the villain everyone had made him out to be. And perhaps he was. "If you refuse to listen to my words, I will show you. You will come to see the error of your ways—you will *beg* me to restore the Crystal when all is said and done. That is, if you survive the treachery and the carnage that is to follow. Tell me, my poor, sympathetic firefly—what will you do when you see Avalon consumed by violence? Reduced to ash and bone by squabbling forces? Will you come crawling to me, begging for forgiveness? Begging for me to save the world again from your foolishness?"

"I—I don't—" She still wasn't following along. What did he mean? What was he going to do?

"You have been in this world for a little under a week, and you think you know better than I how it should be run? You wish me to be the monster that all others see in me?" He lifted his clawed hand toward the Crystal and clenched his hand into a fist. The room shuddered like there had been an earthquake. "*So be it.*"

Something cracked. It sounded like an iceberg rumbling and giving way. She staggered as the room rumbled again.

It was the Crystal. A dark cleft formed in it, straight down the middle. The crack quickly began to glow a brilliant, opalescent white. It was too bright to look at. "What're you—"

His clawed hand grabbed her around the throat and yanked her closer to him, using his considerable height to loom over her. "I will rebuild it. Soul by soul. Elemental by elemental."

"Mordred, I—"

He wasn't done. "I shall give you a head start, my dear, for I wish you to see the horror that you have unleashed. But pray that when I find you—and I will—I show you the mercy of a swift death." He threw her again, toward the door. "Now *run.*"

The chains holding the Crystal aloft groaned and snapped. Lightning shot from the crack in the Crystal, hitting the wall next to her. She screamed and ducked. "But—but what about you?"

His furious expression flickered briefly. When another one of those bolts shot from the Crystal, he threw his cloak up, the blade-like sections of fabric turning to iron. The magic simply hit him and bounced harmlessly off.

Right.

That.

He smirked. "Run, firefly."

Without any chance to stop and consider what she had done—okay, what Mordred had done, but because of her—she turned on her heel and ran as fast as she could, barefoot, up the stairs. The glowing light from behind her was growing brighter, not dimmer.

Breathless and panicking, she realized too late that she had made a wrong turn. She was on a balcony overlooking the sea, some several hundred feet below the cliff. Turning to go back the way she came, she watched as a beam of that bright and shining light shot down the hallway, destroying several pieces of furniture and sending several of the iron guards flying.

She ran, hearing wreckage and disaster behind her. Something kept ringing in the air that made her ears ache.

She ran as long and as hard as she could. Down the stairs, around the corners, running past the confused guards that were all scrambling to defend the keep without knowing what was happening. Luckily, her frantic exit was the least of their concerns. She didn't stop until she got to the edge of the forest, turning to see what was happening.

Light—opalescent, and every color and none at the same time—was streaming from every window in the castle. There was a rumble in the ground beneath her. She nearly fell over, staggering to catch onto a tree as it shook harder like an earthquake.

It didn't make a sound, the explosion. It didn't even really look like an explosion at all. Something *shifted*, the force pulling inward and then shooting out in a ring from the castle. A wall crumbled and fell, crashing off the cliff into the ocean.

And a blast wave was rushing at her, invisible but distorting the air like the summer sun on hot pavement.

Gwen threw her arms over her face as the force smashed into her, sending her tumbling backwards.

It might have been fine if it weren't for the rock she smacked her head on.

Mordred stared at the wreckage that was once his masterpiece. The shattered Crystal had fallen into the pool of shards, sending them scattering and covering the ground around him. Many of them had likely been pulverized in the collapse, sending their magic careening out like all the rest.

Reaching down, he picked up one of the still-glowing opalescent shards between his claws. He would rebuild. It would not be so difficult, now that he knew what he was doing. But the problem would be the elementals that were now free. They would seek his death. And while magic could not harm him, there were many ways to kill a man that were perfectly mundane.

He was ageless. But not immortal.

Gwendolyn. He sighed. He should have killed her. He should have imprisoned her. He was confident in his ability to conquer Avalon a second time. But it was a risk. And he should not be in the business of taking them needlessly.

He had not thought he had a heart left to break. But there it was, in ruins, like his Crystal.

Turning from the smashed Crystal, he headed up the stairs. His guards were picking themselves up from the ground. Some looked as though they had been blown to bits in the explosion—as had most of his furniture and the windows. He had heard the sound of crumbling stone. It would take time to rebuild.

But he had more important matters to attend to. Heading outside, he lifted the gate to the stables where the hounds slept. Eod came out, tail between his legs, looking up at him with his ears flat to his head.

"Go on. She can't have gotten far." He gestured to the forest.

The dog wagged his tail a little, furtive and wary.

Mordred bit back his rage. He wanted to holler at the dog. But he would not understand. Nor would he have deserved it. But it was clear that even his Eod loved Gwen more than he loved Mordred. It would be too painful to have the mutt around as a reminder. "Go on, dog." Unable to stomach looking at the creature any longer, he turned back to his keep and went to find his remaining two knights.

It was not hard to find them. They were all in their full suits of armor, standing in waiting in the throne room. Mordred did not miss them glancing at each other.

"My liege?" Galahad began. "What—"

"The Crystal is destroyed. The magic and the elementals are free." He summoned Caliburn, which hovered in the air beside him. "For the moment."

"What . . . are we going to do?" Percival asked, obviously hesitant to hear the answer.

"We do what we do best." Mordred sneered. "We go to war."

Acknowledgments

I want to take a moment to appreciate all those who have had a hand in making this series come to fruition. To my readers, my patient editor Jack, and my extremely patient husband, thank you for putting up with me while I take us down these weird roads of the places and people who live in my head rent-free.

The Iron Crystal series is an experiment on many fronts for me—and it has been a wonderful adventure. I hope you fall in love with the characters of Avalon as much as I have.

ABOUT THE AUTHOR

KATHRYN ANN KINGSLEY is a *USA Today* bestselling author and award-winning designer. A storyteller all her life, she delights in spinning stories of the sweetest nightmares to delight her readers with her unique twist of horror and romance. With ten years in script writing for performances on both the stage and for tourism, she has always been writing in one form or another.

When she isn't penning down fiction, she works as creative director for a company that designs and builds large-scale interactive adventure games. There, she is the lead concept designer, handling everything from game and set design, to audio and lighting, to illustration and script writing. Also on her list of skills are artistic direction, scenic painting and props, special effects, and electronics. A graduate of Boston University with a BFA in theatre design, she has a passion for unique, creative, and unconventional experiences. In her spare time, she builds animatronics and takes trapeze classes.

You can learn more at:

KathrynKingsley.com
Facebook.com/KathrynAnnKingsley
Instagram @KathrynAnnKingsley